MW00723314

THE QUOTIENT CLUB

JAY HILARY

Copyright © 2004 by Jay Hilary

ISBN 0-7414-2163-1

Published by:

PUBLISHING.COM

1094 New DeHaven Street, Suite 100
West Conshohocken, PA 19428-2713
Info@buybooksontheweb.com
www.buybooksontheweb.com
Toll-free (877) BUY BOOK
Local Phone (610) 941-9999
Fax (610) 941-9959

Printed in the United States of America

Printed on Recycled Paper

Published October 2004

For Mom and Dad

ACKNOWLEDGMENTS

The author wishes to acknowledge the
assistance of the following people:

Beth Mansbridge, Mansbridge Editing & Transcription;
Monica Dias and Richard Goehler, Esq.,
Frost, Brown, Todd LLC.

<1>

Chet Warner pushed his five-foot-nine-inch body up from the damp grass alongside the park trail. Both knees cracked as he slowly stood up. It was a familiar sound to him that had come with age. Regardless, he still thought he was in good shape for a man of forty-five.

He tucked his long-sleeved white Nike shirt into the back of his black running shorts and then pressed the start button on his Timex. He started down the crushed gravel path at a slow jog, then straightened his body as he began to run faster. It was a cool spring evening and though the days were getting longer, daylight-saving time had not yet begun. He knew it would be dark soon.

He looked down at his feet to double-check the car key was still tied to his shoelace. He would do it several more times throughout the run. Sometimes he thought maybe he was obsessive-compulsive, but had convinced himself just about everybody was, about one thing or other.

It had been a long day at the office and an even longer week. *Thank God tomorrow's Friday*, he thought. *By the end of the day I'll be finished with the company that's been a thorn in my side for the past couple years and my chairman will be proud!*

He had helped make his information technology company one of the most profitable and fastest growing in the technology corridor as well as the entire country, for that matter. In fact it was Chet's astute financial decision making that had put him on the most recent cover of *Finance Today Magazine*.

He didn't need to consult with anyone; he made financial decisions like this one daily. Should products be added or dropped, should services be outsourced, should their equipment be leased?

The fact of the matter was, he was in charge of the corporate aircraft and it was time to make a change. He had looked into the necessary arrangements for alternative travel and all he needed to do now was place the calls.

The airplane wasn't for Chet's use anyway. It was for the chairman and several other executives of the company who had flown the same trips over the past five years. Some for business in Mexico and some for travel to the chairman's second home in the Cayman Islands. The remainder was primarily for domestic travel across the United States.

The company had never owned a plane before, so the chairman didn't know any different. But Chet had friends at other companies who told him he should make a change. He respected his peers and consulted with them frequently. They kept telling him the company should buy its own aircraft or at least try one of the other fractional ownership programs.

When Chet had first heard about the StratoShares fractional ownership program, he thought it was a great concept. A company or individual could purchase a portion of an aircraft based on their air transportation needs. They would pay an acquisition price for their fraction that was comparable to what it would cost them for that same aircraft in today's market. They were then only responsible for the operating costs associated with owning their portion of the plane and were guaranteed access twenty-four hours a day, 365 days a year. It was like timesharing and his company owned two shares in two separate aircraft.

That's the way it was supposed to work and would have been a great concept if it actually did work. It should have been a CFO's dream come true, but unfortunately for Chet, that wasn't the case.

He had been threatening StratoShares for the past couple years that he would leave their program if the service didn't improve. They always came back with some feeble excuse. On the next trip, things would be better. But shortly thereafter it would happen all over again.

He never could understand it. Most of the problems occurred on the domestic legs, while in contrast the international flights to the islands or Mexico always went without a hitch.

Chet thought to himself, *Who does StratoShares think they are, anyway? They've practically strong-armed my company for the last several years.* He couldn't count the number of times they'd made mistakes in scheduling or deviated from the original flight plan.

Well, tomorrow I'll make the change and literally save the company about a million dollars a year. That was just the tangible number he had come up with. It didn't include the intangibles, like the loss of productivity that had become so common with their service. He also figured the decision would remove a lot of daily stress for him and probably add ten years to his life.

Then on Saturday he could start spring break with Cindy and the kids. The children sure were growing up fast. Starting this fall Billy would be in middle school, Nate would be in the 4th grade, and Sarah would be going full time to first grade.

They were going to spend a week at their condo on Hilton Head Island. Cindy and the kids sure loved it there. One of their favorite things to do was go down to the lighthouse and listen to the guy who sang John Denver songs on Friday nights. The kids would come from all across the island and gather in a circle to join him in song. Even the younger baby boomers like himself, who had grown up listening to John Denver, enjoyed it.

Cindy would always kid him by saying he and John must have gone to the same barber. They both had that straight brownish-blond hair.

Yes, he had a lot to be thankful for: a successful career, a beautiful wife and three wonderful, healthy children. He had a three-quarter of a million-dollar home in Falcon Ridge, a summer home in Hilton Head, and the coolest car—a Lexus SC 430. His mom and dad, as well as his in-laws, were all in good health. Life was certainly good.

Chet glanced down at his watch and forced himself to pick up the pace. He pushed his body harder and willed his legs to take larger, quicker strides. He had only been running for about five minutes, but could feel the perspiration beading uncomfortably on his forehead and in his mustache.

He ignored the irritating sensation as he continued to admire the dense woods of the northeastern Virginia park located less than a mile from his home. He loved running here several evenings a week. Of course, that was only when he didn't have a soccer, baseball or basketball game to attend, or some type of scouting or church activity. Cindy and the kids had always come first and he couldn't imagine life without them.

Cindy had her part-time job at the bank where she had worked for five years. The bank had been asking her to work full-time, but she had too many other commitments. She belonged to the women's club, sang in the church choir and volunteered once a week at the local children's hospital. The rest of her time was spent catering to him and the kids.

She was the CFO of their house and he left most of the personal finances to her. Though he still kept a close eye on things and occasionally would drop financial hints or sugges-tions, she always did a great job.

He looked over his left shoulder, realizing he hadn't seen any other runners. The park was usually crowded and often attracted many foreign-speaking tourists visiting the nearby capital, but today the area was deserted.

Actually he found the solitude comforting since it gave him the opportunity to enjoy the sights and sounds around him. He noticed a rotten tree lying on the damp ground. A gray squirrel rustled in the fallen dark brown oak leaves and pine needles. Chet slowed his pace to watch the creature run down the length of the tree trunk and scurry inside the hollow log.

Somewhere in the maze of branches came the relaxing notes of a small songbird as it looked for seeds in a loblolly pine. This, however, was interrupted by the intrusive sound of another of the park's more permanent residents, a red-headed woodpecker. The large bird hammered diligently, searching for insects on the bark of a nearby tree.

Chet also heard the gurgle of water flowing across the moss-covered rocks in the creek bed alongside the trail. Though he was now running on the same level as the stream, there were places along the path where it was a sheer cliff and the drop to the water was nearly a hundred feet.

He leaned forward and worked his arms and legs harder as he attacked the upcoming hill. He tried to visualize himself running through it. It was a technique he had learned in college. Hills were the reason he loved this park so much. He had run his best races in both high school and college on hilly courses and would always pass other runners while going up the hills. Unfortunately he had a tendency to hold himself back and going down the other side he would ultimately be passed again.

Chet took deeper breaths as he intensely worked the hill. He could smell the greenish-white blooms of the flowering dogwoods along the trail as well as the almost acidic scent of last year's fallen leaves. He soon reached the top of the first hill where the trail leveled off again. He had now climbed forty feet above the creek on his right.

He couldn't help but notice he still hadn't passed anybody. The sky was overcast and the air unusually cold for the beginning of April. Maybe the weather was keeping some of the other runners away. The elements had never made a difference to him though. He ran religiously. He often thought of himself like the mail carrier. *How did the old saying go? "Through sleet, snow, rain, etc." . . . or something like that.*

He had gotten to know this park over the past several years and felt like it was a part of him. This is where he would come to think and get some of his best work done during long-distance runs. Rarely would he go for more than several days without coming back. In fact he probably knew the park better than anyone else, except for maybe the rangers who managed it on a daily basis.

Chet finally noticed a young runner in a George Washington University sweatshirt heading toward him. He was tall and lanky, practically a stick who looked to be about nineteen years old. They nodded as they passed each other.

Enjoy it while it lasts, kid, Chet thought. *Just wait until you get a little older and your metabolism changes. Then you'll be fighting the battle of the bulge, just like me.*

He didn't have that so-called spare tire around the middle, but he knew the potential was there. Right now he was winning his battle.

He ran around a puddle in the center of the trail and remembered the words of his college cross-country coach. Always run through a puddle, never around it. At the same time he would think of probably the only thing he still remembered from geometry class: the shortest distance between two points is a straight line.

These things were instilled in him as a young man while competing in high school and college. They would have added seconds to his race time and might have cost him a place or two at the finish. He'd remember these things while running, whether competing or not.

They were probably good axioms in the business world as well. Some of us were just born to be more competitive than others, he thought. *It must have been a result of having grown up in the late sixties and early part of the self-seeking seventies.*

He quickly brought his thoughts back to the present and looked to his left. It was the part of the trail that went through a grassy field and was relatively flat for the next three hundred yards. He would often see deer at this point along the path, especially in the evening just before sunset. The wildlife here was overpopulated and sometimes he would literally have to run around them. There were also a few sporadic trees and an occasional large rock scattered about. He noticed last year's thistle, dry and brittle, bowing before him as he passed.

He also noticed a man sitting on one of the large rocks alongside the trail. He was dressed in a black warm-up suit, an Orioles ball cap and dark sunglasses. His back was to the trail and he was looking across the meadow through binoculars. He appeared to be watching a small wooden birdhouse on a pole in the middle of the field.

Chet thought the man was dressed rather oddly for a bird watcher, but then again he wasn't exactly certain what an ornithologist would wear. He ran past the man, who paid him no attention.

As Chet re-entered the woods shaded by its thick canopy of trees, he heard the distinct crackle of a walkie-talkie somewhere behind him. The park rangers often used the two-way radios or similar equipment to communicate. He glanced over his shoulder but only saw the birdwatcher walking away.

He put his head down and leaned forward as he approached the next big hill. He shifted his thinking back to the office and grinned as he thought about replacing the company that presently provided their aircraft service.

Surely, StratoShares will take me seriously this time. First thing tomorrow, I'll contact our company's legal counsel to take our business elsewhere. If the arrogant company doesn't agree to purchase back our shares at an amount greater than fair market value, I'll fight them. After all, it's the least they can do considering all the screw-ups my colleagues have suffered.

The trail leveled off again and he was now ninety to a hundred feet above the rocky creek bed. He looked at the sheer cliff face of gray rock on his right where an occasional tree grew straight out from the small canyon wall. He could still see water in the creek but could no longer hear it.

A few trees with fresh green buds were scattered along the trail between him and the ravine. He recognized a mixture of common blue violets and the deeply notched white petals of chickweeds intermingled along the moist ground. The start of other spring growth included poison ivy, briars, and numerous plants indigenous to the area.

Chet took a longer stride as he straddled a large branch lying sideways across the width of the worn dirt and gravel path. *It would make a great walking stick,* he thought. His kids loved to pick them up and use them as they hiked.

He only had another quarter mile to go before he reached the end of the trail where there was a bluff and vista of the valley. *That's where I'll turn around and start back.* He glanced at his watch, and then at his right foot to make sure his shoelace hadn't come untied. He confirmed the car key hadn't fallen off.

When he looked up, two husky looking men appeared, coming quickly down the trail toward him. They looked like football linebackers running abreast. Chet thought their sudden emergence seemed odd because he was now running a six-minute pace per mile and had been on the trail for the past twenty minutes. Since the path ended in a cul de sac, he knew he should have already seen the runners at some point and felt there was no way the two burley men could run so fast.

As they got closer, he saw they both were wearing black warm-ups and dark sunglasses, much like the guy he had seen earlier. Since the sky was overcast and it was even darker in the woods, there wasn't a need for sunglasses. He suddenly felt his stomach tense and knot when he realized they looked more like thugs from a Mafia movie. He knew he was probably just being ridiculous and letting his imagination get the better of him, but decided to hold as close to his side of the trail as possible, just to be safe.

When they closed their distance to within several feet of him and he realized they were going to collide, he felt the rush of adrenaline spread through his body.

He shouted, "What are you do—" as the men lowered their shoulders and plowed headfirst into him on both sides of his chest. He reached out to grab at them but only brushed the dark nylon fabric of each man's jacket. He felt himself leave the ground as he flew backwards through the trees and over the edge of the ravine.

Chet tried to scream as he fell but was unable to catch his breath. They had knocked the wind out of him.

He flailed and grasped at nothing as he fell backwards through the sky. He could see the gray, overcast clouds through the branches of the trees above. He felt a piercing blow across his kidneys as his lower back struck a large branch of a tree growing on the side of the ravine. This slowed his fall only briefly and caused his body to spin. Instantly his mind filled with terror as all he could see was the rocky creek below.

He continued to fall as he saw his parents at the Little League game where he hit his first homerun, his high school graduation, his brother and sister and nieces and nephews, his college graduation, his wedding day with Cindy, the birth of Billy, Nate, and Sarah, the kids at Christmas, the kids at Disney World, his parents' fiftieth anniversary, Cindy and the kids again.

How could so many things go through his mind in such a short time? His brain was processing massive amounts of information and working much like the high-tech software his company sold.

But Chet felt like he was falling in slow motion, the hundredths of seconds feeling like minutes. He still couldn't catch a breath and could now see the rocks below more clearly. He realized it would all be over soon. *This has to be a dream. Please tell me I'm going to wake up before I hit the bottom,* he prayed. *I love you, Cindy! I love you, Billy, Nate, Sarah! Please God, take care of them!*

He barely heard a sound or felt any pain as his entire body became engulfed in a warm sensation—then instant darkness.

Chet lay face down in the rocks of the cold creek. He couldn't hear the sound of the walkie-talkies above or the shuffle of feet through the wet leaves as the two men ran back in the direction from where they had come.

<2>

J. Edward Chambers II slammed down the telephone and pushed himself back from his large mahogany desk. His leather chair tilted forward and rose about an inch as he lifted his aging body from the seat. He removed his gold-frame reading glasses and tossed them onto the cluttered desktop. He could feel his pulse racing and hear the blood rushing as he massaged his gray-haired temples. He felt like his head was about to explode and his heart jump out of his chest.

He wondered what a heart attack or aneurysm felt like. Most of his friends and peers had already had one—some of them, two or three. Yet he was seventy-five years old and had never spent a day in the hospital.

He walked to the corner window and looked out at the City. Behind him, across his spacious Manhattan office, a mahogany grandfather clock chimed 10 P.M. From the fiftieth floor he had a view of most of the City on one side and the Hudson River and Upper Bay on the other. It was snowing lightly. Rather unusual for late October, but he had seen this several times before.

He took a deep breath and tried to relax as he watched a forty-one-foot Coast Guard utility boat moving slowly along the Upper Bay. Its primary use was for search and rescue or law enforcement. It made Edward remember the years he had spent in the Coast Guard. Most of it during World War II, reporting to the Navy. None of it was during peacetime when it was administered by the Department of Transportation. The word "transportation" brought back his thoughts to the conversation he'd just had.

He had called for Tony Folino, but got some kid instead. *Who does that young punk think he is, talking to me that way! He'd said his title was Vice President of Communications. Vice President of Communications, my ass. The kid's probably never had to work a day in his life. He most likely*

10

graduated from one of the nearby Ivy League schools and sits behind his desk every day with the door closed, surfing the net and jacking off.

From what J. Edward had seen, most of that company was made up of Generation Xers. *Shit, even the pilots look like kids.*

Hell, I should have called William Price's office in San Francisco. Bill is one of the wealthiest men in America and made most of his fortune from the computer and cable industry. Why he ever bought a company like QCI, Chambers didn't know. Especially with the recent rumors he had heard about Folino from other associates in the investment banking world. *Yeah, I should have just called Price.* Chambers owned enough shares of Price's Class A stock that he would have taken the call.

Edward turned from the window and walked across the plush Oriental wool rug he had purchased during his most recent trip to the Far East. He stopped at the mahogany china cabinet to remove a fresh cup. He poured himself some coffee and replaced the pot on its small burner. He held the cup in both hands and took a sip.

It wasn't too hot so he took a larger gulp. He immediately scrunched his tired, wrinkled face. *If this job doesn't kill me,* he thought, *the coffee will. What should I expect, though.* His secretary, Barbara, had made it almost five hours earlier before she left for the night. He plodded back to his chair and rolled it forward.

At least his heart had stopped racing and his head had quit pounding. *I'll take care of everything tomorrow. I'll contact the treasurer in the morning and have him start the process of finding another operator and demand that the Quotient Club, Inc. (QCI for short) buy back their Cessna Citation X and Falcon 900 shares in the StratoShares program.*

He was certain his decision would come as a surprise to the other executives, especially since the company had been with StratoShares for almost six years. His associates never seemed to be the ones affected by QCI's ineptness, though.

Maybe it was because most of their travel was domestic and his was international; he wasn't certain. All he knew was that he still called the shots and no one was going to stop him.

That's what he so much as told that young VP of Communications. He also told him to make sure Tony Folino got the message and not to bother calling back.

This evening had been the last straw. He had called his customer service team at StratoShares, requesting to move tomorrow afternoon's departure to earlier in the morning. He knew his request was within his contractual rights. An hour later he was contacted by his team and informed they could only do the trip at the later time. They said there was no way they could provide an aircraft any earlier.

It was just one of more than a dozen occurrences over the past couple years. Excuses for their delays or limitations ranged from only being able to clear customs at certain times, needing to locate or wait for a life raft, inability to change departure or arrival slots, or the plane was having mechanical problems or was in maintenance.

Many times, representatives from StratoShares would practically hound him to confirm his international trips. Then they'd become downright rude if he changed the reservation. There were even a couple trips he had cancelled yet still received invoices for them.

When he'd joined Folino's program a half-dozen years ago, StratoShares only had a couple competitors in the fractional ownership industry. Now there were many companies to choose from and even though Folino had comp'ed some of their flights, no price was worth the inconveniences he had seen. *Tomorrow I'll put an end to their ridiculousness, once and for all.*

J. Edward picked up his reading glasses again and put them on. He flipped through the stack of pink telephone messages that Barbara had laid on his desk earlier in the day. *It's too late to call any of them back tonight,* he chuckled to himself.

There was one from his first wife. That could wait; he placed it aside. *What does she want now,* he wondered.

Probably more money. He had learned a hard lesson from her and quickly became educated about prenuptial agreements after his first marriage. About the only thing she didn't get back then was his Aston Martin V8 Vantage. He couldn't help it if he liked the fastest of everything.

He quickly flipped through the remaining message slips. There was one from his yacht broker; maybe he had a buyer. Also a message from StratoShares, one from his second wife, and one from Liz, his girlfriend. *How did I miss that one*, he mused. He continued looking and found another from his first wife and finally one from his son.

He took the entire stack and threw them in the gold-plated wastebasket under his desk. He would call Liz and Edward right now. His yacht broker could wait until tomorrow and as far as StratoShares and his ex-wives, well, they could all go to hell.

His conversation with Edward was brief and after a half-hour of talking to Liz, he hung up the phone. He felt his heart racing again. The difference this time was it felt good. What did he care if Liz was half his age. Plenty of guys had trophy wives, so why couldn't he. He'd have to call his attorney tomorrow and see how the prenup was coming along.

He glanced down at the well-designed yellow-gold Patek Philippe wristwatch, a gift from Liz. The time was just after eleven. He pushed back his chair and stood up. He lifted his black suit jacket off the back of the chair and put it on. Reaching across his desk, he removed a Hoyo de Monterrey Double Corona from the humidor and shoved the Cuban cigar into his inside suit pocket. He'd have time to smoke it in the car on the drive to his home on the Upper East Side.

He walked across his office and turned off the burner to the coffee pot. He flicked off the light switch and closed the large wooden door behind him. Stopping at Barbara's desk, he jotted a quick message on a yellow Post-It note and left it for her to find in the morning.

As he proceeded down the long carpeted hall toward the reception area, he realized he had finally had enough. He knew it was time to retire. He had been in investment banking for fifty years and seen just about everything. He had worked with them all. You name them and he knew them.

He just couldn't do it anymore. He suspected his health was failing and wanted to enjoy the remainder of his life. He wanted to go out on top. It was time to turn it over to his son, J. Edward Chambers III.

As he neared the office reception area he could see through the outer glass wall, a uniformed night watchman standing in the hall near the elevator. Edward walked over and pressed several numbers on the security keypad. He activated the alarm and then exited through the large glass double doors.

He approached the elevator while he patted his pockets to make sure he had his wallet, keys, and cigar.

The young Italian security guard greeted him with a friendly "Good evening."

Edward looked at him indifferently and replied with a monotone "Hello." After pausing a second, he added, "I assume the elevator has been fixed? I had to take the stairs down to forty-five earlier today to catch an elevator."

"It's been fixed," the guard replied with a distinct Brooklyn accent. He pressed the Down button and stood there chewing his gum, smiling at Edward.

Edward eyed him curiously. "I don't recognize you. Are you new?"

"Nah," he replied, "I usually walk the lower floors and that's mostly on weekends."

Edward was there on weekends but didn't recall ever seeing the young man. *Oh well,* he thought, *it's a big building.*

Edward looked down at his watch as the elevator doors slid open. It was 11:15 P.M. As he said good night and started to step forward, he raised his head and felt his heart skip a beat. His body paralyzed as his mouth dropped open in disbelief. He blinked a couple times and reached up to find he was wearing his reading glasses. He tore them off and blinked again.

He knew his vision was failing, but confirmed he wasn't imagining what he was seeing. He was staring into an open elevator shaft, at gray steel cables and bare concrete walls.

What Edward didn't see was the butt of the security guard's revolver come crashing down on his right temple.

The blow instantly knocked Edward unconscious as he closed his eyes and crumpled forward in pain into the darkness of the elevator shaft.

The guard momentarily stopped chewing his gum and stood silently waiting. Seconds later he heard a faint, distant echo as the old man's body collided and became one with the top of the elevator car at the bottom of the building.

The guard pressed the wall button and the elevator doors closed on the now makeshift mausoleum. He turned and walked away as he resumed chewing his gum. He smiled and thought to himself, *The boss is sure gonna be pleased.*

<3>

Johnnie couldn't believe how beautiful the northern California weather was for the third week of March and he was enjoying the unseasonable warmth. Spring was just a week away and he had the fever. He was going to take advantage of the wonderful climate and make the long drive down the coast with the roof off his Mercedes Benz Roadster.

The forecast for the entire weekend was perfect, with the National Weather Service calling for no precipitation, sunny skies and near record temperatures. It was the perfect weekend for a drive south to L.A.

It was now early morning and his trip would take the majority of the day traveling mostly along State Highway 1. He always enjoyed the breathtaking scenery and found the coastal road relaxing. He hadn't made the drive in quite some time and was looking forward to the change. Besides, he didn't need to be at the charity benefit until 7:00 P.M.

He could have requested to take their StratoShares plane out of Napa County Airport, but knew what a joke that would have been. Actually, that was the very reason he was making the drive. He needed time to relax and gather his thoughts.

He had spent most of the previous night on the phone trying to reach Tony Folino, who was never available to speak with him. He left several messages for the man to call, but never heard back. When he finally got Folino's personal voice mail, he left his message loud and clear. He played it through in his mind one more time, as best as he could remember.

Tony, this is Johnnie Perrino at Perrino Winery up in Napa Valley. I've had it with your program and want out. Your company continues to wreak havoc on my daily schedule, especially with regard to international flights. I've sent

16

numerous letters and placed hundreds of phone calls to your company over the past nine months. Rest assured I'll be contacting my attorney upon my return from L.A. this weekend. I'll be driving there in my car since I've found it more reliable than your planes.

Also I'll be calling any of the other owners I know in the Valley, across the country, and in Europe as well. In addition I'll be placing calls to all my friends and associates that I've passed to your company as referrals.

You can reach me on my cell phone, but I may be in and out of range as I'm driving through the mountains along the coast.

That was it and he had hung up the phone. He thought the tone of his voice should have made it obvious there was nothing at this point Tony Folino or his company could do to appease him.

He glanced to his left at the dark waters of San Pablo Bay as he headed west on 37 toward 101 South. He thought back on his relationship with StratoShares. It had been exceedingly rocky for the past year.

He supposedly had an agreement with the chief marketing executive, Ross Nickels. For every prospect or referral he gave them, they would compensate him with free flight time. These were supposedly things that StratoShares didn't do for everybody.

Well, that was a joke, because they didn't do it for him either. Whenever Johnnie would go back and ask Ross for compensation, he would invariably be told that they had already been working that lead from another source and that his relationship had nothing to do with them joining the StratoShares program.

Next Johnnie started thinking about his actual trips, more specifically the international legs. Their trips to Marseilles in the Provence region of France were regular and always on StratoShares aircraft. They had vineyards just a short drive northwest of the capital city. It was only if he tried to change something, like add a leg or depart sooner or later, that StratoShares would become uncooperative and give some excuse as to why they couldn't do it.

On his last trip back from the south of France, the crew practically interrogated him before they would allow him on the plane. They wanted to make sure he wasn't carrying any illegal contraband. *Even the customs agents back in the states didn't typically blink an eye or show any interest. So what if he had a couple boxes of Cuban cigars?*

Then he recalled all the trips when he didn't even get a StratoShares aircraft. They would subcontract his flight to another operator and send him a different airplane. The aircraft were never as new and the interiors were typically badly worn. In addition he was continually questioning the safety of their operators.

He shook his head in disbelief and took a deep breath as the thought of StratoShares continued to annoy him. He didn't need the aggravation and neither did his father. Johnnie was thirty-nine years old and president of the company. The vineyards were all he knew. His father had been grooming him for the position his entire life.

He was a good-looking young man with short, wavy brown hair, dark brown eyes, and chiseled features. He always appeared suave and debonair. In fact, he was the most eligible bachelor in the Valley and had even made it on some national lists that once included John Kennedy Jr.

Johnnie reached across the passenger seat, opened his CD holder, and removed a disc with his favorite collection of classical music. He slid it into the sound system and adjusted the treble and bass. The sound wasn't quite the same with the varioroof down, but it was still enjoyable.

He pushed himself deeper into the black leather seat while zipping up his white cotton windbreaker. He pressed his black-rimmed sunglasses more firmly against his face as he applied more pressure to the gas pedal of the silver SLK 320. The 6-cylinder engine responded immediately. He relaxed and listened to the music of Richard Wagner as he headed for San Francisco.

Fifteen minutes later he exited the Waldo Tunnel in Marin County, just north of the city. The panoramic view of San Francisco was breathtaking, with the Bay Bridge bordering on the left and the Golden Gate Bridge on the right. He reveled at the city's skyline and only briefly glanced away to notice Alcatraz in the bay. He never got tired of the view.

After crossing the bridge, he exited U.S. 101 onto Highway 1 and drove through the Presidio. Before changing lanes he glanced in his rearview mirror and saw a black Lincoln Continental following closely behind. This was the second time he'd seen the car, but didn't think anything of it.

Within minutes he was through San Francisco and driving south along the Pacific Ocean. He passed the Point Montara Light Station and headed for Half Moon Bay. He was relaxed, enjoying the scenery of the road winding along the mountain's edge and rough waters crashing to his right.

It had been an hour since he had last seen the black Lincoln when suddenly it appeared again. This time he watched intently in his rearview mirror. He didn't move his head, but observed the vehicle from behind his sunglasses as he shifted his eyes back and forth between the road and the mirror. He didn't take his eyes off the curvy cliff road for more than a couple seconds at a time.

He could make out what appeared to be two men in dark suits, wearing sunglasses. He looked back at the winding road and wondered if they could be federal agents and if so, why would they be following him?

When he looked back again, he was startled to find they were now less than a car-length behind him. He could see the guy on the passenger side talking on a cell phone.

Johnnie pressed his foot harder on the accelerator and immediately felt the car's two-hundred-sixteen horses kick in. *These guys can't be Feds*, he thought. He glanced back again and saw he had widened the gap. At the same time, he noticed the passenger had his arms extended upward and was loading what appeared to be some type of automatic weapon.

Johnnie sank lower in his seat while reaching up to adjust the rearview mirror. He wasn't certain what he was going to do. Because he was familiar with this rural stretch of road, he knew there wasn't anyplace to stop for help. It consisted only of twisting pavement, old guardrail, and sheer cliffs.

At least my car should handle the road better than their Lincoln, he thought. *I should be able to outrun them. Thank God the road is dry.*

He glanced in his mirror to find they were now about fifty yards behind him. The goon on the passenger side was hanging out the window.

Johnnie's body tensed when he heard the sound of bullets whizzing past. Either the guy was a terrible shot or he was intentionally trying not to hit him.

Johnnie reached over with his right hand and lifted his cell phone off the passenger seat. While trying to control the vehicle, he quickly punched in the recall number for his father. He tilted his head and placed the phone between his left shoulder and ear. He placed his free hand back on the steering wheel and tightened his grip. He got his father's voice mail and left a quick message. He then started pressing 911.

Ahead on the road he could see a sharp bend to the left. What he couldn't see was the fully-loaded logging truck that had just backed into the road around the curve.

He downshifted the Roadster and lightly touched the brake as he approached the turn. In his mirror he saw that his pursuers were a couple hundred yards behind him. When he shifted his focus back to the road, it was too late to stop.

He yanked the steering wheel hard to the left and stood on the brake. The car turned sideways and traveled under the trailer bed that was sitting lengthwise across the road. The windshield shattered as the vehicle spun completely around and Johnnie was instantly decapitated, his head landing in the passenger seat.

The car continued sideways through the guardrail and the engine roared as the Roadster sailed down the side of the mountain, into the rocky shore and crashing waves.

<4>

The repeated ringing of the telephone interrupted Joe's shower. *I must have forgotten to reset the answering machine after listening to the last message,* he thought. *Can't a guy even take a relaxing shower after a long workout?* He had biked for nearly an hour and then run hard for another forty-five minutes. He didn't want to interrupt the pulsating spray of hot water massaging his well-built, muscular shoulders and back.

"Crap," he groaned as he quickly turned off the water and blindly reached outside the white vinyl shower liner and curtain. He grasped a burgundy bath sheet from the porcelain bar and dried his face. He wrapped the towel around his trim waist and slid back the curtain as he stepped outside the shower. Almost immediately he created a puddle on the cold, white ceramic tile floor.

He hurried his dripping body into the bedroom and across the carpet toward the pine nightstand where the phone continued to ring loudly.

He sat on the queen-size bed and picked up the handset. He caught it as it slipped from his wet hand, then held it to his ear and clumsily said, "This is Hara."

When Joe heard the voice of Frank Buchanan, his former LAPD police chief, his eyebrows raised. They hadn't spoken in several months and Joe wondered why he'd be calling.

As the chief began to speak, Joe appraised himself in the mirror above the nightstand. Through dark brown eyes he admired his handsome Japanese-American features and yellow-tan complexion. He was good looking and at forty-seven years old, still turned the ladies' heads even though his short, coal-black hair was graying over the temples. He ran his right hand through the crew cut, spraying water droplets onto the nightstand. He wiped away the moisture with the side of his right fist.

"Joe, I need to ask a big favor of you."

"Sure, Frank, what can I do?"

"Well, I know you're retired now and primarily focusing on your triathlon competitions, but I could really use your help on a case."

Joe waited while the older man paused, then continued. "You see, Joe, I just flew back from the funeral of a very close personal friend. Do you know who Johnnie Perrino is?"

Joe thought for a moment. He'd heard something about his death just yesterday on the radio. He was one of the wealthiest, most eligible bachelors in the country. "He makes Perrino wines, doesn't he?"

"That's right. He and his father, Nicholas, ran the Perrino Winery up in Napa Valley. Nicholas and I grew up together just north of San Francisco, near Novato. We went to high school and college together and our families are close friends. Anyway, I watched Johnnie grow up. He was practically family, almost like a son to me. Carol and I were his godparents."

"What happened, Frank?" Joe interjected.

"The coroner said he ran his Mercedes Roadster under a flatbed hauling timber on Highway 1 just south of San Francisco. He was instantly decapitated."

Joe heard Frank's voice begin to crack. He scrunched his face at the gruesome thought and waited as Frank paused to take a deep breath.

"He was driving down here on Saturday to join me at a charity benefit for the city's underprivileged youth. Johnnie contributed to similar charities in the San Francisco area as well."

Joe heard a rustling noise on the other end of the line.

"Just a minute, Joe."

He could hear Frank blowing his nose in the background. He had never known the chief to get so emotional.

22

"Sorry, Joe. Anyway, after he passed under the truck, his car continued through the guardrail and over the cliff."

"I'm sorry, Frank. For you and your family. I know it has to be difficult, but I'm not certain I understand where I come in. What can I do to help?" Joe glanced down at the beige crush-resistant carpeting. There was a trail of watery footprints leading from the bathroom to the side of the bed where he was sitting. He smoothed out the prints closest to him with the underside of his right foot.

"You can help by finding out who killed him. This wasn't an accident. Johnnie was being chased by a couple of thugs. If the kid's head had ended up in the front seat any other way, I would swear this had ties to the mob."

"How do you know he was being chased?"

"Because Johnnie called his father while it was happening, and left a message on his voice mail just minutes before his death. The last thing he tried was to reach the California Highway Patrol, but died before he could get through. Nicholas asked me at the funeral if I knew of anybody who could find Johnnie's killers. I told him, 'Only the best homicide detective the LAPD has ever had.'

"So, can you help me, Joe? Nicholas Perrino will pay any amount of money, plus all your expenses. No cost is too much."

Joe didn't hesitate. "Anything for the Buchanan family, Frank. You know that."

"Thanks, Joe. You don't know how much this means to me. I know you'll get these guys. You always do."

Frank knew that Joe, as a detective on the Homicide Task Force, had personally investigated close to four hundred murders in a period of about fifteen years and cleared over ninety percent of them. Joe Hara was truly the elite of the elite.

"When can you get down here? I'll give you everything we've got and put you in contact with the folks up north who are heading up the investigation."

Joe looked at the large, round alarm clock with two large chrome bells on the nightstand in front of him: 4 P.M. With late afternoon traffic, he could possibly get to the precinct in about an hour.

"If I leave now, I can probably be there by five."

"That's great. I'll get everything together and be ready to brief you when you get here."

"Okay then. See you in a bit, Frank."

He hung up the phone and continued to sit on the edge of the bed. He stretched out his right leg and smoothed another footprint in the carpet. He wondered if he would ever get to enjoy his retirement. He had only been off the force for six months and was already involved in his second case.

Granted he had literally stumbled into the first one. He was just in the wrong place at the wrong time. Actually, when he thought about it, it was more like the right place at the right time. His involvement led to the overthrow of a small faction in the Japanese military.

He knew this case couldn't be nearly as involved and he'd be back to his retirement in no time. Besides, he had Boston to keep training for in three weeks and an age group title to defend this October in Hawaii at the annual Ironman World Triathlon.

He rose from the bed and quickly got dressed.

<5>

Joe sat in the old wooden chair beside Frank Buchanan's cluttered desk. Like he had done so many times before, he looked at the assortment of pictures in metal and wooden frames. There was a photo of Frank's silver-haired wife, Carol, a picture of their two gorgeous daughters alongside their handsome husbands, and another of the four beautiful granddaughters.

He glanced around at the organized clutter from thirty-five years of service with the LAPD. Most of Frank's furniture was old, but occasionally he'd add a new piece. Joe noticed a yellow, four-drawer horizontal file behind the desk.

"New filing cabinet, Frank?"

The chief snickered. "Yeah, it only took a year to get. They gave me the same old bureaucratic gobbledygook every time I asked where it was."

Frank was sitting behind the desk in a worn-out brown leather chair, looking through a manila file folder. He was a big man who stood about six feet, four inches tall and weighed close to two hundred thirty pounds. He was dressed in a black suit with light pinstripes and was wearing a white button-down dress shirt and black tie with small white dots. His full head of snow-white hair accentuated the leathery features of his mature, tanned face. He was fifteen years older than Joe and had been on the force ten years longer. Pushing thirty-five years with the LAPD, he would retire at the end of the year.

Even though Frank was considerably older, the two were a lot alike, with an unending passion for the force. They both loved the challenge of solving a murder and the thrill of the hunt.

The biggest difference Joe could see was that he needed to be more hands on; he could never have been chief of police. He wasn't good at delegating authority. He needed to be in control of the situation and couldn't just sit back and wait for someone else to do the job. Frank had that ability, Joe didn't.

That's why Joe liked competing in triathlons so much. It was an individual sport where he could control his destiny.

Frank placed the open file on the desk. "Here's what we've got to go on."

Joe sat and listened intently as Frank handed him a photograph of Johnnie.

"Johnnie called Nicholas from his car phone during the last moments of the pursuit. He got his father's voice mail and left a brief but distressed message. He said a black Lincoln Continental Town Car with two guys wearing dark suits and sunglasses was chasing him. He couldn't make out the license number, but said they were California plates.

"They were discharging some type of automatic weapon around him. You can hear it on the recording in the background, the crackling repetition of the weapon, as it's being fired. He asked his father if he knew of anybody who would want to kill him, then said he thought he could shake them and would call again when he felt he was safe.

"He apparently punched 911 just before colliding with the truck. The California Highway Patrol found it saved in his cell phone's memory."

"What did the truck driver say?" Joe asked. "Did he see the black Lincoln that was chasing Johnnie?"

"The truck driver was pretty shaken. He was a young man in his late twenties. He witnessed the whole thing through his side view mirror. He'd never seen anything like it in his life. Hell, most people never have, for that matter."

Joe noticed Frank's bright blue eyes tear up slightly before he rose from his chair and turned to look out the window.

Frank continued speaking, his back to Joe. "It was the young driver's first time at that logging facility, so he had never backed into the road before. There was a turnaround further back down the road, but the recent rains made it impossible for him to use it.

"It wasn't his fault. There are signs posted along Highway 1 coming from either direction saying to watch out for trucks entering the roadway. There's a reduced speed limit of twenty-five miles an hour for that very reason. Supposedly, even when the trucks pull out forward, they still sometimes cross the double yellow lines as they maneuver themselves onto the roadway.

"It wasn't the kid's fault. I feel bad for him." Frank released a heavy sigh, his eyes focused on the landscape.

Joe sat patiently and waited. He knew this was hard for the chief.

"The highway patrol determined Johnnie must have been going close to sixty when he came around the curve. They said if Johnnie had been doing the posted speed limit, he would have had plenty of time to stop."

Frank turned around and sat down at his desk. "To finally answer your question, Joe, no. The kid didn't see the black Lincoln. He was in shock when the police arrived. Apparently, another motorist coming from the south stopped to see what happened. He's the one that called them. He didn't see anything either.

"After Nicholas played back the voice mail for the local authorities, they went back and searched the roadway for shell casings from the weapon, but didn't turn up anything. They also looked in the nearby wooden guardrail posts and road signs to see if any bullets had become lodged during the shooting. They even checked Johnnie's car, but couldn't find evidence of bullets there either."

"When exactly did Nicholas play the recording for the police?"

"It was probably early that evening, sometime just before dark. Because of that, they didn't send anybody out to look until the following morning."

"So somebody could have gone out there later that afternoon or evening and picked up any shell casings that might have been lying around," Joe commented.

"Yeah, I guess that's always a possibility."

"Okay. So what else do you have?"

"Well, police up in the Valley contacted Johnnie's phone service provider and got a printout of his most recent calls. The only thing that appears unusual is that he seems to have spent most of late Friday afternoon and early evening on the telephone with several people from QCI."

"What's QCI?"

"One of the largest fractional jet ownership companies in the world. As Nicholas explained it to me, they have a program called StratoShares that sells companies and high net worth individuals a fraction of an airplane, then guarantees them access to an entire fleet virtually anywhere, anytime. All the owners do is pay a percentage of the operating expenses proportional to the share size they own.

"Nicholas said they've been in the program for several years now and he's never really had any problems. On the other hand, he stated that Johnnie was always having problems. So much so, that he was apparently very vocal on Friday night and threatened to leave the program. That's why he was driving to L.A. He didn't want the hassle of trying to get their StratoShares plane."

"So you think this QCI might have something to do with Johnnie's death?"

"Nicholas didn't know of anybody that would want to hurt Johnnie. The young man had never been in trouble his entire life. It's a mystery to us all."

"Hmm. Well, I have to allow my judgment to be slanted by recent events and that would involve his conversations with QCI the day before."

"I have to tell you, Joe. QCI is owned by William Price and run by Tony Folino, the great entrepreneur and media mogul."

Joe raised his eyebrows in surprise as the chief continued.

"We're not actually certain if he spoke to the chairman or not. He placed several calls to Folino's office and there was one rather lengthy call to his direct line. That could have been a voice mail, though. We don't know for sure.

"Anyway, the police in Napa Valley called QCI and left a message with Folino's secretary. A guy named Ross Nickels called them back. He's their chief marketing executive or something. He said Folino was out of the country and doubted Tony had even checked his voice mail."

"Do you believe this Nickels guy?"

"We've got no reason not to."

"And you said William Price, huh? That guy's an investment genius. Then add Tony Folino to the mix." Joe thought a moment, then said, "That's gotta be a lot of money."

"That's a lot of political clout," Frank replied. "You need to be careful and remember the type of people we might be dealing with here. You know, I just remembered something else," he added. "If my memory serves me right, my friend Max Wells told me he uses StratoShares to supplement the airplane they use to transport their Hollywood bigwigs around. He's the chief pilot for Adventure Studios."

"So what's your idea, Frank?"

He handed Joe a seven- by ten-inch black and white advertisement that appeared to have been torn from a *World Business Gazette*.

"I've seen these ads before," Joe commented. "There are a whole bunch of companies doing this sort of thing."

"There's an 800 number on that ad," Frank pointed out. "I want you to give them a call and request some information on their company and services. That's what Nicholas did when he first looked at the program.

"He said they'll send you a marketing packet of information. I'd call as soon as possible and have them overnight it if they can. After you familiarize yourself, you should give them a call and see if they'll bring you into their facility for a tour. Nicholas said they sometimes give demonstration flights at no charge, especially if you're coming to see their operations facility."

"And under what guise would I be doing this?"

"I thought maybe you could say you had a private investigation agency based in Los Angeles and you needed a private jet for your travels."

Joe raised his eyebrows. "Hmm, that might work. I could also say I have a second home and family in Hawaii and travel internationally for triathlon competitions."

Joe's great-grandfather had come to Hawaii in 1885 along with seventy thousand other Japanese when Hawaii's king signed a treaty with Japan allowing large-scale immigration. Joe's nearest living relative was his grandfather, who lived on his family's land on the Island of Oahu.

Frank's phone rang. "Excuse me a minute, Joe." He picked it up. "This is Buch. Yeah. Uh-huh. No shit? Really? What a dumb fuck! Will she testify to that in court? Okay. Well, call me back if you get anything else. Yep, sure." Frank put the phone down. "You gotta love interrogations. Don't you miss them, Joe? Don't you miss everything—the stakeouts, the canvasses, all that stuff?"

Joe shook his head. "No, not yet. I guess I haven't been away long enough." He laughed as he thought about the question some more.

He really didn't miss it. You'd think that after having ate, drank and slept the LAPD for twenty-five years, he would be going through some type of withdrawal. But that wasn't the case. Part of the reason might be because even though he had been retired for six months, he still somehow managed to be involved in a case.

Frank said, "So where were we? Oh yeah, I remember. Your cover. Anyway, we need you to look into QCI's program and maybe even join it to find out everything you can. I'll free you up some help on this end. I'll make Froberg available."

Daniel Froberg had been Joe's partner during his last ten years on the force. Joe was a fifteen-year veteran when they paired Froberg with him. Daniel had only been on the force four years, but the department had high hopes for him.

Together they looked like "the odd couple." Joe was about five-feet-ten, short, thick, and muscular with coal-black burr-cut hair. He was always neatly groomed and overly conscious of his appearance. His mother had always told him he was worse than a girl.

Danny, on the other hand, was ten years younger than Joe. He stood a lanky six-foot-six and had windblown, curly blond hair. Dan, who never particularly cared about his appearance, was very fair compared to Joe's dark, tawny complexion.

As partners they complemented each other and made a great team. They were practically brothers now.

"Where is Danny today?" Joe asked.

"He's here. That was him who just called a couple minutes ago. He's been interrogating a couple of murder suspects for the past two hours. The guy's Latino wife finally cracked. Says she saw the whole thing. Her husband knocked off the mother-in-law. She says he hit her in the head with a cast iron skillet, then dumped her body in an abandoned cistern behind their garage. She didn't tell anybody because she was afraid he would do the same to her. Can you believe that? What kooks!"

Joe grinned as the chief shrugged his shoulders.

"Anyway, back to QCI. The police in the Valley have launched an investigation. Nicholas will give them your name. You should find them most helpful if you need assistance on that end. And don't hesitate to call me for anything. So, I guess that's about it. I know it's not much to go on, but you've worked with less."

"You'll brief Danny?"

"Absolutely."

"Then do me a favor and ask him to have somebody start researching Folino and Price's family histories. Let's see if we can find any skeletons in their closets."

"Okay, but I seriously doubt they'll find anything. You don't become a couple of the wealthiest men in the country and not live your life under a microscope. Kind of like the President of the United States."

"You may be right, but we'll still give it a try. Also see if we can get somebody to check out that stretch of Highway

1 about one hundred to five hundred yards north of where Johnnie collided with the truck. If he was being chased on that two-lane stretch of highway with that guardrail all around, there probably isn't anywhere they could quickly turn a large Lincoln around without putting a couple tires off the road. I know it's a long shot, but with all the recent rain there might be some tire tracks we can trace."

"It's done."

"Oh, and one more thing, Frank," Joe said as he got up. "Why don't you or Danny give your friend a call. What's his name—Max Wells?"

Frank nodded.

"Give him a call or go out and see him. Find out how long they've been in the program and what their experience has been with StratoShares."

Joe looked again at the advertisement in his hand. "I'll call this number right now. Tell Danny I'll give him a ring in a day or so to see what he's found. And I'll keep you posted."

"Thanks, Joe. I can't tell you how much this means to me."

Joe reached across the desk and shook Frank's large hand. The chief came around the corner of the desk and with his left hand, patted Joe's right shoulder a couple times.

Joe turned and left the office. He stopped in the boisterous squad room to use the phone at a vacant desk. He looked around at the room filled with white and gold shields and noticed many familiar faces along with several new ones. He acknowledged the numerous friendly hellos and banter.

Everything appeared pretty much the same. It was crowded and noisy, as usual, with both uniformed and plainclothes police officers moving about exchanging files and information. He was sure the cases were probably the same, just the names and faces were different. He'd probably seen it all although he had to admit, the one Frank just told him about, the guy killing his mother-in-law with the skillet, was a first.

The desk area in front of Joe looked like all the rest, with standard issue computer stuff, except to the side was an old manual typewriter on a wooden cart. The metal desk had a brown fluorescent lamp with flexible post and two stacked plastic trays marked IN and OUT set on the front right-hand corner. The pencils, all with worn erasers, and pens were crammed in a tin can-shaped holder, alongside a plastic Rolodex and several personal items that included a Dodgers autographed baseball.

He lifted a large, thick pen from the can. It was transparent and filled with liquid. He looked at the young lady inside, sunbathing in a scanty pink bikini on a California beach. He turned the pen upside down and her bikini fell off. He turned it back over and she was clothed again. Joe shook his head and smiled. He hadn't seen one of these since he was a kid.

He punched in the number to StratoShares. The phone rang twice, then a recording came on saying the phone call may be monitored to insure quality customer service. It rang a couple times before a young man answered.

"StratoShares marketing, this is Jeff. Can I help you?"

"Yes, I'd like some information on your program." Joe rolled the wooden chair closer to the desk as he pressed the silver button on the pen and readied himself to write.

As the young man spoke, Joe quickly became transfixed in the conversation.

6

Joe drove past several airplane hangars and fixed base operators, or FBOs, as the pilots called them. An FBO was a facility where passengers could arrive and depart on their private jets. The services they provided for both passengers and pilots typically included activities such as aircraft refueling, catering, pilot and passenger lounges, briefing areas, maintenance areas, conference rooms, rental cars, classrooms for flying schools, offices and so forth. They were usually located on the other side of an airport, away from the main terminal and the commercial carriers. The passengers could then comfortably get in and out in a matter of minutes. It was the only way to travel.

After speaking to security, he parked his Lexus LS 430 in the gated parking lot just outside Callahan Aviation at Los Angeles Van Nuys Airport. He guessed he probably could have flown out of Santa Monica Municipal Airport which was much closer to his home, but when the customer service representative at StratoShares asked if there was an FBO he preferred, Callahan was the only one that came to mind. He had flown in and out of there several times before.

The department had chartered a plane for him on two other occasions while he was working a couple cases. The other time was when he was being wined and dined by a large sportswear manufacturer. Since he was a world-class triathlete, they had wanted him to wear their product line as well as be a spokesperson.

He removed his luggage from the trunk, and then activated the car's security system. He crossed the pavement of the circular drop-off area. He could hear and see several aircraft towering above the black wrought iron fence that separated the terminal apron from the access road and automobile area. He proceeded toward the large white two-story hacienda-style building topped by an attractive clay tile roof.

He placed his baggage just inside the double glass doors and glanced around the large waiting area. The room had warmth about it with its wood-beam ceiling, ceramic tile floor, wood-burning fireplace, and Santa Fe décor.

He noticed a couple pilots talking together as well as several passengers sitting on sofas in the lounge. He approached a young woman with Asian features standing behind the counter.

"Hi, I'm Joe Hara. I'm here to catch a StratoShares plane. We're going to New Jersey."

"Yes sir, Mr. Hara," the young woman said. "Your pilots are right over there. I think they're ready to go."

"Thank you," he replied as he turned and walked toward the two young pilots. They were dressed in navy blue blazers, white dress shirts, dark blue ties with gold aircraft tie clips, and khaki pants. They abruptly ended their conversation when they noticed him headed in their direction.

"Mr. Hara?" the sandy-haired pilot asked.

"Yes, but just call me Joe," he stated as he reached out and shook the pilot's hand.

"Hi, Joe. I'm Randy Weber. I'll be your captain on today's flight and this is my first officer, Donnie Folino."

Joe turned toward the dark-haired, muddy-complexioned young man. He held out his hand. "I'm pleased to meet you. Any relation to Tony Folino?"

"Why, yes sir, Mr. Hara. He's my uncle."

"Oh, so this is a family business?" Joe chuckled.

"I guess you could say that, Mr. Hara," the young man replied with a smile.

"Please," he said with a laugh, "call me Joe. Mr. Hara is my father."

"Well, if you're ready to go, Joe, the plane is waiting," stated Randy. "Do you have any additional bags other than your briefcase and duffel?" His eyes shifted their focus toward the two bags closest to Joe.

"Yes, as a matter of fact, I do. I also have a soft-sided suitcase and my bike box. I left them over there by the door," he said with a nod.

Because he was a triathlete he would always bring his bike with him so he didn't miss a workout. He transported it in a special bike box to make sure it didn't get damaged. His was a Trico Iron Case box. It had a Triconium shell that was cocooned in three layers of foam. The box was bulletproof and very light, only weighing about thirty-one pounds. It wasn't the most expensive bike box on the market, but it had worked well for him on his travels.

Randy said, "I'll get your stuff, then we'll rock and roll."

Donnie reached out to take the black duffel from Joe. "Here, let me get that for you."

Joe followed both pilots as they walked through another set of wood and glass doors and exited onto the executive terminal ramp where the roar of various aircraft engines greeted them. He looked around in amazement. Although he wasn't an authority on jet aircraft, he did take a passing interest in them. He had taken several private lessons as a young man and knew just enough to be dangerous.

It was 7:45 A.M. and there was a bustle of activity on the ramp. Joe noticed a half-dozen aircraft being prepared for morning departures. Several pilots were doing a walk around their aircraft and other preflight preparations. Another pilot was moving back and forth between the cargo compartments of the nose and tail of one long, slender aircraft. He had at least six bags of golf clubs and ten bags of luggage scattered across the ramp. The pilot stopped and stood scratching his head as he tried to figure out how to make it all fit.

An Exxon tanker truck had just finished fueling a similar looking aircraft and its driver was busy disconnecting the grounding cables. Joe noticed a large Gulfstream aircraft with its trademark oval windows taxiing into the area as they briskly continued walking toward their aircraft.

He could see the plane sitting on the ramp directly in front of them. The Citation X was a magnificent machine, the fastest business jet in the world that could reach speeds of .92 mach. When he received StratoShares' marketing material, he had called and spoken to the chief marketing executive Ross Nickels. His business card had been in the packet.

After they spoke for a half-hour, Ross determined that a combination of aircraft was the best match for him. Joe had told him he frequently traveled from L.A. to New York and Hawaii, as well as internationally. The executive recommended the Citation X and Falcon 900EX as the best aircraft for his missions.

Ross extended an invitation to come to New Jersey and take a tour of their operations facility. Joe gladly accepted and was going to demo the Citation X today, then return on the Falcon later in the week.

Both pilots stopped and stood on each side of the aircraft stairs. Randy made a sweeping gesture with his right hand and motioned for Joe to climb aboard.

"Thank you," he replied, and proceeded up the five steps. He bent down as he stepped through the door and into the 5'7" stand-up cabin. Once inside, he still had to stoop a little to keep from hitting his head.

He looked down the short, narrow aisle of the metal fuselage and was hit with a sudden anxiety attack. Memories of his last trip on a business aircraft came rushing back. Although it had been five months earlier, he would have preferred to forget it.

He had been flying from Hawaii to Los Angeles on the aircraft of a major sportswear manufacturer. The huge Japanese company had approached him after he won his age group of the Ironman Triathlon, saying they would like him for a spokesperson. They supposedly wanted to seize the moment and have him do a television commercial endorsing their products. Since he was already wearing their line of apparel, he figured, why not.

So, after speaking with his attorney by phone, he agreed to the arrangement. The following day found him flying back to Los Angeles for the commercial shoot. The Challenger

601 aircraft was beginning its descent from about 41,000 feet when at 30,000 feet the cabin started to lose pressurization. Joe's oxygen mask didn't deploy and neither did the captain's. Luckily, though, the copilot's did.

Joe was eventually able to break loose the cover on the ceiling panel and release the oxygen mask above his seat. The copilot immediately extended the spoilers and landing gear and began an emergency descent. In less than two minutes they were down to 15,000 feet, a survivable altitude. Had the process taken a second or two longer, though, the consequences could have been severe.

Though the copilot had quickly gotten the aircraft to a safe altitude where they could breathe without the assistance of masks, Joe always wondered if the incident had been an accident or an attempt on his life.

His thoughts were interrupted by the captain's voice behind him. "Is something the matter, Joe?"

He quickly perked up. "Oh, no, Randy. I was just admiring the magnificent cabin."

"So you like it, then? It is nice, isn't it?" asked the forty-something captain.

"All the comforts of home," he replied as he sat down in one of the tan leather seats facing forward. He slid the seat out and away from the fuselage wall, raised the soft armrest, and reclined the seat backwards a couple inches.

After Joe was comfortable, the captain went through the safety features of the aircraft, explaining everything from the location and operation of the seat belts and shoulder harnesses to the use of oxygen masks in case of depressurization.

He found himself thinking, *Been there, done that.*

Randy continued with the life vests, fire extinguisher, and exit doors. Joe nodded his head in acknowledgment, all the while thinking how miserable it was to always start flights in this manner. Nothing like being reminded of all the possible things that could go wrong during your flight, with each one as horrible as the previous.

"Well, make yourself comfortable, Joe."

That's easy for you to say, he thought.

"If you get thirsty or hungry, you can find everything you need in the refreshment center up front, just behind us. If nature calls, the lavatory is behind you in the tail of the plane. It has a sliding door for privacy as well as a sink and vanity. We'll have about a hundred-knot tailwind, so we should be into Newark in about four hours."

"Thanks, I'm sure I'll be fine."

He glanced out the window at the thin, wispy cirrus clouds hanging high in the sky. He understood about the winds from the flight lessons he'd had. Going east you would typically have a tailwind behind you, causing your flight time to be faster. But going west you were flying the nose of the plane into the wind, almost always causing travel to be slower.

"We'll keep you updated en route, but if you have questions, just pop your head in the cockpit. We'll be on our way in just a few."

Randy turned around and after closing and securing the cabin door, joined Donnie who was already busy in the cockpit with several last-minute preflight preparations.

Joe glanced up at the beige ultra-suede ceiling and reached out to push gently on the panel where the oxygen mask was stored. *I hope I don't ever have to see you again,* he thought.

He fastened his seat belt into the gold-plated clasp and pulled the shoulder harness down, connecting it so it fit snugly across his broad chest. He shifted his body and pushed himself deeper into the soft leather seats, trying to relax and make himself more comfortable.

He still found it hard to believe he was about to fly on an airplane that was possibly owned by Hollywood celebrities, high-ticket sports athletes, and the wealthiest people in corporate America.

He reached across the aisle and lifted the day's *World Business Gazette* off the adjacent seat. He noticed a headline on the front page under the "Top News" section. There was a short paragraph about Johnnie Perrino's tragic death, with a page number for the article inside.

He looked up the aisle toward the cockpit. The door panels were slid open and he could see inside. He watched as the pilots started the engines and after several more checks of the instruments, began rolling toward the taxiway. He could hear Randy communicating with the control tower as they were cleared for immediate departure on runway three four left.

Joe was familiar with runways from his flying lessons. The three four indicated the approach direction of the runway in relation to magnetic north and was rounded off to the nearest ten degrees. The "L" indicated left for parallel runways. Since the winds were predominately out of the northwest and airplanes almost always take off and land into the wind, their departure route made perfect sense to him.

The plane moved onto the active runway as they pointed the aircraft to the north and aligned it with the dashed white center line. The engines started their forceful roar as the pilots applied full power and began the takeoff roll.

Their speed continued to increase as Joe was immediately pushed farther back into the soft Italian leather. The two powerful Allison engines hurled them forward down the length of the runway. As the plane lifted from the ground, he tried to relax by closing his eyes.

Though he was nervous and anxious about the flight, he was also excited. He thought of Captain Randy Weber's earlier comment, "We'll rock and roll," and that's exactly what they did.

<7>

Joe bent down as he exited the aircraft cabin door and went down the stairs into the bright afternoon sunlight. Just like Van Nuys, the ramp at Newark was a bustle of activity as aircraft were busily being readied to return passengers home from another day of work in the City.

The flight was uneventful and had taken about four hours, just as Randy had said. During that time, Joe read the story in the *Gazette* about Johnnie's death, an article about Tony Folino's company, and a story on fractional ownership in an old aviation magazine.

He then spent the rest of the flight perusing the Strato-Shares marketing packet that Ross Nichols had sent him. He had reviewed the financials of the different aircraft the day before and was surprised at the pricing. Even the smallest share in the smallest airplane would initially cost an owner close to half a million dollars just to acquire the asset. Then a person had to pay roughly another $150,000 annually just to cover the operating expenses.

He even glanced at some of their competitors' packets. He found it very odd that after his initial phone call and Internet request for information, he also received a plethora of marketing materials from other companies doing the same thing. It appeared to him that StratoShares might have a leak within their company. He thought he should probably mention the possibility to Ross Nickels.

Randy had joined him in the cabin about halfway through the flight. He asked Joe questions regarding his travel profile, specifically his destinations and their frequency, the number of passengers, and amount of baggage he would typically carry. Joe got the distinct impression Randy was assisting somebody in the qualification process.

Upon reaching the bottom of the steps, he once again stepped onto a red-carpeted runner where Randy and Donnie simultaneously welcomed, then thanked him.

"I hope your flight was good?" Donnie asked.

"Everything was great," replied Joe.

He noticed an overweight young man with blond hair dressed in a hunter green StratoShares windbreaker and beige Dockers standing alongside the pilots, holding Joe's duffel bag. Another man was loading his luggage and bike box onto the back of a golf cart.

"Well then, at this point I would like to turn you over to our Director of Tours and a good friend of mine, Travis McGee."

Travis held out his plump right hand. "Welcome, Mr. Hara!"

Joe noticed only the slightest hint of a New Jersey accent with a predominantly Southern dialect.

He reached out with a strong grip and vigorously shook the young man's hand. He firmly believed in an energetic handshake; after all, handshaking was a masculine activity and a way to silently display competitive power. The kid's handshake felt soft and clammy.

"Travis McGee, like the John D. MacDonald detective?" Joe asked. He had read several of the late author's books.

"Yeah, my mom was a big fan. She named me after him."

"It's nice to meet you, Travis. You can call me Joe."

He continued to assess the young Mr. McGee, who in no way resembled MacDonald's sexy, fearless adventurer. Joe thought the kid looked no older than his mid-twenties. He was short and chubby with the complexion of someone who suffered from acne; not at all the type of person Joe thought a company the stature of StratoShares would want to leave with the responsibility of that all-important first impression.

Travis turned to Donnie and said, "Give me a call when your tour is over. We'll go hang out in the City."

"Sure thing, Travis."

Travis then turned and started to walk toward the facility. Joe raised his right hand to say farewell. "Thanks again, gentlemen."

As they walked toward the building, Joe began the conversation. "So, how long have you worked for Strato-Shares?"

"About nine months now."

"Where did you go to school?"

"University of Tennessee," replied Travis. "My major was marketing."

"So you're a volunteer, are you?" Joe ribbed.

"No, they pay me to do this," he said, then laughed at his own joke. It was a fake-sounding laugh, much like the young man's personality. Joe wanted to reply with his best Three Stooges impersonation as he heard himself saying inside his head, *Oh, a wise guy* ... but figured, *why bother— this kid probably doesn't even know who the Three Stooges were.*

He looked in the direction they were headed. It was the first time he noticed the building. It was the largest structure on this side of the airport compared to all the other hangars and buildings. The front had a sloping glass roof that descended from the fourth floor to the second. Its all-glass façade was glistening in the bright afternoon sun and looked like a large greenhouse.

It was a known fact that both Tony Folino and Bill Price had very deep pockets. This building was a prime example, as they had spared no expense constructing it.

"Let me tell you a little bit about the history of our company, Mr. Hara."

The kid proceeded with his memorized spiel and in just a few moments, Joe could tell that his first impression was accurate. The kid was a bullshitter. *He should be selling used cars, not airplanes,* he thought. Joe wished he had brought his boots because it was getting deep, quick. He couldn't help but think it was going to be a long afternoon.

He shifted his focus back to the facility. Travis continued speaking as they walked off the ramp and through the automatic glass doors.

"It's a state-of-the-art facility with all the latest and greatest technology. The hangar area and attached four-story structure measure approximately 400,000 square feet."

"Is Tony Folino's office located here?" Joe asked.

"No, Tony's office is in Manhattan. Everybody else, with the exception of the pilots, is located here."

Joe couldn't help but notice the way the kid used Folino's first name, like they were best friends. He suppressed his amusement and continued to probe. "So, where are the pilots located?"

"They reside anywhere they want. They just have to be able to report to their aircraft when needed. Since they know their schedules a month in advance, it's never a problem."

"How do they know their schedules that far in advance? I thought the whole point of this program was the fact a person could call with as little as a few hours' notice and get their airplane."

"It is and they can. What I meant is that at least they know what days they will be working, not necessarily where they will be going."

"Is that typical of the other fractional ownership programs? I mean, are their pilots also located all over the country?"

"I'm not really certain," Travis replied. "So, what does your company do, Mr. Hara? Ross told me a little and asked me to send his apologies for not being able to join us today."

"Well, I'm primarily a one-man operation. I was on the LAPD for twenty-five years, with twenty of those as a homicide detective. I now run a private investigation firm back in L.A. Most of the travel would be for me, but I'll occasionally hire someone from elsewhere in the country to assist with an investigation. Sometimes I take care of their travel."

He raised his voice as a nearby aircraft's engines roared. "I have a home in Los Angeles and a second home and family in Oahu. I also compete internationally in numerous marathons and triathlon events."

Travis interrupted, saying, "Ross was telling me you won the Ironman last year."

"Not quite, but he's sort of correct. I won my age group." Joe smiled.

"Wow, that's, like, really incredible. I tried running in high school, but was never very good at it. Physical education wasn't my strongest subject. My father could never understand," he said with a frown, "but Mom was always supportive."

Joe silently grinned. Somehow it didn't surprise him. He could see Travis participating in organizations like the chess team and computer club. *Hell, the kid probably has a plastic pocket protector under his windbreaker.*

As they stepped into the building's large atrium, his face felt a sudden blast of warm, moist air. He was immediately awestruck at the sight. The atrium resembled a jungle or rainforest with thousands of tropical plants and trees, some climbing nearly three stories in height. He squinted up at the glass-paneled sloping ceiling that was allowing the sunshine to radiate on the plants below. In addition there were several small ponds with rocks and a couple miniature waterfalls intermingled within the vegetation.

He noticed a woman in a white knit polo shirt and brown khakis on a small wooden stepladder, tending to several trees and shrubs. She was obviously some type of horticulturist. Her services and expertise were no doubt needed since there appeared to be every type of plant imaginable. He admired the ivory-white-veined and glossy, dark green leaves of a cluster of zebra plants. He could identify weeping figs of varying sizes scattered about. There were numerous rubber plants, paradise palms, and polka dot plants with their deep olive green and pink freckle foliage.

He also noticed several exotic birds amongst the thick foliage. He pointed to one with vibrant green feathers and a long tail sitting in a tree.

"What type of bird is that?" he asked.

"That's a quetzal. It's a rare perching bird usually found in tropical rainforests from Mexico to Costa Rica."

"I thought quetzal was a form of money," Joe queried.

"It is," Travis said, "but it's also the national bird of Guatemala and what they call their currency."

Joe's eyes were suddenly drawn to a bird with smooth, brilliantly colored reddish orange feathers. They were accented by its dark, perfectly round eyes and curved, long and narrow orange-yellow beak. Its long black back and tail feathers gave it the appearance it was wearing a cape. He immediately recognized it as an endangered Hawaiian 'I'iwi.

The only reason he was familiar with it was because he had grown up on the islands where the 'I'iwi was often referred to in ancient Hawaiian chants and its feathers were used in Hawaiian capes and feather work. In addition several years back, *National Geographic* had placed the bird on the cover of their magazine with the headline of "Hawaii's Vanishing Species."

He knew there were laws protecting endangered species and wondered if Folino was abiding by them. "So, what's with all the birds?" he asked.

"Tony is an avid ornithologist. He collects them from his travels around the globe. I guess it has something to do with the theory of flight. He just seems to have a fascination with things that fly."

Again the kid called the chairman by his first name. Joe looked down at the gray slate tile floor made to resemble stone, then around at the several sitting areas. There were large brown leather sofas with rustic-looking end tables and coffee tables. The lobby looked like a Disney resort, except more tastefully and elegantly decorated.

In the middle of the room, behind a half-circle reception desk was a wide-open double-spiral staircase that rose to the upper floors while encircling a glass elevator. The young woman sitting behind the desk had long blonde hair, obviously enhanced with bottled color, and was chewing gum like a cow chews its cud.

Travis placed Joe's duffel bag in the cabinet behind the reception counter. While he had the door open, he asked, "Would you like to leave your briefcase here too?"

"That would be fine." Joe handed over his attaché.

Travis locked the door and dropped the key in his pants pocket.

"What about my other suitcase and bike?"

"Jim is carrying everything inside right now and Tiffany here will keep an eye on it for you. Oh, Mr. Hara, this is Tiffany, our receptionist."

Joe decided he wasn't going to insist Travis call him Joe because he didn't particularly care for the kid.

Tiffany held out her right hand tipped with long, maroon fingernails, obviously artificial. "Pleased to meet you, Mr. Hara."

The nasal pitch and tone of her voice left no doubt in Joe's mind she had been born and raised in New Jersey.

He politely shook her hand. "Nice to meet you too."

"Do you want to take the stairs or the elevator, Mr. Hara?" Travis asked.

He noticed the way Travis pronounced "stairs." It sounded more like "steers."

"Let's take the stairs. I could use the exercise. I've been stationary long enough."

As they climbed the open stairwell and spiraled the all-glass elevator to the fourth floor, Travis once again started the sales pitch in his annoying mix of New Jersey and Tennessee dialect.

"What you are about to see, Mr. Hara, is our customer service area. Have you ever been on the trading floor of the New York Stock Exchange?"

"No, I can't say that I have, but obviously I've seen pictures of it."

As they reached the top steps, he could feel the temperature turn several degrees warmer as the heat rose to the higher level, closer to the sloping glass ceiling. He glanced back over his shoulder at the treetops and plants below. It was a spectacular atrium.

They crossed the white and gray marbleized tile floor of the hallway as Travis opened the door. The din of the room instantly drowned out the sound of the waterfalls behind them. They stepped inside as Travis pulled the door closed.

Joe was impressed yet again. It was like the stock exchange, only smaller. There must have been at least four hundred people on the floor where telephones were ringing and customer service representatives were shouting to each other.

Travis could see the surprise on his face. "Welcome to StratoShares, Mr. Hara," he said, chuckling.

He led Joe around the outer edge on the right side of the room. They walked along the glass wall as Travis pointed to the outside ramp below. Joe counted twelve aircraft of several different shapes and sizes sitting on the ramp.

They walked the length of the room to the far end where the wall was glass from three feet above the floor to the ceiling. They looked out over a huge maintenance hangar where mechanics were working on everything from small Citation aircraft to larger Airbuses.

"You don't fly Concordes, do you?" he asked jokingly, assuming he already knew the answer.

"No, we don't. But we all joke that someday Tony will sell shares on the space shuttle."

Joe smiled as he quickly counted fifteen aircraft in the hangar, with room for several more. "How many airplanes does StratoShares have?"

Joe turned back and looked down the length of the room. It was brightly illuminated by fluorescent lighting recessed in the ten-foot ceiling. Several clocks on the far wall where they had entered showed the different times across the globe.

"I think the fleet presently consists of around seven hundred and fifty aircraft with about five hundred more on order from several manufacturers. I'd have to check because the number changes a couple times a week. We take delivery of a new or used aircraft on average about every three or four days."

"That's incredible," Joe commented. "Are they all jets?"

"Mostly all, with the exception of a couple regional programs down south in Texas and Florida, where we operate smaller turbo-prop aircraft and several helicopters."

"Why are the turbo-props and helicopters only regional?"

"Because of their shorter flying range, it would be logistically impossible to guarantee response times similar to those of the jets. They just don't have the range or speed. It would require an extremely large fleet and the cost to operate them would be tremendous."

"I see. Well, about how many owners are there in the program?"

"Roughly, close to forty-five hundred owners. That's everywhere, not just in the United States."

"What types of people make up the majority of your owners?" Joe leaned on the short wall while looking down into the maintenance area.

"Over half the owners are private individuals with second or third homes located around the globe. Many of them use it primarily for their personal travel, not just for business."

Suddenly there was a buzz of activity behind them along the outer wall facing the ramp area. Many employees were gathered and looking down at something.

"What's going on?" Joe asked.

"I'm not sure. Let's go check it out," replied Travis.

Travis led the way and Joe followed. They looked outside. A large black Mercedes limousine was rolling to a stop on the ramp. The driver hopped out, walked to the back door and opened it for a large, burly man in a dark Armani suit and sunglasses. The driver walked around to the other side and opened the other door. A similar-looking fellow got out, followed by Tony Folino. Joe recognized him from the pictures he'd seen.

Folino was a shorter man that Joe guessed stood five-foot-nine or so. He had a high forehead and a slightly receding hairline of thick, wavy black hair that was perfectly combed back. His skin appeared tan and leathery, and he was adorned with several articles of gold jewelry. The hot afternoon sun glistened off his jewelry and the gel in his hair.

Joe thought he looked younger than all the photographs he had seen. One of the articles Joe had recently read said Folino was fifty-five years old. Of course, it was hard to tell since Joe was standing four stories above and about thirty yards away. Joe hoped he would get an opportunity to meet the man.

The two men alongside Folino were obviously his bodyguards. Joe noticed his pilots from earlier that day, Randy, and Folino's nephew, Donnie. They approached Folino and spoke briefly with him. Tony and his security then climbed on board the waiting Citation X aircraft.

"I hope I didn't leave the aircraft a mess," Joe commented. "That wouldn't give too good an impression with the chairman."

Travis laughed. "It wouldn't have mattered anyway. The pilots clean the airplane between each flight. It's all part of the program. When the next passenger gets on board, he should never know there was anybody on the plane before him."

"Does everybody always react this way when Mr. Folino comes through?" Joe asked.

"Yeah, pretty much so. He's a very generous man. We all adore him and appreciate our jobs and everything he's done for us. He also gives a lot to the community and local charities. His employees practically worship him. They never like to miss an opportunity to get a glimpse of the man who has done so much for them."

Joe noticed what appeared to be a photo shoot occurring at one end of the ramp. At the other end, he watched a young family of four with two small children. The parents looked to be about the same age as Travis. They also were climbing on board a waiting StratoShares aircraft.

As the crowd of about twenty employees dispersed and headed back to their work cubicles, Joe asked, "Do you know who that family was getting on the other airplane? Were they also owners in StratoShares?"

"No. The guy was a StratoShares employee. They're probably going somewhere for the weekend on a ferry flight."

"A ferry flight?" Joe asked, puzzled.

"Yeah, that's what really makes the program work. You own a fraction of one or more specific aircraft, but have an entire fleet of identical aircraft at your disposal all the time. That's how we can guarantee availability, twenty-four hours a day, three hundred sixty-five days a year. Sometimes when you request an aircraft, we have to send or ferry the nearest one."

Travis paused until Joe nodded that he understood. "Anytime that occurs and there is not an owner on board, StratoShares employees are welcome to fly themselves and family or friends on the airplane." Travis laughed. "There's only one problem, though. They have to be ready and willing to drive themselves home or spring for an airline ticket if they can't find a ferry flight back. That can be expensive." Travis motioned for Joe to follow him.

Joe overheard one of the customer service representatives saying something about selling off one of the StratoShares owners that wasn't on Folino's special list, so that Mr. Folino could take his trip.

"What's a sell-off?" Joe asked Travis as they walked between the low, walled cubicles toward the center of the room. Phones rang around them as the bustle of activity increased.

Travis stopped and turned to face Joe. He raised his soft voice to a low shout. "A sell-off is when we have to locate another operator and aircraft in order to do a trip for a StratoShares owner."

"How often does that occur?"

"I'm not really sure. It depends on the owner and the aircraft type he owns, as well as his trip mission or destination. If I had to give you an average number, I'd probably have to say it happens less than ten percent of the time. It's actually all part of the program. That's just part of how it works," Travis stated.

"Who decides who gets sold off and who gets the StratoShares aircraft?"

"It's basically first come, first served."

Joe heard an employee sitting nearby snicker at Travis' comment.

Travis started into his company spiel again as he commented on the customer service area and other supporting departments that made up the large room. He pointed out the dozen or so offices that were lined up along the far left wall. "This is where the supervisors and directors of each department are located."

Joe only heard pieces of what Travis was saying as he strained to hear the conversations of several other employees at work around him.

Joe suddenly realized that Travis was asking him a question. Joe scanned his brain and tried to remember what he had just heard Travis say in the background. Thinking the last part was "Any questions, Mr. Hara?" Joe responded, "No, Travis, I think you've explained everything quite well."

A young, muscular blond-haired man holding a small white notepad and pen approached Joe. "Excuse me, sir, but aren't you Joe Hara, one of last year's Ironman champions?"

Joe smiled. "Why, yes I am." Joe was surprised. Even though he did advertisements for the apparel company, it was rare that anyone recognized him. Triathlons were still a particularly obscure sport.

"Do you think I could have your autograph? I'm a big fan of the sport and hope to someday compete in the Ironman."

"I'd be delighted. What's your name, son?" Joe took the young man's pad and pen.

"Joe, sir," the young man replied.

"That's a great name, kid. I like you already." Joe scribbled "Best wishes, Joe. Hope to see you at the Ironman. Joe Hara."

"Have you competed in any triathlons yet?" Hara asked.

"Yes, sir."

"What's your personal record in each event?"

The young man replied and the two got into a discussion about running. After several minutes of waiting, Travis interrupted and tried to end their conversation.

Joe added, "Bring me one of your business cards before I leave and I'll send you an autographed copy of my book when I'm finished writing it."

After the last Ironman race, Joe had been approached by a writer who suggested that Joe should write a biography. He thought that Joe's unparalleled success as a homicide detective on the LAPD along with his triathlete achievements, particularly the Ironman, would make a good read.

"Radical! What's your book gonna be called?" the kid asked with great enthusiasm.

"Well," Joe said, embarrassed, "I didn't come up with the title. My editor did. It's called *Far from a Regular Joe*."

"That would be great, Mr. Hara!" the young man said.

Joe placed his hand on the man's shoulder. "Please, just call me Joe."

The young man smiled and headed back across the room.

"Let's go down to the boardroom, Mr. Hara. We have some refreshments waiting and there are several people that I'd like you to meet," Travis said.

"Okay, let's do it, but I'd like to visit the restroom first."

"Right this way. I'll show you where it is."

They proceeded out into the hallway where again Joe noticed a change in the temperature. It had been very comfortable in the customer service area but was very warm in the outer atrium area. They took the elevator down to the third floor. Joe once again admired the tropical plants and the birds.

Travis and Joe stepped out of the elevator and crossed the hall. Travis opened the wooden double doors to a large conference room. They stepped inside and were again greeted by a more pleasant and cooler temperature.

The room was nearly as large and set up similar to the customer service department, which was located one floor above. The right wall was all glass and looked out onto the ramp. The far back wall looked out over the hangar. A retractable divider was sometimes used to halve the room for separate but simultaneous functions.

A long and large boardroom table surrounded by burgundy leather chairs appeared to seat no less than thirty people. There was also the latest and greatest teleconferencing equipment as well as monitors for video conferencing.

Just like upstairs, the wall behind him with the door had numerous clocks showing the time around the world. The entire room was carpeted, with the area to the left remaining open.

In the far left-hand corner was a small kitchen area that vaguely resembled the galley of an airplane. Travis said that they often entertained owners, guests, and prospects in this room. The far left wall was decorated with an assortment of framed photographs; they appeared to be some of the many StratoShares owners. Joe gravitated toward the photos as Travis began to explain what Joe was already seeing.

He noted numerous professional athletes: golfers on the PGA, LPGA and Senior PGA tours; drivers in Formula One, CART, IRL and NASCAR; and future Hall of Famers from the NBA, MLB, NHL and NFL.

The Hollywood crowd was also pictured, with some of the most famous producers and directors, actors, actresses, and musicians. There were also photos of chairmen and CEOs of many national and multinational companies. Countless pictures were signed With Best Wishes, or something similar, to either Tony Folino or the staff of Strato-Shares.

Travis was talking like he personally knew every one of these people and how he practically single-handedly brought them into the program.

Jesus, Joe wondered, *does this kid ever get tired of listening to his own bullshit?*

"We call this our Wall of Fame," Travis said proudly.

Like he had something to do with all their success, Joe thought, then asked, "If I join the program, will you put a picture of me on the wall?"

"Absolutely!" Travis exclaimed. He added, "But only if you want us to. Obviously, this isn't all of our owners, just a couple hundred of them. We understand and respect the privacy of all our owners. Some choose to keep a low profile and would prefer that nobody even know they own a jet."

Joe noticed a picture of Johnnie Perrino and his father, Nicholas, standing in front of a StratoShares jet. Joe glanced farther down the wall looking for other recognizable faces and noticed a picture of J. Edward Chambers II, the investment banker. Joe recalled seeing on the news and reading an article in a magazine late the year before, about his tragic death.

"I guess you should probably be taking down the pictures of Johnnie Perrino and J. Edward Chambers II, since they're no longer in the program."

"Yeah, I guess maybe we should, but actually their companies are still in the program. Johnnie's dad still flies with us and so does Mr. Chambers' son. He took over the company after his father died."

"Could I get a list of the people who own shares with StratoShares? I'd like to contact some of them and get their opinion of the service."

"Certainly, Mr. Hara. I don't see any problem with that. Besides, it's public information that can be obtained from the Federal Aviation Administration."

Walking toward the boardroom table, Travis said, "I'm just gonna call now and see if everybody is ready to join us."

He reached down and pressed a couple buttons on the conference phone. Joe heard the high-pitched, whiney voice of the young receptionist that he had met earlier.

"Tiffany, this is Travis, in the boardroom. Can you please call the list that I gave you earlier and see if everyone can join me and Mr. Hara in the boardroom now?"

"Sure thing, Travis," she replied.

Joe turned toward Travis. "Can you direct me to the restroom?"

"Certainly—I forgot. Go out the double doors and turn right, past the elevator. You'll see the doors just across from the balcony on the same wall that you went out."

"Thank you." Joe exited, turned right, and headed down the hall, spotting the restrooms just ahead.

He looked out over the glass balcony at the tropical jungle below. It really was impressive. *The upkeep and overhead for this botanical garden must be incredible,* he thought.

As he turned toward the men's room, he didn't see the woman hastily exiting the ladies' restroom. He suddenly felt the softness of ample breasts and two arms wrap around him to lessen the impact as their bodies silently collided.

Joe was startled and turned to find himself face to face with a gorgeous woman. She appeared to be in her mid to late forties. Joe was transfixed as he stared into her dark brown eyes. She released her hold on him and he stepped back.

He felt his face flush as he began apologizing profusely. "Excuse me, I am so sorry. I was just admiring the plants and wasn't watching where I was going."

She smiled a beautiful smile, and Joe felt his heart skip a beat.

"It's quite all right," she said, continuing to smile.

She appeared to be sizing Joe up and seemed pleased with what she was seeing.

She held out her right hand. "I'm Jill Riley."

Joe extended his right hand and they exchanged a long, firm handshake.

"I'm Joseph Hara. You can call me Joe." Joe wondered what part of the country she was from. She didn't have the Northeast dialect that most everyone else had.

"Do you work here, Joe?" she asked.

"Me, no. I'm here from L.A. as a guest of StratoShares. I'm considering purchasing a share in their program."

"Really? Well, I'm a journalist with the *World Business Gazette* writing a story on the wealthy and their toys. How long are you here for, Joe? I would love to interview you for my article."

"I'll be staying in the City tonight and then I'm heading up to Boston in the morning to have a practice run on the marathon course." Joe glanced down at her hands to see that they were free of any diamonds or gold bands.

"What a coincidence," she said. "I'll be staying in the City tonight also and am headed to Boston for another interview in the morning. Perhaps we could get together later tonight or possibly tomorrow in Boston."

Joe found the journalist very attractive. The ecru-colored sleeveless silk blouse she was wearing accentuated her shoulder-length, dark brown hair and bronze skin. Through the top's thin fabric, Joe could see a matching lacy camisole. She had the first two buttons undone, showing just enough of her smooth, unblemished skin to keep Joe's heart racing.

"We could probably do that," he replied.

She reached into a pocket of her charcoal-gray slacks and removed a card. "Here's my card, Joe. It has my cell phone number and my pager number. Just give me a ring and I'll get right back with you. I look forward to talking further. Well, I really should be getting back to Mr. Nickels."

Joe looked puzzled. "Ross Nickels?" he asked.

"Yes, do you know him?"

"Well, we've spoken a couple times on the phone," Joe replied. "How long have you been here today?" he asked.

"Oh, since about eight this morning. We're just wrapping things up. I've got some photographers taking pictures out on the ramp as we speak."

"Well, I'll give you a call and we'll coordinate getting together either later tonight or tomorrow," Joe said.

"Thanks, Joe, the pleasure will be mine." She turned and walked down the hall past the elevator and boardroom.

As he watched her, Joe couldn't help but think the pleasure would be all his.

He turned around when he realized he was staring, and quickly entered the men's room. He returned to the boardroom a few moments later to find a half-dozen people gathered with Travis at one end of the table.

A young woman was pouring coffee and tea into gold-trimmed, white china cups. A large silver platter of assorted gourmet cookies had been set in the center of the table.

Travis said, "Please, Mr. Hara, come join us. I have several people that I would like you to meet. I think they can answer all your questions."

As Joe walked the length of the room, he glanced at the so-called Wall of Fame. Something was different. There were now vacant spots on the wall where the Johnnie Perrino and the J. Edward Chambers photos had been hanging moments before. Joe also noticed a couple other bare spots and wondered whose pictures had been there and what happened to them. *Travis sure hasn't wasted any time taking them down,* Joe thought.

Travis began introducing everyone as they each rolled back a leather chair and took a seat at the large oval table. They began fielding Joe's questions.

<8>

The next morning Joe was driving north toward Boston on I-95, along Long Island Sound. He had left the City about 8:00 A.M. and the traffic, as usual, was horrendous. It was now going on noon and he was just passing through Providence, with still another fifty miles to go. He was driving a blue Lincoln Town Car he had rented from Hertz. Joe adjusted the cruise control when the traffic thinned out.

His meeting and tour at QCI the day before had lasted another two hours. He had spent an additional hour in the boardroom speaking with several other executives from the company including the chief financial officer, the vice president of maintenance, vice president of contracts, the chief pilot, and the head of security.

One of the most interesting things Joe learned during that time was that all StratoShares pilots were not trained through SimuFlight or Flight Safety International, like most of corporate America's pilots.

Tony Folino had his own training facilities around the globe. Within the states there was one located near Miami and another in the mountains just outside of Durango, Colorado. At both locations he had private resort-type training facilities that included thousands of acres of land and his own private airstrips.

In the U.S. the nearly fifteen hundred pilots would rotate between each location every six months for both simulator and ground school recurrent training. Just like their work schedules, the training was automatically planned in advance.

Internationally, Folino had training facilities in Italy, the Middle East, the Pacific Rim, Brazil, South America and Mexico.

Folino's rationale was that the U.S. and internationally based training companies could not accommodate the number of pilots that he employed, nor could they meet his higher standards for safety and customer service. His own private facilities afforded him the opportunity to give special attention to his pilots and at the same time reward them for their services. He liked to think of it as an executive retreat and believed that his pilots left invigorated and regenerated.

Joe had also found out something else that was very interesting. He had been curious how StratoShares kept so many planes in such good condition between each trip. Obviously, certain owners were probably not as neat in the cabin as others. With so many owners, how could they always keep them so clean as they traveled around the country? Joe had asked who detailed the aircraft.

He was surprised at the way in which Travis McGee responded. Joe sensed an obvious displeasure or bitterness toward the aircraft cleaners.

Travis informed him that StratoShares had employees located at their operations facility in Newark and at other key FBOs across the country to handle most of the detailing. They were responsible for the exterior washing, polishing and paint protection of the aircraft as well as the interior upholstery and carpet cleaning. They would also do the surface detailing throughout the cabin interiors. Oddly enough, the detailers also trained at the two pilot training facilities.

When Joe asked Travis why, Travis said it was because of the importance that Tony Folino placed on the service aspect of his programs. He said that was where Mr. Folino always wanted to be better than his competitors, because he felt they were selling a *service* to their owners and not a product.

Joe had asked why customer service didn't train there also.

Travis response was that because it would be too cost prohibitive to send so many people to those facilities for training. Besides, customer service personnel didn't need recurrent training.

This prompted Joe to ask what type of recurrent training did the cleaners need, and he was again surprised at Travis' response.

He said, "You know, I'm not really sure. Maybe it has something to do with the union."

"Union?"

"Yeah, the pilots, mechanics and cleaners are all union."

"Has there ever been a strike or work stoppage?"

"I was told, just one time. It was apparently about three years ago. The pilots had been working for some time without a contract and for whatever reason, none of them showed up for work one day. Nobody knows for sure. Rumor has it that one day cost Folino a lot of money. The very next day the pilots had a new contract. A couple weeks later the company started construction on the two new training facilities in Colorado and Florida."

Joe sensed there was some resentment from Travis and probably many of the other employees as well. Joe didn't see Travis as somebody who kept his opinions to himself. No doubt if Travis had a problem with something or somebody at the company, he would probably rally the troops.

Joe thought about it and guessed he could understand their possible feelings of envy or jealousy. After all, if Folino's training facilities actually were as described, who wouldn't want to go spend a week in the Colorado mountains or on the beaches of southern Florida?

As Joe speculated about the information, he couldn't help but feel that it seemed odd. Pilots in any company always had a tendency to place themselves on a pedestal. They had to let the whole world know that they were the greatest. The cleaners of the airplanes, on the other hand, had a tendency to be blue-collar people. Joe couldn't see these two different groups of people mixing well as they shared a training facility for a week.

Travis had added that whatever the reason, Mr. Folino obviously knew what he was doing. The pilots, mechanics, and cleaners being union was really a non-issue. The turnover across the industry for both positions, pilots and cleaners, was very high, he said. But Tony Folino had an almost unblemished retention rate. In fact, he said Mr. Folino had only lost two pilots in the past three years.

Joe asked why they had left the company and was informed that both pilots had died in a car accident at the training facility in Colorado. The rental car they were sharing apparently slid off an icy road and struck a tree head-on. They were killed instantly.

After the chief pilot had finished his briefing of the StratoShares pilot training, he asked Joe for detailed specifics regarding his international travel. When Joe was done, Travis took the last hour to show him the remainder of the facility.

They went down to the second floor, which consisted of the lavish executive offices. Everybody in the company, with the exception of Tony Folino and Bill Price, were located there. Joe couldn't recall ever having seen so much mahogany and gold in his life. He still didn't get to meet Ross Nickels, but did meet most of his staff.

Travis finished with a tour of the maintenance facilities as well as a walk through the interiors of the entire fleet of StratoShares aircraft. They had a showroom on the first floor that included full-scale mock-ups of all their airplanes.

The only other time Joe had seen such mock-ups was several years back when he attended the National Business Aircraft Association Convention in Long Beach. An ex-girlfriend of his, a private pilot with multiple ratings, was considering purchasing her own plane. All the manufacturers were there and many had models like the ones he had seen yesterday at StratoShares.

Afterward, Travis told Joe he would have someone get back with him with flight times for several of his anticipated trips. Joe told Travis he would have his legal counsel peruse the set of contracts he had given him, as well as call several owners on the list provided. Joe said he would keep in touch as he compared the other programs.

Travis reminded Joe they had a backlog of people waiting for aircraft and if he wanted to hold a delivery position, he should put down a deposit. He also told him, though, that they had several options where he could start flying immediately in the program while he waited for his airplane to be delivered. Joe didn't quite understand that option but thought it would be a good reason to call Travis back later.

Travis called for a limousine to take Joe to his hotel in midtown Manhattan. He was staying at the Hilton Times Square. Joe had dinner reservations at Above, famed Chef Larry Forgione's newest restaurant located in the hotel's Sky Lobby.

Joe was just a culinary novice who liked to play around in the kitchen, but Forgione was a culinary visionary. Joe even had his cookbook. Whenever Joe was in the City, he would frequent his other restaurant, An American Place, located over on Lexington Avenue at Park and Madison Avenues. The square room was usually packed at lunchtime, but not quite as crowded at dinner. Reservations were always necessary.

Eating was one of the benefits of being a world-class triathlete. Dedicated triathletes could require as many as six thousand calories a day just to maintain their body weight. So, having an occasional meal prepared by the man hailed as the Godfather of American cooking, never hurt. Joe still kept a close count of his carbohydrate, fat and protein intake, but nonetheless enjoyed his meals.

The previous night was no exception. Though Joe would have preferred not to have dined alone, he still thoroughly enjoyed Larry's latest innovation of exotic fish from the Caribbean and organic vegetables. The flavorful food was both spicy and crisp. So what if he felt a little stuffed during the show.

He had two tickets to see *Phantom of the Opera* at the grand Majestic Theater in the Times Square district. The show was good but couldn't compare to the performance he had seen some years back with its London stars, Michael Crawford, Sarah Brightman, and Steve Barton.

He had called Jill Riley on the drive into the City and invited her to join him for dinner and the show. Unfortunately she said her editor had moved up a deadline for another story she was working on, and she needed to get it finished. She asked for a rain check and told him to call her the next afternoon to see if they could arrange getting together in Boston. Joe had to admit to himself that he was disappointed, but was looking forward to the possibility of tonight just the same.

Joe had also coordinated another demonstration flight with one of StratoShares' competitors, a company called Jet Divide. Tomorrow, after he had finished in Boston, they were going to fly him from Logan International to their operations facility in Indianapolis, Indiana. Joe had coordinated a couple other stops from there with other fractional companies as he made his way home. The last leg would be on another StratoShares aircraft going from Dallas back to L.A.

All of the companies were willing to pick up the expense since he was coming to take a tour of their facilities. Some of them sounded a little skeptical when they found out they would be taking him to tour a competitor's facilities as well, but realized it was in their best interest to do the trip. If they hadn't, it would have certainly appeared they were trying to hide something.

Even though Joe didn't particularly care for Travis McGee, the young man did provide him with a wealth of information yesterday. *Man, that kid could sell you a pile of shit with a ribbon tied around it and make you think you got a great deal!* Now, all Joe had to do was figure out what was truth and what was shit. Joe figured he was probably going to get a lot of that over the next couple days. In a multimillion-dollar industry like this, there was no way around it.

Joe reached into his brown tweed sports coat and removed Jill Riley's business card. He punched in her number on his cell phone. The phone rang twice.

"Yes, this is Jill," answered a flustered voice.

"This is Joe Hara, Jill. Is everything okay?"

"Oh, hi Joe. Uhm, well, no not really. You startled me."

"What's the matter?"

"Well, it seems my lunch interviewee kind of just checked out."

"You mean he stood you up?"

"No," Jill said, as if Joe should already understand. "I mean he's dead."

"Where are you now?" Joe could hear a dog barking in the background.

"Well, I'm standing in Randall Johnson's bathroom watching him do the dead man's float in his bathtub."

"Have you called the police yet?"

"Well, no. I literally just walked in and found him when you called."

"Can you tell what happened?"

"Well, it appears that he knocked his radio into the tub and electrocuted himself."

"Don't touch anything, Jill. Hang up the phone and call the police immediately. You should probably go back out to your car and wait for the police to arrive. Is anybody else there?"

"There doesn't appear to be. Just his white Maltese, whose incessant yelping led me to him."

"This isn't the Randall Johnson who is chairman of the largest biotech firm in the country, is it?" Joe asked.

"The one and only—or at least he was."

"Where is his home?"

She gave him the address in Back Bay.

"Okay, I know the area somewhat. I'll figure out how to get there. In the meantime, you call the police and wait in your car. I should be there in about an hour and a-half."

"Okay, Joe, thanks."

"One last thing, Jill," Joe added. "Was Randall Johnson an owner in the StratoShares program?"

"Yes, he was. Why do you ask?"

"Oh, no reason in particular. I was just curious. I'll see you in a bit." He turned off the phone and placed it on the seat beside him.

Joe reached down and removed the in-car navigation system from its mounting bracket on the dashboard. "Okay, NeverLost," he said, "let's see if you can live up to your name."

NeverLost was Hertz's on-board satellite navigation system that uses the Global Positioning System, or GPS, which is similar to the type used on airplanes.

Joe pressed a few buttons and received the female voice prompts and visual directions. He first chose a language and selected Japanese. He always liked to stay fluent whenever he had the opportunity.

Next he selected his destination by pressing a few more buttons and entering the specific street address. Under the Route Method menu, Joe chose the Shortest Time icon and pressed Enter.

Joe pressed a few more buttons and adjusted the volume before placing the unit back in its bracket on the dash. From here, the system should do the rest by giving him turn-by-turn directions with its automated voice and visual maps.

Joe picked up his cell phone again and quickly punched in Daniel Froberg's cell phone number back in L.A. He was going to see if Danny had found anything on Tony Folino, and also give him some additional work to do.

The phone rang twice. "This is Froberg."

"Hey kid, it's Hara. Did you find anything on Folino?"

"What, Joe? No hi, how ya doing, or how's the weather? I'm hurt," Danny kidded.

"Sorry, kid, how ya doing? Now, what did you find on Folino?"

Danny just laughed. "Real sincere, Joe. I'm convinced. I'm fine, how are you?"

"Come on, kid, quit yanking my chain. This is serious." Then Joe laughed. They did this to each other all the time.

"That's more like it," Danny said. "Damn, Hara, you're just too intense sometimes. Okay, I haven't found much yet, but I'm still working on it. I got a little on Folino's family history, though. His grandfather, Mario, grew up in Sicily and was part of a mass immigration of Italians and Sicilians that came to the United States in the middle of the nineteenth century.

"So far, we can't find any evidence to tell if he was part of the Cosa Nostra that was based in Sicily. The Cosa Nostra is by far the most powerful and ruthless of the Italian Mafia gr—"

"I know what the Cosa Nostra is," Joe said. "For all we know, he might have been fleeing Italy to get away from the Octopus. That was also quite common back then. Octopus is what the Italians called the Mafia," Joe shot back.

"Well, I've got some people doing more research on the Cosa Nostra, as we speak," Danny said.

"So, what about Tony and his father?" Hara asked.

"Nothing out of the ordinary yet. We haven't been able to dig up anything on either of them. But we're still working on it."

"Well, I have another project for you. I've got a list of owners in the StratoShares program. Travis McGee gave it to me. He said that it was basically public information and anybody could get it through the FAA. I sent it last night from the hotel by overnight FedEx. You should get it later this morning. I need you to crosscheck that list and find out the names, titles, and cause of death for any employees that might have died while working at those companies during the past few years. Then I need you to research and do the same thing with any of the other three fractional providers that I've been looking at."

"We can do that," Danny said. "It will take a little time, but I'll see if I can get the chief's approval to put a couple extra people on it."

"I'm sure he'll say yes. Perrino was his godson. I know Frank's not going to rest until he finds out who killed him," Joe added. "Also see what you can find out about the laws and policies that apply for obtaining an animal or more specifically, a bird that is on the Endangered Species List. You can probably contact the U.S. Department of the Interior or the U.S. Fish and Wildlife Service. There probably is an Endangered Species branch or division that they can direct you to. I'm curious to see if Mr. Tony Folino is registered or listed as having any endangered species in captivity.

"And one more thing, Dan. See what you can find out about J. Edward Chambers II's death about six months ago.

If you don't know, he was one of the biggest investment bankers in the country who died late one night after leaving his Manhattan office. He fell fifty stories down an elevator shaft that was under repair."

"It seems to me I recall hearing something about that. I'll see what we can find."

"Okay, Danny, keep up the great work. Well, I have to be going now. I've got to meet up with a beautiful journalist in distress, who's with the *World Business Gazette*," Joe practically crooned.

Danny laughed. "Big surprise there, Romeo. You never did have any trouble getting the women."

"You're just jealous," Joe replied.

"Yeah, whatever. I'll give you a call when I've got some more information. Don't work too hard, old man."

"I'll be talking to you soon, kid. Thanks." Joe laid the phone back down on the seat beside him as the wheels in his head started turning even faster. This case was getting interesting fast.

He reached inside his sports coat and pulled out his soft leather address book. He flipped through several of the gold-leafed pages until he found the number he was looking for. He picked up his cell phone again and pressed the number for Brock Henry in New York City. Henry had contacts in the underworld and had gotten tips from organized crime chiefs before. If there was dirt to be found on Tony Folino, Brock would have it.

<9>

A little over an hour later, Joe followed the voice prompt command and turned his rental car down the street where Randall Johnson's private mansion was located. It was no surprise that the chairman of one of the largest biotech firms in the country lived on the coveted lower blocks of Commonwealth Avenue in the Back Bay area.

It wasn't just the wealthiest neighborhood in Boston but one of the wealthiest in the country. Some of the Georgian Revival homes, built in the mid-nineteenth century, now sold for close to ten million dollars.

Joe wondered what it would be like to have so much money. He thought it might be nice to see how it felt for maybe just a couple of days. But too many times he had witnessed what money and wealth could do to people, and Randall Johnson was probably just another example.

Joe found several police cruisers and the local television media parked in front of one residence. There was a truck from Channel 12, the local CBS affiliate, along with trucks from Channel 9 and 10, the respective ABC and NBC affiliates. A small crowd of gawkers gathered behind the yellow and black police tape that encircled the sidewalk across the front of the home. Reporters from numerous TV, radio, newspaper and wire services waited, focused on the front entryway.

Joe observed a car pulling away from the curb a few houses ahead so he clicked on the right turn signal as he drove past the house and the bustle of activity. He executed a quick, perfect parallel park between two blue and white Ford Crown Victoria police cruisers.

Joe tossed an empty fast-food bag from the passenger seat onto the floor. He had stopped for some gas just south of Boston and decided to grab a couple of burgers, or a "heart attack in a sack," as they had always called it on the force.

Joe walked back toward Johnson's mansion. It was a beautiful afternoon for the last week of winter. The birds were singing in the budding trees along the sidewalk, and flowerbeds and some window boxes were blooming with yellow daffodils.

Joe noticed Jill Riley standing just inside the taped-off yard, talking to a local reporter. She was dressed in a double-breasted pinstripe suit. If Joe had to guess, he'd say it had probably come from an expensive shop like Loro Piana in New York. Jill obviously had very fine taste and wore it well. He stopped several feet short of the tape and waited for her to finish.

He thought back to the phone conversation of just a while ago with Brock Henry. He said he knew of Folino, but not personally, and wasn't aware of any illegal activities or charges that had ever been brought against him.

Jill acknowledged Joe's presence and motioned with her finger that she would be occupied another minute.

Joe smiled and nodded as two young white boys on bicycles brushed past and rode up to the yellow tape. They rolled their front tire wheels under the plastic boundary until the tape was hitting them directly across the chest.

Just like kids to push the envelope, Joe thought.

They craned their heads toward the front stairs as they tried to get a look inside.

No doubt hoping to catch a glimpse of some graphic carnage or mass destruction, Joe thought. He wondered why they weren't in school.

Jill finished speaking to the young reporter and lifted the crime scene tape to allow him to exit the area. She motioned for Joe to come forward and step inside while she continued holding the tape. Joe took a couple steps and bent under the police tape, wondering how many times he'd crossed under that line to enter a crime scene.

As Jill released the tape, she looked directly into his eyes and said, "I don't think you've been completely honest with me, Mr. Hara."

"I'm not quite sure I know what you mean," Joe said.

She took Joe by his right arm and walked him closer to the front door, away from the crowd gathered at the perimeter of the tape. The two stepped off the walkway to the front door, onto the grass. Joe sniffed at the distinct smell of chemicals from a recent herbicide application to the professionally manicured lawn. A couple uniformed police officers were walking down the sidewalk, having just exited the house.

She looked at Joe seriously. "What I mean is that I don't believe you were at StratoShares yesterday because you want to join their program."

Joe continued to act puzzled but knew the gig was up. He was clearly dealing with a very intelligent person. "And why would you think that?" he responded.

"Oh, you are good, Joe Hara. But I'm a journalist. We have a lot in common." She paused as the two officers walked closer to them.

Joe nodded his head to greet them as they passed.

Jill said, "Just like a good homicide detective, I ask a lot of questions and do my research."

Joe stared blankly at her and didn't speak. Jill couldn't detect any expression on his face. The silence continued as Joe didn't blink. He could see the look on her face changing to one of concern. She suddenly appeared uneasy.

She said, sounding sheepish, "I hope you don't mind."

Joe turned the tables. "I think it's you that hasn't been completely honest with me. You're not writing a story on the rich and their toys, are you!"

She let go of Joe's arm and looked up at him, her dark brown eyes betraying hurt feelings. "I don't know what you're talking about, Mr. Hara. Why would you think that?"

They looked at each other waiting for the other to speak. Joe finally cracked a grin on his stern, rigid face. Jill did likewise. Their grins quickly turned to smiles.

"You are good, Mr. Hara," she repeated.

"And your interrogation technique needs some help," Joe said, chuckling.

"Thanks for the kind words," Jill said. "How about we both just stick to what we do best? You detective," she said, pointing her finger at Joe, "and me journalist. Deal?"

"Deal," Joe replied as he thought to himself, *Me Tarzan, you Jane*. He pictured Jill in leopard skin.

Jill interrupted Joe's thoughts. "And no more secrets."

"Uhm, okay. That's fine, but you first."

"We'll talk as we're going through the house."

They proceeded up several concrete stairs toward the front door of the Victorian mansion. It was a magnificent residence with a graciously bowed front.

Joe wondered if the crime scene unit had arrived yet. The first officers or detectives at a crime scene were not allowed to touch anything, especially the body, until CSI showed up. The unit usually consisted of two experts whose job was to record the scene first. They would do this by using everything from photos to notes and sketches.

Next they'd collect any physical evidence—that could be practically anything and included any type of body fluid, ballistics, hairs, fingerprints, footprints or tire marks.

Finally they would reconstruct the scene from the physical evidence, along with any information that other officers might have acquired through the questioning of witnesses or canvassing of the area.

"Has the crime scene unit already processed the scene?" Joe asked.

"I think so but I'm not really certain. I'll introduce you to the officer in charge. So, what makes you think I'm not just writing an article about the rich and their toys?"

"Years of observation. I quickly surmised that you were a woman of great wisdom and superior intellect."

"Flattery will get you nowhere, Mr. Hara." She added, "Well, almost nowhere. So, cut the bullshit."

Joe laughed. He really liked this woman. "Okay, it was just a lucky guess. It hadn't even occurred to me until you started questioning me. I figured if you suspected my motive for being at StratoShares, there was a good possibility you were probably doing something that would be of interest to me."

Before stepping inside the front door, Jill stopped suddenly in front of Joe and turned to face him. "You don't think the fact that I was going to interview Randall Johnson had anything to do with his death, do you? I mean, his dying truly could have been an accident, couldn't it?"

"I don't know. I guess it depends on what you were really writing about and who knew you were going to be here."

They both turned sideways to allow an older detective in a dark suit and gold shield to pass between them and exit the house.

"So, what *are* you writing about?" Joe asked.

Jill, standing across from Joe, pressed her back against the wooden doorframe. In a soft voice she almost whispered, "My guess is it's the same thing you're investigating. My newspaper has reason to believe that several of the recent— recent being within the past couple of years—deaths or accidental deaths of high net-worth individuals across the country haven't simply been a coincidence."

Joe shifted his weight as he looked at Jill. He was more impressed by the minute. "You obviously have some additional information," he said, keeping his tone low.

"I do." She smiled. "I also know that you and I are both looking into the same thing. Like I said before, I do my research. When I heard the story about Johnnie Perrino's death, I waited until after the funeral to contact his father. I finally got through to him yesterday evening and told him about the story I was working on. He told me that he had hired you to do the investigation and that he would appreciate it if I would share my suspicions with you. I told him we had already met and would probably be having dinner tonight. We're still having dinner, aren't we?"

Joe stood there, chewing on his bottom lip. He would like to have played a little harder to get, but knew she had him. She had just hooked the big fish and was now reeling him in.

Joe smiled and said, "You know, Ms. Riley, I think you were wrong before. You're the one that's good."

She raised her voice to a normal level. "Why, thank you, Joe. So then, I'll take that as a yes. I'm sorry again for not being able to join you last night at Larry Forgione's new restaurant. I've been to his place at the Beekman Arms in Rhinebeck. It's charming. But since you are obviously a connoisseur of fine cuisine, I'll make dinner reservations at, let's see, there's Locke-Ober Café. They've got great lobsters, or . . . I know—Radius over on High Street. Have you ever been there?"

"No, can't say that I have."

"Michael Schlow, their chef, recently won the James Beard Award for Best Chef in the Northeast."

The James Beard Award, Joe thought, *that's impressive.* He was certain he would like the place. "I look forward to it," he replied.

Jill smiled as she turned to go inside. Joe followed closely behind and could smell the sweet scent of her perfume. But it was soon overpowered by the smell of fresh paint emanating from somewhere in the house.

Joe placed both hands in his pants pockets as he started to observe his surroundings. It was a technique he had learned many years back when he was a young detective just starting out. He picked it up from one of the gray-haired veteran detectives on the force. This helped him insure that he didn't touch anything, at least not until the crime scene unit was done with their investigation. He had never intended to continue doing it, but it was something that had stuck with him.

The first thing Joe noticed was the large dimension of the townhouse. It was unusually wide and very deep. The plaster ceilings were tall and intricately cast. The newly waxed hardwood floors were stunning and accented by rich mahogany molding throughout. The house was furnished primarily with antiques or replicas from the same era as the architecture.

To the left was a large living room with a white baby grand piano in the farthest corner. Further back, past the living room, Joe could see a formal dining room with an antique crystal chandelier hanging over the center of a long table.

Directly in front of him was a wide set of wooden stairs, carpeted with an Oriental runner that covered all but about one foot on each side. To the right of the stairs was a long hall with doors on each side and at the end was the doorway to a large kitchen. The hall door to the kitchen was open and Joe could see all the way through to the mansion's back door. He glanced to his right at a large and lavishly furnished sitting room.

"Do you know when this place was built and how big it is?" Joe asked.

"Of course I do. I did some research before I came here today. I wanted to seem at least somewhat intelligent about his home and neighborhood. In answer to your question, the house was built in 1866 and is approximately 9,700 square feet. It has fourteen rooms, with five bedrooms and five full baths. It has walk-in closets throughout, eight fireplaces, a full basement, as well as a four-car garage. Let's see . . . there's also a wine room, mahogany library, rooftop terrace and garden, a media room, and a Jacuzzi spa room. Do you want to hear more?"

"No, I think I get the picture. Did anybody else live here with him?"

"Nope. Just him and that little white dog that looks like a hairy rat."

Joe laughed. "Can I quote you on that?"

"Very funny."

"So, walk and talk me through everything you did when you got here."

They stopped and stood in the large foyer.

She turned to face Joe. "I'll tell you the same things I told the other officers and detectives. When I first arrived, it was about five minutes before noon. I was supposed to meet Mr. Johnson here to start the interview, then we would continue elsewhere over lunch. He said he would make the reservation."

"Did he know what you were actually writing about?"

"No. When I called him yesterday morning around nine and asked for the interview, I told him the same thing I told all the others. I said I was doing a story on wealthy and affluent Americans and their toys. You know, planes, yachts, cars, second and third homes, those types of things. And do you know what he said to me?"

The way she asked the question, Joe knew he was going to like what he was about to hear. She definitely had his attention. "What?"

"He said that would be fine. 'As a matter of fact,' he added, 'it just so happens that I might be getting some new toys. I'm reviewing the contracts as we speak, for my own airplane and my own yacht.' He said I could meet him here about noonish. He would give me a tour of his home, then take me to lunch nearby."

"So he was thinking about leaving the StratoShares program and selling back his aircraft shares."

"Airplane and yacht shares," Jill added.

"Yacht shares?"

"That's right. Didn't you know? Folino has a program based in West Palm Beach called OceanShares. It's a subsidiary of QCI and it's just like the StratoShares program, only with boats. Really big boats."

A couple detectives were proceeding slowly down the stairs, closely observing things as they walked. The younger of the two said, "Excuse me, Ms. Riley" as they reached the bottom of the stairs, then walked past and continued down the long hallway toward the kitchen.

"That's very interesting," Joe commented.

He didn't recall seeing anything in the StratoShares literature about an OceanShares program, but it was possible he had simply overlooked it.

Joe said, "Okay, so it's five till noon and you just get here."

"Yes. I walk up the front steps and ring the doorbell. I could hear the dog barking from somewhere in the house."

"Was the front door open?"

"Do you mean, like, wide open? This is one of the richest neighborhoods in Boston. People don't just leave their front doors open in a neighborhood like this."

In a monotone, Joe said, "I have to ask. I can't assume anything or take for granted what should be the obvious."

"No, the front door wasn't open, and it wasn't unlocked either, because I tried it. After several minutes of waiting between rings, I tried the doorknob but to no avail. I couldn't see very well through the door curtain, but could still hear the dog barking its head off."

"So then what did you do?"

"I backed down the steps and glanced up at the front of the house. There didn't appear to be any activity in any of the windows and none were open. So I checked my pager and the voice mail on my cell phone to see if maybe Mr. Johnson had left a message saying he needed to cancel our meeting."

"And you've already told all this to the Boston police?"

"Oh yes. They said they were through with me for now. Just to let them know if I think of anything later that I might have forgotten."

"Let's go outside so you can show me what you did next."

Joe noticed the security system keypad to the left of the doorframe as they walked through the open front door and proceeded down the steps. Joe squinted as he pulled his hands from his pockets and reached into his sports coat to get his sunglasses. The glare from the mid-afternoon sun was almost blinding.

"Jill!" a young man's voice shouted from the sidewalk.

Joe looked into an even larger crowd gathered around the tape.

Jill recognized the young Italian man who had called her name. "That's a friend of mine, Paul Stavale. He's a reporter with *Boston Today*. Excuse me for a few minutes."

Joe turned and looked back at the mansion. Out of the corner of his eye, he noticed a lawn care technician arriving in the adjoining yard to Joe's left. Joe walked across the grass and introduced himself.

Jill noticed Joe speaking to the technician. At one point she saw Joe go back inside the house, and noted his return about ten minutes later with a tall and stocky detective that she at once recognized. As he'd stepped into the afternoon light, the sun glared off the detective's gold shield and shiny bald head.

Joe introduced the detective to the technician and then stood by silently while the other detective questioned him.

Another five minutes passed before Jill finished her conversation and walked toward Joe. Joe nodded at both men and turned to walk away as Jill approached.

"What's up?" she inquired.

"That's Detective Wilson, one of the homicide detectives investigating the scene. But I guess you already knew that."

After briefly speaking with the lawn technician, Joe had gone inside the mansion to look for one of the detectives that was handling the investigation. Joe introduced himself and spoke briefly with Wilson, telling him that the lawn technician had been at Johnson's house earlier that morning and probably should be interviewed.

"Yes, of course," said Jill. "Detective Wilson questioned me earlier. I was going to introduce you to him. So, what did the lawn care kid have to say?"

"Not much. Says he spoke briefly with Johnson this morning before he sprayed the lawn. Johnson had some extra stuff he wanted him to do, so he ended up being here about a half-hour."

"That's all?"

"Yeah, pretty much."

"Well, let me take you around back so I can show you just what I did."

After exiting the cordoned-off area, Jill and Joe walked past several houses further down to the end of the block. She took him halfway down the side street to the alleyway that ran behind the houses.

Since the townhouses were side by side, the only way to access the back was to either go through the house or around the block. The two walked down the narrow lane and approached the rear of Randall Johnson's mansion. They quickly strode across the tiny backyard and up the back steps. Joe noticed a concrete nail sticking out of the brick mortar just to the right of the doorframe and about two feet above the porch landing. They walked through the old wood and glass back door and entered the freshly varnished kitchen.

"Wow!" he exclaimed. Joe was instantly envious of the large state-of-the-art kitchen. It was equipped with the finest Viking commercial-type cooking equipment. Joe may have only been a greenhorn at cooking, but knew enough to know that home kitchens didn't get any better than this.

All the appliances were built-in along the walls and richly finished in stainless steel with brass trim. For cooking there were several ovens, a large cooktop, a wok, warming drawers, and a micro-chamber. For refrigeration there was a bulky side-by-side refrigerator-freezer, an under-counter refrigerator as well as a wine cooler. A dishwasher and trash compactor made for easy cleanup. The kitchen had it all.

Jill seemed unimpressed and somewhat preoccupied as she continued reenacting her day's earlier actions. Joe, still in awe of the kitchen, listened intently while he inspected everything around him. He noticed an empty cereal bowl, a single spoon, juice glass, and coffee cup and saucer resting in the left basin of the kitchen sink. His highly trained eyes were looking for things that most people would never notice. Occasionally Joe would take out his notepad and write something down. He noted the security system keypad located to right of the kitchen door.

When Joe had come inside earlier to find the detective in charge, he saw that both the medical examiner and the crime scene unit were still processing the scene. For that reason he was still careful not to touch anything.

Joe noticed Jill extending her hand toward the refrigerator, about to lean on it.

"Don't touch anything," Joe quickly reminded her.

Jill winced. "I knew that," she said, obviously aggravated at her own absentmindedness.

Joe noticed some scratches on the recently varnished door to the hallway, as well as the door to the dining room. The scratches were on the kitchen side of both doors, about two feet up from the baseboard. Joe made a note of this as he asked Jill several more questions.

They then walked from the kitchen, down the hall, and toward the foyer and front door.

Passing a closed door on the same side as the stairs, Joe looked at it and said, "Basement?"

"That would be my guess," she replied. "But remember, I never did get a tour."

As they reached the front entry hall and were about to go up the stairs, they stopped and took a step back. The body of Randall Johnson was being carried downstairs on a steel gurney. The medical examiner followed directly behind.

Towering above this scene was Detective Wilson, who was in charge of the homicide investigation. If Joe had to guess, he would say Wilson stood close to six-foot-eight and weighed around two hundred forty pounds. Joe guessed his age to be in the late forties. He was obviously a seasoned veteran and his stark appearance gave him a commanding presence that could have scared guys in World Wrestling.

Two members of the crime scene unit and several uniformed officers followed him. One of the younger officers was holding Johnson's dog in his arms. When the dog began to growl, he rubbed her coat as he tried to console the small white Maltese. The other officers paid no attention as they continued down the stairs discussing their plans for lunch, after having just worked through that all-important meal.

Detective Wilson stopped at the bottom of the stairs as they wheeled Randall Johnson's body out the front door and down the steps. The rest of the group filed past. Jill watched as the young officer and the agitated little dog proceeded by.

Wilson said, "Mr. Hara, feel free to continue to canvass the area and look for witnesses and clues. We're done here for now. Give me a call later and we'll compare notes—though it appears to us that this probably was an accident."

He then looked at Jill. "Thanks for your assistance as well, Ms. Riley. I'm sorry we had to meet under these circumstances. Once again, give me a call if you remember anything that you might have forgotten to tell us."

"Absolutely," Jill replied. She reached out and shook his large, thick hand. "It was a pleasure meeting you." Jill paused as she looked at the officers exiting the front door. "What's going to happen to the dog?"

"We're taking her downtown for questioning. We think maybe she saw something." The hulking detective gazed down at Jill Riley as he kept a straight face and didn't blink an eye. He watched a perplexed look come over Jill's face.

After several seconds, she finally said, "Right!"

Joe chuckled and Wilson finally smiled.

"I had you going there for a minute, didn't I? You were at least thinking about it. Actually, we're taking her to see the police department vet. She's somehow gotten injured. After that, Ms. Gonzales—that's Johnson's housekeeper—she'll take care of the dog."

The bald-headed detective looked at Joe and said, "Later, Hara."

He turned to catch up with the others. As he walked out the front door and slipped his sunglasses on, the detective said, "A steak hoagie and onion rings, that's what I'm in the mood for."

Joe and Jill proceeded up the two flights of stairs as they continued retracing her steps. She explained how she had followed the sound of the dog's barking. When they got to the bathroom, she provided Joe with an account of everything she had seen and exactly what she had done afterwards. Joe wrote down more notes as she spoke.

Joe had witnessed the crime scene only momentarily when he had come looking for Wilson earlier. It looked very different now. He would need to speak with Wilson later, since any evidence they found had been removed.

Jill went on to explain how the bathroom door had been standing wide open and she could see the small dog barking frantically as it sat in the middle of the room on the large braided rug. "The damn dog never quit barking and wouldn't let me get past her. I guess it really didn't matter. I could tell Mr. Johnson was already dead. When one of the officers arrived, he was finally able to calm the dog down."

Joe asked her several more questions, including the position of Randall Johnson's body when she first found him. He also asked if she had noticed anything unusual around the bathroom. Jill said she hadn't. Joe really didn't expect her to have noticed anything. Most people are so overwhelmed at the sight of a dead body that they suddenly get tunnel vision. They aren't trained and don't know to immediately start looking for clues.

Joe happened to be in the bathroom earlier when the detectives had looked in the wastebasket beside the toilet. It had been empty except for a single flattened soapbox and the plastic wrapper that had surrounded it. This explained a water trail that the detectives had been discussing when Joe first entered the room. They noticed dried hard water stains on the ceramic tile floor of the bathroom. It started at the tub and went to the towel closet, then across to the wastebasket and back to the tub.

It was about that time when Joe introduced himself to Detective Wilson. He told the detective he had reason to believe that Johnson's death wasn't an accident, but that it might be connected to a series of other mysterious deaths. He quickly briefed him on his investigation and informed him of the lawn technician outside. Wilson agreed he should go interview the young man.

After fifteen more minutes of asking Jill questions and looking around the bathroom and bedroom, the two returned downstairs. As they were leaving, Joe noticed a laundry chute in the wall beside the towel closet. Earlier, Detective

Wilson had informed Joe they had found Johnson's clothes in the basement's laundry room at the bottom of the chute.

Joe once again walked down the hall to the kitchen and looked around some more. He occasionally stopped to jot down a note as Jill silently followed behind him. She only spoke when spoken to, although she craned her neck several times to try and sneak a peek at what Joe was writing. He exited the kitchen through the dining room, proceeded into the living room and back into the front entry hall as he completed the circle at the base of the stairs.

"So," she asked, "what do those rooms have to do with anything? I mean, if Randall Johnson's death was an accident."

"I'm not certain they do, but we can't leave any stone unturned. I have to consider all the possibilities."

Joe looked at his watch. The time was close to 2:00 P.M. "Well, Jill, I hope you don't mind, but I need to check into my hotel and get in my afternoon workout."

"Where are you staying?"

"At the Hilton Back Bay. Not too far from here."

"I am too. Why don't you go get yourself settled in and do whatever you have to do? How about I meet you in the hotel lobby at, let's say, six-thirty?"

Joe quickly determined he could be ready within that timeframe. "I can do that."

"Great. I'm looking forward to dinner tonight. I know you'll like Radius."

"I'm sure I will."

They exited the now empty mansion and headed for the street. Most of the crowd had dispersed, but the black and yellow police tape remained. Joe briefly spoke to a uniformed officer who was standing on the sidewalk. He let the young man know they were finished inside.

Joe said goodbye to Jill, and she headed up the sidewalk in the opposite direction toward her car. Joe once again caught himself staring as she walked away. *She certainly is beautiful,* he thought.

Joe turned and headed for his rental car. He had a couple calls to make, along with one to Detective Wilson. Joe was almost certain Randall Johnson had been murdered and felt that Wilson probably knew the same. The comment a few moments ago was purely because Jill Riley was present. Wilson knew she was media and because of that, didn't want her putting anything in print that might alert the perpetrator. This way, at least, if the media reported Randall Johnson's death as an accident, they might still be able to catch the killer off guard.

Joe smiled and whistled a lively tune as he put on his sunglasses and pulled away from the curb.

<10>

Joe eased into a brown leather wingback chair near the window of his room at the Hilton Back Bay in Boston. He had just finished the day's workout, having run the second half of the marathon course. After a quick shower he had pulled on some Dockers, a knit polo shirt, and a pair of burgundy loafers. He was now ready to relax. He still had an hour and a-half before he needed to meet Jill in the lobby.

Joe liked staying at a Hilton because they were more of a traditional hotel. So many of the other hotels, like the nearby luxurious Fifteen Beacon, were now targeting Generation X. Even the stodgy Ritz Carltons were changing their décor to attract more Xers. Sure, Hilton had made some changes too, but not like some of the other hotel chains. At least, that's how it appeared to Joe.

He briefly admired the artistic presentation of the fresh fruit and warm banana bread on the plate that room service had placed on the end table beside him. He picked up the china plate and silverware, set them on his lap, and began eating. His appetite was voracious. He glanced out the window at the city below and took his mind off the case by reflecting on the afternoon's run.

The marathon was always on Patriots Day, which was a Monday in mid-April. The race was one-way and traveled 26.2 miles down Route 135, through the quaint New England village of Hopkinton, Massachusetts, with its old frame houses, to Route 16 and the towers of downtown Boston.

Joe caught a taxi from the hotel and had the driver take him to about the twelve-mile point on the course where there's a sign marked Entering Wellesley. This was just before the halfway mark at 13.1 miles.

Joe had paid the cabbie before leaving the hotel and left his room key with the clerk at the front desk. All he had with him was the running gear that he was wearing. Though spring was still several days away, the weather was unseasonably warm. The mid-afternoon sun beat down on Joe as he stepped out of the cab wearing his black and green polyester running shorts and a white and black singlet tank top. The lightweight material of both articles of clothing made running much more comfortable.

He had stretched out in the grass alongside the road as he did his pre-run warm-up. Whenever time allowed, Joe did flexibility exercises before he ran. First, he did sit-ups for his stomach muscles. Next, he lay flat on his back and did some leg exercises to stretch his hamstrings and calf muscles. Then Joe found a tree and faced it with his palms against it. This worked the muscles in the back of his legs. Finally Joe lay on his back again, doing more leg exercises to stretch his hamstring muscles.

After about a half-hour of stretching, Joe was ready to begin his run. He started out slow for the first mile, to adjust as his body temperature rose and circulation increased.

As Joe passed through the town of Wellesley, he increased his pace. Joe had been here before; he had run at Boston five other times. The first half of the course was mostly downhill or flat. He had chosen to practice on the back half of the marathon course today because it was the most difficult. Joe turned onto Route 16 and headed for Wellesley Hills.

About twenty minutes later, or three miles farther, Joe crossed the Charles River after a long downhill run. He had reached the start of a series of four hills known collectively as Heartbreak Hill. It was the toughest part of the course. The hills over that five-mile stretch would come at the absolute worst time in the marathon.

Joe had tackled the hills aggressively today, only having run the back half. It was a good feeling, though he knew he wouldn't be able to do that in the race. In a couple weeks he would need to taper back after having run twice the distance.

Joe ate the final strawberry and the last piece of bread. After he placed the china plate, napkin, and fork on the table, he glanced at his watch and realized he had better get a move on. He was supposed to meet Jill in just over an hour and he wanted to look good.

He also still needed to call Detective Wilson so they could compare notes. Joe had been thinking about Randall Johnson's death since leaving the crime scene. It had consumed his thoughts during his afternoon run as well as the remainder of his day. In his mind he had already started to develop a rough idea as to what might have occurred. Hopefully, with a little luck, Wilson and his guys at the BPD could fill in some of the blanks.

The Boston Police Department was the oldest in the country and their state-of-the-art facility at One Schroeder Plaza was equipped with some of the best and most advanced ballistics identification equipment in the country. From the evidence Joe had seen that afternoon, he felt certain they could piece together exactly what had happened. Figuring out who the perpetrator was—well, that was another thing.

Joe pushed himself up from the soft leather seat. He was excited about tonight. *So what if I'm pushing fifty,* he thought. He still felt like a young man, and a beautiful woman like Jill Riley always helped that feeling. He walked over to the closet to look for just the right clothes to wear.

<11>

As usual, Joe was punctual, and met Jill in the hotel lobby at exactly six-thirty. They caught a taxi in front of the hotel and rode the two miles to the restaurant. They enjoyed casual conversation during the short drive but even though her beauty smote Joe, he still found himself thinking about Randall Johnson's death. His phone call a short while earlier to Detective Wilson had proved to be very fruitful. They arrived at Radius in ten minutes.

Typical, he thought, *obsessed with another case. If I'm not careful, it's going to cost me another relationship before it even has a chance to get started.*

After they were seated in the radial-shaped dining room and he consulted with Jill, Joe ordered a bottle of California Chardonnay. Their waiter, who was wearing a loose-fitting gray linen suit, promptly delivered the bottle. Joe went through the customary wine tasting ritual. He checked the color of the wine, smelled the bouquet, then sipped and swished the wine in his mouth to ascertain its taste and feel. The fine wine met with his approval and Jill's as well.

They quickly became involved in conversation, but none of it relating to work or the Randall Johnson case.

Joe glanced around the noisy dining room. The walls had no noticeable art except an occasional shiny red circle. They were seated near eighteen boisterous guests at a large communal table used primarily for single diners or those without reservations. Jill raised her voice so Joe could hear her over the hubbub.

She started with a condensed version of her life story and how she had grown up in the Midwest, more specifically Chicago. This explained her accent, or lack thereof. Ever since their meeting the day before, Joe knew she couldn't be a native Northeasterner, and that was fine with him.

She said her parents were devout Roman Catholics. Her father was a sergeant on the Chicago Police Department. His family was Irish. Her mother was a freelance writer. Her family was Italian. Jill's dark features obviously favored her mother's side of the family. It was because of her father's work on the force and her mother's freelance writing that Jill became interested in police reporting.

She went on to talk about receiving her master's degree in Journalism from Northwestern University, and how she had spent her earlier college years working for the *Chicago City Paper*.

She described herself as a shy, awkward and gawky youth who was very plain looking and unsure of herself. Joe found it hard to believe that the beautiful and intellectual self-assured woman now sitting across the table from him could have ever been that way.

She had been married once, but only briefly. As she told it, she was young and restless, in her second year of college, and he was ten years older. He had his juris doctorate at the time and was already a partner in his father's law firm.

After a whirlwind romance of several months, they were married. She thought he was the man of her dreams. But Jill quickly became disillusioned to find that her new husband, her prince—or Italian Stallion, as she put it—was the center of his own universe and only interested in domesticating her. He was possessive and controlling. After the most miserable year of her life, they had the marriage annulled. Her fairy tale dream of a husband turned out to be a nightmare.

As far as relationships went since that time, Jill did not elaborate except to state that she had dated.

She went on to say that she finished college while she continued working full-time at the *City Paper*. But she wasn't happy there. She longed for something more. About two years after graduating, she called a friend living in Palm Beach who knew someone at the *Miami Journal*. They normally didn't hire anyone with less than five years' experience, but they apparently took into consideration her four years of employment during college. A few weeks later she was packing up and moving to Florida. That was in 1980.

Joe didn't ask if her friend in Palm Beach was male or female. He was certain he knew the answer. A woman as beautiful as Jill Riley probably had all sorts of male friends. He said, "So, how long did you stay there?"

"About five years, I guess," she stated as she continued to reflect.

"That means you were there during the riots and all the drug cartel violence?"

"Yep, I saw a lot. It was quite an eye-opener for a green kid just a couple years out of college. But it really fueled my passion. I mean, it just made me love my work that much more."

"So, did you know Mike Martinez? He and I touched base many years ago regarding a couple different homicides and some cases involving the Medellin cartel."

"Really? What cases were those? I might have been writing about them." The mention of Joe's involvement seemed to pique Jill's interest.

"Well, one of the cases included automaker John Z. DeLorean's attempt to finance his failing auto company with cocaine. Another case dealt with the stockpiling of cocaine in Los Angeles for the 1984 Summer Olympic Games."

"And that's it?" Jill asked.

"Yeah, pretty much. My involvement was mostly just helping by keeping my eyes and ears open for him. I was never really too involved on the L.A. end."

"Oh, well, I remember the cases but I didn't write any-thing on them. I mostly wrote stories about sex crimes, missing persons and, of course, the homicides. There were so many murders to write about," she said, shaking her head as she remembered. Thinking back now, she still found it hard to fathom and believe the homicide rate that existed in Miami during the early eighties. It was the highest in the nation.

"So why'd you leave?"

"Things really settled down in Miami after the federal posse moved in, and well, my friend in Palm Beach knew somebody at the *Empire State Tribune*. He called me and said they needed another police reporter in New York. You know, somebody to work the police beat. They offered me an increase in pay that was great, so I said sure."

"So, in the words of the Godfather, they made you an offer you couldn't refuse. Is it true that the Mafia owns or has ties to most of the major newspapers, or at least controls what goes into print?"

Jill shifted in her seat and rolled her eyes as she shook her head. She dryly replied, "No, Joe, they don't." Obviously agitated by his comment, Jill said, "I think now would be a good time for you to tell me a little more about yourself."

"But what about your friend?"

"My friend?" Jill asked, confused.

"Your friend that got you the jobs."

"Oh, him," she replied. "Well, we stay in touch. Now," she practically growled, "about you?"

The tone of Jill's voice made it obvious to Joe that he would be pushing his luck by asking more questions of her right now. He probably shouldn't have been so direct. Being a cop, he usually mistrusted strangers, particularly the press, but he felt comfortable speaking to her.

After the main course was served, Joe reciprocated. He started with a brief summation of his life history. He explained to Jill how his family also was Roman Catholic, though Joe had not practiced the faith in quite some time. His great-grandfather had been a member of the oldest Christian church in Japan. Built in Nagasaki in 1864, Oura Tenshu-do, or Oura Catholic Church, was now a designated national treasure.

In 1885, at a very young age, his great-grandfather immigrated to Hawaii. In 1900, Joe's grandfather was born, then twenty years later, his father. Joe's father had fought in World War II and was a member of Hawaii's highly decorated all-Japanese 100th Infantry Battalion. The Veterans Act provided education funds for returned service members, so his father enrolled for several years at UCLA, where he met Joe's mother. She was an American majoring in political science and over the course of four years of college they fell in love. They married in Los Angeles and then returned home to Hawaii.

Joe had heard countless stories about the war from his father, and though his parents would have preferred it, he had no desire to pursue a military career. Back then the military was Hawaii's largest industry. But tourism had surpassed it. He loved the islands with all their beauty and splendor but he, much like Jill, had still yearned for something more.

Joe had longed to visit the mainland as far back as he could remember. As best he could recall, it probably began after Congress granted Hawaii statehood in 1959. He yearned to see the country that his father had fought so bravely for, the country that had accepted their island nation as part of its own.

It was Joe's interest in running that carried him to Los Angeles. Even in high school he had been a strong runner. His success enabled him to obtain a scholarship and attend his father's alma mater, UCLA. He even got to compete against some of the best runners ever, including the great Steve Scott. Even as exciting as that was, Joe found something that interested him more.

The thing that fascinated Joe most of all was the amount of crime on the mainland. He had never before seen anything like it on the islands. He was amazed and excited at the same time. It was then he decided to pursue a position in law enforcement. After obtaining his bachelor's degree in Psychology, he remained in Los Angeles, took the police department test, and was accepted in the LAPD.

Joe followed an accelerated career path to become a Los Angeles detective and obtain the coveted gold shield.

Joe had known that his nationality had helped get him both the scholarship and the job on the LAPD. Even at that time, he understood the politics involved and knew that each place had minority quotas to fill. Though he worked the system, he never let it bother him. In a very short period, his performance and record always spoke for themselves, whether in the classroom, on the track, or on the force.

Joe had every intention of moving back to the islands some day, but it never worked out that way. He would go back once or twice a year to visit his parents and grandparents and run in the Ironman Triathlon. That was while they were still alive. His mother, father, and grandmother were now deceased, but his wise old grandfather still lived on the Island of Oahu, not far from Pearl Harbor. Joe's father had been a very astute investor and left Joe, his only child, everything. A portion of that money had allowed Joe to retire early from the force.

As far as relationships went, Joe hadn't had much time. Sure, he had some regular girlfriends over the years, but his passion for the force and his love of running always seemed to get in the way. He told Jill the same thing she had told him, that he dated occasionally.

Joe didn't share with Jill that he was just getting over the most serious relationship he had ever been involved with. Granted it had been six months since their breakup, but Joe still found himself occasionally thinking about Susan.

He had spent the past three years involved with only one woman—Susan Graham. Susan had her juris doctorate from Stanford University Law School and was a partner at the largest law firm in the city, Stout & Patterson. Joe thought he was ready to make a commitment but on the weekend that he was going to propose, she had told him it was over.

They had only spoken a couple times since. Joe wasn't exactly certain what had happened, but suspected it had a lot to do with the amount of time he spent on the force and training for competitions. Joe had read once in a book, before getting started in triathlons, that it was important to consider the social consequences. It said the importance of training to some triathletes had been cited as the cause for the breakup of their marriages. When he read it, Joe had just laughed. But he was over her now and had convinced himself it was time to move on. At least that's what he kept telling himself.

Joe took the last bite of prime rib and set down his utensils, savoring the morsel. He had begun his meal with the seared Japanese Hamachi and finished with the slow-roasted prime rib eye. The main course had been delicious: potato puree, baby carrots, pearl onions, haricot vert, and red wine sauce. He took another sip of wine and placed the half-empty glass back on the white linen tablecloth.

Jill was right; Joe did like the restaurant. Even though the portions were somewhat small, the modern French cuisine was magnificent. He could easily see how the chef, Michael Schlow, had recently won a James Beard Foundation Award.

Joe watched Jill finish the last of her confit of pork. Earlier he'd noticed the way she held her utensils, with the fork in her left hand and the knife in her right, the European way.

"So, how much time have you spent in Europe?"

"Now, where did that come from?"

"Well, I was just noticing the way you hold your utensils. You've obviously spent considerable time in Europe."

"You are very observant. Yes, I have."

"Business or pleasure?"

"What is this, an interrogation?" The utensils clinked as she set them across her empty plate. All that remained were a couple flageolet beans in jus de cumin.

Joe laughed. "No, I was just curious, that's all. Calm down. I'm sorry if you thought I was prying."

Jill lifted the white linen napkin from her lap and softly dabbed at both corners of her mouth as the waiter quietly removed their plates.

"Well, you know the saying, 'When in Rome, do as the Romans do.' "

"But we're not in Rome."

"I know, but it just sort of stuck with me. I think it's more elegant anyway. The American style is quite eccentric," she said.

"Well, I'm sorry if I think the American way of zigzagging is more practical and efficient. Anyway, I actually prefer chopsticks." Growing up Japanese American, Joe had eaten many meals with chopsticks during his youth.

That mental image brought a smile to Jill's face. "My travels are mostly business, but some pleasure as well. I've traveled all over Europe. I wrote several years for the *Empire State Tribune*, but have been with the *Gazette* based out of New York for the past five. It's been with the *Gazette* that I've done most of my business travel."

"What's your favorite place?"

Jill smiled. "Oh, without a doubt, it would have to be Italy. I find it enchanting and irresistible."

Joe noticed that Jill's brown eyes seemed to light up at the thought. "Then you've spent a lot of time there?"

"Oh no, not a lot . . . but enough to know I would love it there. I remember my first trip was during the summertime between my junior and senior years of college. It was just after my divorce. I still have my copy of Georgina Masson's *The Companion Guide to Rome*. As it turned out, I really didn't use it much."

"And why was that?"

She grinned, blushing. "Well, let's just say I met my own personal Italian tour guide and we didn't stay long in Rome. He took me farther south to Naples, then all the way to Sicily. Have you ever been to Italy, Joe?"

"Only once, but it really doesn't count. I was vacationing in Switzerland after a triathlon competition in Europe and decided to drive across the border into Italy for the day. Milan was the nearest big city and that was as far as I went. I'm a big fan of the Renaissance artists. I got to see da Vinci's *Last Supper*. That was pretty much the highlight of my trip. I honestly wasn't overly impressed with Milan. But I'm sure the other parts of Italy must be beautiful."

"Oh Joe, I truly believe it has to be the most beautiful place on earth! You say you like the Renaissance artists. Have you ever been to the Isabella Stewart Gardner Museum?"

"I've heard about it but have never been there. Here in Boston, right?"

"That's right. It's only about a mile and a-half from our hotel. The museum building is called Fenway Court and is designed in the style of a fifteenth-century Venetian palace. Many people believe it's a dismantled Venetian palazzo that was brought over and reconstructed here. But that's just a myth. Isabella Stewart Gardner only bought some of the architectural details like window frames and balconies from actual Venetian buildings."

Jill's eyes sparkled as she continued. "Bernard Berenson, who was an authority on Renaissance painting, became advisor and agent for many of the museum's most valuable paintings. In fact, Botticelli's *Tragedy of Lucretia* was his first acquisition for Isabella. You really should go see it. The museum has art galleries on three floors that overlook a central courtyard filled with plants and flowers. It's quite beautiful."

The mention of Renaissance paintings made the museum sound like a place Joe would enjoy. Since Jill seemed to like Italy so much, he wondered if she had ever been to probably the finest Italian restaurant in America. It was located a few miles from where Joe lived. "Have you ever been to Valentino in Santa Monica?" he asked.

"Oh God, yes. It's my favorite place. Max took me there a couple times. They put white truffles on everything!"

They sat and smiled at each other, Jill appearing to be off in another world.

She softly said, "Viva Italia."

Joe wasn't certain what to say next. He didn't know who Max was and didn't care. "So how about a cappuccino?" he asked.

Jill's smile instantly turned upside down. "Real Italians would never drink a cappuccino after supper. It's a morning drink."

Okay, Joe thought to himself. *That was European faux pas number two. One more strike and I'm probably out.*

Without thinking he said, "Perdoname," as he made a poor attempt at an Italian accent. Realizing she might not see the humor, he quickly changed the subject and continued in his normal tone of voice. "So, do you want to know exactly what happened back at Randall Johnson's house today?"

Jill raised both eyebrows in surprise as her eyes became larger and brighter again in the dim light of the dining room. "You know?" she asked as she daintily wiped at the corner of her mouth again and placed the napkin back on her lap.

"Well, here's how I see it. All off the record, of course. I can't take a chance of this getting into print. It could jeopardize our catching the perpetrator."

Jill took a quick drink, more like a gulp, and finished her glass of wine. She leaned forward and replied, "Of course."

"Johnson had apparently just finished his breakfast at about 08:30 this morning when he turned off the security system and let the dog out the back door to go do his business. The housekeeper, Carmela, established that was his normal routine. The dishes in the sink confirmed he had finished his breakfast.

"Anyway, the dog had just, well you know, in the backyard grass when Mr. Johnson stepped onto the back porch and removed a small black metal shovel he kept hanging on a nail near the doorframe. It's what he used to scoop up the dog's waste—the same kind you'd use to shovel out a fireplace.

"About that time the front doorbell rang. He called for the dog and together they went back inside the house. Johnson was still carrying the makeshift pooper-scooper. In his rush to answer the front door, he left the back door unlocked. As he exited the kitchen, he realized he was still carrying the shovel and placed it somewhere in the hallway.

"He answered the front door and was greeted by his lawn care technician. Randall Johnson joined him on the front stoop where he discussed some things he wanted the young man to do. After a brief conversation, the technician went about his work and Randall returned inside, locking the door behind him."

Jill sat in awe. She closed her mouth when she realized it was slightly open, and leaned further back from the table so as not to appear too enthralled, even though she was. *Where did he get all of this information?* she wondered.

Joe continued. "Randall Johnson then proceeded upstairs to take his morning bath. He apparently didn't realize he left the back door unlocked and also forgot about the dog's mess. His forgetting to lock the door wasn't all that unusual, though. He apparently did it all the time. Carmella said she always had to keep close tabs on the security whenever she was there. Unfortunately, she had the morning off. There was a death in her family and she was across town at the funeral.

"Anyway, Johnson went upstairs to the third floor to the master bedroom. He started the water for his bath. He tossed his clothes down the laundry chute, then partially closed the door to the bathroom. He left it slightly ajar so that Lady could come and go as she pleased. Lady is, and I quote, 'his little white dog that looks like a hairy rat.' "

Jill smirked as she shook her head and rolled her eyes at the detective.

"After turning on the built-in stereo and intercom, he laid his cordless phone beside the tub and climbed into the freestanding tub. He submerged himself in the water, then apparently realized there wasn't any soap.

"Randall stood up and climbed out of the tub dripping wet. He didn't bother to towel off. He went to the linen closet across the bathroom and took out a fresh bar of moisturizing soap. He walked across the room, leaving a trail of water as he went. He threw the box and plastic wrapper into the wastebasket beside the sink, then walked back to the tub and climbed in again. He submerged his body and laid there with his back to the door."

Joe stopped for effect while he took a sip of wine. He hoped he was impressing her. He noticed Jill's empty glass. "Can I pour you another glass?"

Jill stared in amazement. "Uhm, yes please. Thank you."

Joe poured, then replaced the bottle in the clear thermal-insulated wine chiller on the table.

"Meanwhile, the lawn care technician finished his work in the front yard and drove his truck around the block to take care of the grass in back. As soon as the technician was finished and had left, somebody wearing gloves opened the unlocked back door and stepped inside the kitchen. After closing the door behind him, he apparently surprised the small dog, probably causing her to start yipping. He looked around and realized he could close the dog up in the kitchen. He pulled the door to the dining room closed, then apparently kicked Lady across the kitchen as he headed for the hallway. He exited through the hall door, closing that behind him as well. Somewhere in the hallway between the kitchen and the front door, the killer picked up the shovel that Randall Johnson had set down earlier. The dog continued barking and started scratching at both newly varnished doors, trying to escape its confinement.

"The killer walked down the hall, toward the front door, and checked to make sure it was locked. He proceeded up the stairs. Upon reaching the second floor he probably could hear the loud music coming from the master bedroom located one floor above. He continued up the stairs and followed the music to Johnson's bedroom where he walked in and found the bathroom door slightly ajar.

"The killer opened the door and saw Randall Johnson sitting in the tub with his back to him. He crept across the marble floor, raised the shovel and struck Johnson with the flat backside of the blade. The blow to the top of Mr. Johnson's head knocked him unconscious. His body slid under the water and he drowned.

"Looking for a way to make it seem like an accident, the killer apparently located the portable CD unit at the top of the stairs and decided to use that. He carried it into the bathroom where he found a wall outlet close to the tub. He plugged it in, then tossed the stereo into the tub. After several seconds of sparks and smoke, the mansion's main circuit breaker threw.

"The killer didn't notice because he was already on his way back down the stairs with the murder weapon in his gloved hands. He went through the living room and dining room to exit through the kitchen, instead of down the hall."

"Why?" Jill asked, looking concerned.

"My guess is because the dining room door was much closer to the back door and he wouldn't have to battle the dog as he crossed the length of the kitchen. Anyway, as he was passing through the dining room, he apparently noticed the shovel was missing from the fireplace tools hanging alongside the fireplace. He put the shovel back, not knowing that it actually didn't belong there. He exited through the kitchen, possibly kicked the dog again, then went out the back door. He left the dining room door open and the dog no doubt ran out then.

"Randall Johnson died at approximately 9:17 this morning and his murderer was in and out of the house in less than ten minutes. When the circuit breaker threw and the electricity went off, the clock on the kitchen stove stopped at 9:18."

Jill was speechless. It appeared to her that Joe had figured everything out. It all seemed to make perfect sense. She shook her head and simply uttered, "How?"

"Okay, so I found out a couple things that you weren't aware of," Joe said, and smiled.

"Like?" Jill asked impatiently.

"Well, the lawn care tech told me that as he waited for Mr. Johnson to answer the front door, he could see him through the cheesecloth-type curtain that hung over the door's glass. He said Johnson was walking up the hall from the kitchen and appeared to stop about halfway to bend over and put something down. He then continued on to answer the door.

"The young man also said that when he went to the backyard to do his work, he noticed a fresh pile of waste that the dog had recently deposited. He said he thought that was kind of odd, knowing that Randall Johnson was, and I quote, 'anal about that sort of thing.' I have to admit I laughed at the kid's pun. Anyway, he knew there was the metal shovel hanging on the back wall just for that purpose, so he went to get it. When he got to the back door, he saw the nail was empty and the back door was slightly open, so he pulled it closed. He said he didn't want Lady to get out. He was only in the backyard for maybe five minutes.

"As he was leaving, he said he noticed a silver-gray Mercedes with New Jersey plates and dark-tinted windows sitting behind Johnson's garage. It was parked on the back street that runs behind the house. He said he couldn't tell if anybody was inside it or not. The only reason he noticed was because when he went to leave in the company truck, it was a very tight squeeze back there. He didn't want to scratch the Mercedes."

"Was the person already in the house?" Jill asked.

"No, not yet. He was apparently waiting for the lawn care technician to leave. Once he pulled away, the guy got out of his car and walked up the back sidewalk to the kitchen door. That would have been sometime after 9:10 A.M. The reason we know that is because the lawn technician writes down the time that he arrives and when he leaves."

Joe's conversation was interrupted when the waiter asked if they cared for dessert or an after dinner drink. They said coffee would be fine.

As soon as the waiter left, Jill asked, "What about some of the other details? How did you know all that?"

"Detective Wilson also talked to Carmela Gonzales, his housekeeper. You've probably spoken to her when you've called."

"No, I haven't. Mr. Johnson always answered the phone himself."

"Well, it turns out that the CD-radio boom box was hers. The stereo and intercom system built into the walls through-out the house only had an FM stereo. She had favorite music on compact discs that she liked to listen to so she carried the boom box with her throughout the house while she cleaned. She said she always finished her cleaning on the third floor and would leave it on the table at the top of the stairs. Apparently Randall's killer needed something quick and logical to throw in the tub to make it look like an accident, and that was the closest thing.

"Also, Randall Johnson was, like most of us, a creature of habit. Carmela said he would take a bath about the same time every morning. He had partial hearing loss and refused to get a hearing aid, so he would always turn his music up loud so he could hear it. He would also turn on the intercom in case Carmela needed to reach him. He'd also carry his portable phone with him.

"As you know, when the detectives flipped the breaker, the in-house stereo in Johnson's bathroom came on very loud. For that reason, we assume he didn't hear Lady's barking or scratching downstairs. Also, the volume setting on the CD-stereo was too low for him to have been able to hear. In addition, there was no disc in the unit and the radio was tuned to a Latin music station. Finally, why would he have both the in-house stereo playing along with the boom box?"

The waiter returned and turned their cups over, filling them from a pot of steaming coffee. He then placed the check on the table between them and stated that he would take it for them whenever they were ready. As the young man walked away, Jill picked up the check.

"I insist," she said. "Besides, it's a business expense."

Joe was hoping it was more than business. Dismissing the thought, he continued where he'd left off. "Carmela also said that she had just cleaned the bathroom late yesterday afternoon. The hard water stains on the bathroom's marble floor show the path that Randall Johnson took after climbing out of the tub to get a fresh bar of soap.

"They also found some shampoo residue and a gray hair on the back of the shovel as well as a large dent that matches up with the top of his head. I guess the killer thought it would look like he was climbing out of the tub when he accidentally knocked in the stereo, thereby electrocuting himself. Then it would appear that he simply fell afterwards, hitting the top of his head on the side of the tub or faucet.

"What the killer doesn't realize is that the medical examiner will be able to determine that Randall Johnson drowned first, then was electrocuted. As far as the blow to the head, well, he would've had to be hanging upside down from the curtain rod to fall and strike that part of his head.

"Carmella also confirmed that painters had been to the house yesterday and freshly varnished some of the wood in the kitchen; so, the scratch marks I saw had to have occurred today. The housekeeper said Mr. Johnson would have never confined Lady to the kitchen, or anywhere else in the house, for that matter.

"She also said Lady was fine when she left late yesterday afternoon. But the dog winces when you pick her up now. She obviously has a tender spot around the underside of her ribs. My guess is this is where the perpetrator kicked her.

"Finally, the only fingerprints they found on the back doorknob were yours. This tells us that the killer was wearing gloves or wiped everything he touched. If this wasn't the case, then Randall Johnson's prints should have been on some of the doorknobs and the shovel, but they weren't."

Jill said, "Just like that, you've figured everything out. Truly amazing!"

"I wouldn't say I've figured everything out. At least not yet. I still don't know who the killer is. Whoever it was, they obviously knew enough to know that Carmela wasn't going to be there, but probably didn't know about the dog. They probably knew enough to know he was hard of hearing, but didn't know the stereo wasn't his and in their haste didn't check the station or the volume it was turned to. I don't think the person who did this was a hired hit man or professional killer. Although I think it was premeditated, I don't think it was well thought out."

"You know, if you didn't already suspect Tony Folino's operation, I would swear the housekeeper probably did it."

"The same thought crossed our minds as well, but she does have an alibi. We've already checked and confirmed that she was at a family funeral during the time of Johnson's death. There's no motive, either. Detective Wilson said when they informed her of Randall's death, she went hysterical. She adored the man. He was like family to her. The poor dear blames herself for his death. She kept saying, if only she had been there, if only she hadn't taken the day off."

Joe paused as he silently reflected, and then spoke again. "So you still haven't told me. What other deaths are you suspicious of and how did you and your newspaper get turned on to them?" Joe had no sooner finished asking the question when Jill's cell phone rang.

"Excuse me." Jill reached into her purse and answered, "Jill Riley."

Joe nodded at Jill as he excused himself from the table to give Jill some privacy and at the same time use the restroom.

When Joe returned, Jill was finished with her call and had already paid the check. "Are you ready to go?" she asked.

"Ready when you are," Joe responded as he helped her from her chair.

She walked alongside Joe, holding his left arm as they proceeded outside to catch a taxi for the ride back to the hotel. They soon arrived at the Hilton Back Bay.

Joe and Jill stepped out of the cab and walked into the hotel lobby. "Join me for another drink in the bar?" Joe asked as they headed for the elevators. He thought he knew what her answer would be, but was surprised by the response.

"Oh Joe, I really wish I could, but I've got to go back to my room and do some work. That call I received just after dinner, well, that was the paper calling to say that the deadline for another one of my stories has been moved up." She added, "More copy, you know? It's all editors want."

They reached the elevator and Joe pressed on the Up button. "I understand," Joe replied, even though he actually didn't. "Dinner was great. Radius was an excellent choice and I thoroughly enjoyed the food and your company. Thank you. Next time I'll pick the restaurant. Deal?"

"Oh Joe, you're such a gentleman."

The elevator doors slid open.

"Thank you for being so understanding." She lightly pecked Joe on his right cheek. "Goodnight, we'll talk again tomorrow."

Joe stood there as Jill stepped into the elevator and the doors closed. He wasn't sure what had just happened. He thought she had been showing an interest in him.

Joe waited a few more seconds, then pushed the Up button again. He briefly thought about having a drink in Club Nichole, the hotel's sophisticated international nightclub, but then thought better of it.

The elevator doors opened and an elderly couple stepped off. Joe walked in and pressed the button for his floor. He would have a drink in his room. The suite's wet bar would do just fine.

In his room Joe removed his sports coat and hung it on a wooden hangar in the closet on the inside of the door. He loosened another button on his dress shirt and kicked off his shoes as he sat down on the end of the bed. He stared at the bright flowered comforter, wondering what he had done wrong. Was it something he'd said? He knew that was a definite possibility; he had a habit of putting his foot in his mouth, especially around beautiful women. Surely it couldn't have been his lack of European etiquette. He did have to admit she acted rather strangely whenever she spoke of Italy.

Joe got up and headed to the bar. His thoughts were interrupted by a knock at the door. He turned, walked down the short hallway past the bathroom, and opened the door to find Jill standing there.

"There was a message on my phone when I got back to my room. The other story I was working on, well, they scrapped it altogether. Is it too late for that drink?"

Joe smiled as he opened the door wider. "Actually, you're just in time." He closed the door as he thought, *Viva Italia!*

<12>

Tony Folino stared out over Central Park from the terrace of his Fifth Avenue penthouse. He and his wife had just returned from dinner at San Domenico on Central Park South.

A couple of his boys, as he liked to call them, stepped out on the patio into the chilly evening air. Today's warmer temperatures were quickly dropping as another cold front moved through, reminding them that winter was not quite over. The thick clouds blocking out the moon formed a canopy over the City, aglow with its millions of lights.

Tony liked being at the top of the heap and this stretch of Fifth Avenue on New York City's Upper East Side was just that. His years of hard work and ambition had earned him this premier address as well as several others around the country. He had second and third homes located near both of his U.S. training facilities. The estate on South Ocean Boulevard in Palm Beach was a favorite of his daughter's, though they also enjoyed the ranch just outside of Durango. In addition, he had the place in Sicily.

He stood with his back to the two young Italian men, the outline of his body illuminated by a single citronella candle on the table beside him. His shadow was cast on the wall to his left. He listened to what they had to say.

"We have it from a good source, Boss, that this Joe Hara guy has been snoopin' around. He came to your operations facility yesterday for a tour. He says he's looking at the program for himself, but our understanding is he's looking into Perrino's death."

"Please don't call me Boss." Folino's voice was monotone and void of emotion. "Did you find out who killed Perrino?"

"Uh, no Boss, uhm, I mean sir. We haven't, but we're still working on it. Word on the street is that you called the hit." He paused for a moment. "We're also trying to figure out why this Hara guy was at Randall Johnson's house today right after he died."

Folino turned around and faced the two men. Expressionless, he addressed the older of them, whose name was Bruno. "Was Randall Johnson's death really an accident or did someone kill him too?"

Bruno hastily answered Folino's question. "The television is saying he accidentally electrocuted himself while taking a bath. The old fart knocked his ghetto box into the bath."

Jimmie, the younger of the men, laughed. He could see that Folino was not amused and lost the grin. "We're looking into it, sir. We've got our best guys on it. We expect more information by later tonight."

Folino frowned and shook his head. "I don't know if that is gonna be good enough, fellas. I'm very disappointed in both of you. I expected to have some answers by now."

"Yes sir," they replied together.

"Remember, I call the shots around here. So I have to know who took out Perrino and Johnson, if their deaths really weren't accidental. I especially didn't want Randall Johnson dead." He turned and looked again at the park.

They all stood in silence, hearing only the distant sounds of the hectic City far below.

Tony thought, *What fucking rotten luck! Randall Johnson was the only user of the aircraft. I didn't want him dead. The timing couldn't have been worse. And who the hell ran Perrino off the road? Whoever they were, they were sloppy.* Folino finally said, "You've got somebody following Hara?"

Again the older man took the lead. "Yes sir, we do. As best we can. It seems he's making his way back west on some of the competitors' aircraft. He's touring their facilities and looking at their programs too."

A silence followed.

Jimmie, the shorter and younger man, said, "Boss, there's something else."

"Yes, go on, I'm waiting," he snapped.

"Well sir, it seems Ms. Riley, uhm, Jill Riley was at Randall Johnson's house with Detective Hara. She's the one who found his body."

Folino faced the men. "What the hell was she doing there?"

"I guess she was there to write a story for the *Gazette*." He paused and added, "Sir."

Folino stared down, then reached into the inside of his suit coat. Both men tensed. He pulled out a pack of chewing gum and removed a single stick, balled up the paper wrapper and foil, and flicked it over the balcony railing. The men looked at each other as they silently let out sighs of relief.

Folino looked at the two men as he slowly and methodically chewed the gum. "Do you have somebody keeping a close eye on Ms. Riley?" he asked.

"Yes sir," one immediately replied.

"All the time," the other added.

He paused again. "And you know what you're supposed to do on Sunday?"

"Yes sir, we do. We'll make sure everything is taken care of."

"Then, we're done for now. The next time you come to see me, you better have some answers. Now go, show yourselves out."

Folino turned his attention to the park once again.

They both replied, "Thank you, sir," and stepped inside.

Tony stood thinking about his lovely wife, Maria, and their two beautiful daughters, Estelle and Teresa. They were his pride and joy and he always wanted to provide the best for them.

They had always had the finest schooling possible. He had enrolled them in an exclusive nursery school, a prestigious private grade school, and the best prep school money could buy.

He also thought about his mother, who now lived with them, and his deceased father. He missed his father, God rest his soul. He had taught Tony everything he knew. When Tony was growing up, his father had been a hard man to live with. But he was a good man. Tony had always told himself he would be happy if he could just be half the man his father had been. The family had always come first with him. He had wanted to make sure they were always taken care of.

Tony felt the same way. His thoughts revolved around his family. He looked up at the cloudy sky and hoped his father somewhere in heaven would forgive him, because he knew that he wouldn't approve. Tony had been weak where his father and grandfather had been strong. Tony took a deep breath and shook his head as he wondered what the hell he had gotten himself into.

13

Joe briskly exited the hotel elevator as he whistled "I've Got the World on a String." Joe had been a Frank Sinatra fan as long as he could remember. His mother had started listening to the young Sinatra on the radio during World War II. A punctured eardrum had made "Old Blue Eyes" unfit for military service.

When Joe thought back to his childhood as a small boy in the late fifties, he could remember often hearing Sinatra's voice crooning on the radio or emanating from the speaker of his parent's phonograph. He didn't pay much attention at the time and didn't realize that the music was subliminally being embedded in his mind.

He strode toward the hotel lobby's front desk.

A young black woman behind the counter greeted Joe with a huge smile and a sincere sounding "Good Morning." Her gold-plated name badge read Yolanda.

Joe thought her attitude was refreshing. "Good morning, Yolanda. How are you?" Joe was feeling wonderful. He was invigorated after having slept soundly the previous night in the king-size bed. No doubt, Jill Riley was just what he'd needed.

"I'm fine, thank you. Wuz everything satisfactory during your stay?"

Joe couldn't help but notice the way she pronounced the word "was." "Everything was fine, thank you." Joe said, emphasizing the correct pronunciation. He found it refreshing to receive service with a smile, and he smiled back as he placed his room key on the counter.

He always liked to check out at the front desk. He had never been comfortable just doing the express or video checkout in his room. He always felt much better personally watching them charge his account and then walking away with a receipt that has come off the printer. It was just a quirk of his.

"It will be a few moments, sir, while I bring up your account."

Her courteous service made Joe recall a recent trip he had made to the supermarket. He had just gone through the checkout lane and was walking toward the exit when he heard a woman asking a young male cashier if he knew the price of a particular lawn chair that was on display at the end of the checkout aisle. The young man, probably about seventeen or eighteen, replied indifferently, "I have no idea." Very politely, she said, "Do you know how I would go about finding out?" To which the young man replied, "I couldn't tell you."

Joe didn't hear the rest of the conversation because he left, but as much as he hated to admit it, that type of service seemed to be commonplace in today's society.

"Would you like to keep this on your American Express card?"

Joe was scanning the front page of the *Boston Today* morning edition that was on the counter in front of him. "Uhm, yes, that's fine," he said without looking up. He read the front-page story regarding Randall Johnson's death.

He looked up and asked, "Could you please ring Ms. Riley's room? Jill Riley. She's in 415, I think." Joe quickly scrutinized the article.

"Just a moment and I'll ring her room."

The young woman clicked away at the keyboard of the computer terminal. A few seconds later the printer hummed and pushed forward a printed invoice carrying the hotel's insignia along with Joe's account information.

Joe was glad to see that the story in the newspaper made no mention of any suspected foul play in Randall Johnson's death. Although it did say that local police officials were waiting for the coroner's autopsy and report, they didn't feel there was any reason to suspect foul play. Joe glanced at the writer's name and noticed that Jill's friend, Paul Stavale, had written the story.

Joe glanced at the receptionist, who was shaking her head.

She looked up from the monitor and said, "I'm sorry, Mr. Hara, but I just checked the registry and Ms. Riley has already checked out this morning." Yolanda tore Joe's receipt off the printer and folded it before handing it to him. "I hope you'll be stayin' with us again soon."

"Thanks," Joe said as he turned and headed for the front door. Joe would be back soon, having long ago made his reservations for the upcoming marathon. Hotel rooms in the city were always at a premium during marathon weekend.

Joe thought about Jill as he walked toward the valet out front. *She definitely is a go-getter. I guess you don't become a great journalist by sleeping in. She probably had another deadline moved up.*

She had spent the night in Joe's room. He remembered looking at the clock beside the bed after their second time around and saw that it was just after midnight. Shortly thereafter they fell asleep in each other's arms. Joe wasn't certain what time she got up and left. All he knew was that when he woke up at seven, she wasn't there.

Joe wasn't concerned, though. He would try to reach her later on her cell phone.

He handed the valet his ticket. The morning air was considerably cooler than the day before and the sky was completely overcast. A cold front had moved in during the night and dropped the temperature back into the upper thirties. The forecast was calling for a ninety percent chance of rain with a high near fifty degrees.

Joe had dressed more casually today, wearing a pair of navy Dockers with his burgundy tassel loafers and an ecru button-down Oxford shirt. He knew it was going to be chilly so he wore his dark green Ralph Lauren windbreaker. Joe zipped up the jacket as the cold wind whipped through the hotel breezeway.

A short, rotund bellhop grabbed the gold-plated poles of the rolling baggage cart and pulled it closer to the curb where

Joe was standing. Joe noticed his bags and bike box along with several other people's bags on the cart.

After several more minutes the valet returned with Joe's rental car. The valet released the trunk lid before getting out and the bellhop immediately began placing Joe's baggage in the back. Joe tipped the bellhop several dollars and also gave a couple to the valet. He kindly thanked both men and got into the warm car.

Joe pulled the car over, against the curb, several spaces farther up while he programmed his destination into the navigation system. Even though Logan Airport was only five miles away, there were a lot of turns and this would make driving much simpler. Joe could think about the case, or Jill Riley, and let the car tell him when to turn. He smiled as he thought about last night with Jill.

Joe quickly finished the programming, then signaled as he pulled away from the hotel and turned west onto Belvedere Street. Within one hundred yards the female voice prompted him to turn right on Massachusetts Avenue.

About fifteen minutes later Joe turned right and traveled the last quarter-mile to Five Star Aviation. Joe would drop his rental car here and someone from Hertz would come pick it up. As Joe pulled into the facility, he glanced at his watch and saw he was right on time for his flight. He drove into the parking lot and parked the car near the door. Joe reached down and pressed a button on the driver's door trim panel, releasing the car's rear deck lid. When Joe looked up, he noticed the first drops of rain rolling down the windshield.

Joe got out of the car with his briefcase in hand. Out of the trunk he removed his bike box, suitcase and duffel bag. Joe carried the bike box and suitcase to the nearby sidewalk, where he set them down. He went back and got his briefcase and duffel, then proceeded inside the FBO.

At the service counter an attractive young woman holding a piece of paper greeted him and asked, "Can I help you?"

"Yes, I'm Joe Hara. I'm here to catch a flight." Joe pulled from his jacket the itinerary that Jet Divide had faxed him at the hotel. He quickly unfolded it. "Let's see, the tail number is 423JD," Joe told the woman.

"Oh yes, 423 Juliet Delta. They just finished fueling your plane. This is the fuel ticket in my hand. Your pilots are standing right over there, Mr. Hara. Let me go get them for you."

Joe glanced out the window and saw a shiny white aircraft with the tail number 423JD, on the ramp. A three-foot wide and maybe ten-foot long red carpet was rolled out from the base of the airplane stairs. But that wasn't what caught Joe's attention—it was the woman he saw hurrying across the ramp. About thirty yards away, Jill Riley was rushing across the ramp toward a plane.

Joe dropped his briefcase and duffel bag, and ran to the door that exited onto the ramp as a pilot was entering. He half-stepped out of the building while still holding the door and shouting, "Jill!"

She stopped and turned, obviously surprised to see him.

One of Joe's pilots was approaching him from behind as Joe hurried out the door and across the ramp.

"Mr. Hara!"

Joe turned and shouted back at the pilot, "I'll just be a minute. I got a couple things on the curb and two more in front of the counter."

Joe walked up to Jill and immediately noticed her large silk scarf and sunglasses.

She smiled awkwardly and said, "Joe, I'm sorry I didn't get to say goodbye, but . . ."

As Jill was speaking, Joe stepped closer and could see something wasn't right. He took another step and reached out to take off her sunglasses. Jill winced and started to turn away, but Joe gently grabbed her by the right arm. She flinched at his touch.

"Jill?" Joe said, puzzled.

As he removed her sunglasses, he was startled to see a large bruise below her right eye. There was considerable swelling from the contusion and her eye was red with broken blood vessels.

Jill glimpsed down at the concrete ramp, then back at Joe. "I didn't want you to see me this way," she said softly, then forced a slight smile.

"Who did this to you!" Joe demanded. *Who could do such a thing!* Her beautiful face, unblemished a few hours before, was battered and bruised.

"It goes with the territory, Joe. You, if anybody, should understand that."

"What do you mean?"

"Hello," she said, "you've heard the expression 'hard-hitting investigative reporter.' Well, that's me—only this time somebody else did the hitting. I guess the bitch didn't like the questions I was asking." Jill let out a half-hearted laugh.

The rain was now a heavy drizzle. Joe could hear his airplane behind him on the ramp as the pilots started the Citation V engines.

"Another woman did this to you?" Joe asked, surprised.

"Yeah, it's not the first time," Jill said, like it was no big deal. "I also once had a guy punch me while doing a story."

"Where did this happen?" Joe stared at Jill's eye. The woman had to have been big to pack a punch that could deliver a shiner like the one he was seeing.

"Uhm, do you think you could please stop staring at my eye? I mean, here I was worried about you seeing me with bed head this morning, and now this happens."

Joe grinned. "I'd like to see you with bed head."

Jill took the sunglasses from Joe's hand and slid them back on. "I left early this morning because I had an interview with someone regarding another story I'm working on."

"Don't tell me, I know. More copy, right?" Joe said sarcastically.

"I'm sorry, Joe, but it's my job."

"So, what did you ask that got her pissed off enough to punch you?"

"It doesn't matter. It's a long story. I'll tell you the next time we get together, and I hope that's very soon." Jill stepped forward and kissed Joe on the right cheek. "I had a wonderful time last night."

As she stepped back, Joe noticed a pilot standing at the top of the stairs just inside the airplane cabin. Joe instantly recognized the uniform.

"We're ready whenever you are, Ms. Riley," the young pilot stated.

"I'm coming now," she replied.

Joe looked up at the plane's tail. The serial number ended with the familiar letters SS. It was one of Tony Folino's planes.

Jill saw the puzzled look on Joe's face as he tried to process the information. She asked him, "Why do you think my newspaper has such an interest in Tony Folino's company? They own shares in his program. The chairman asked me to see what I could find out. Okay?"

Joe nodded. "Okay, it all makes sense now."

She climbed the aircraft stairs as the pilot took her hand and helped her into the cabin. Joe noted how nice she looked in jeans.

She looked back at Hara. "Well, goodbye, Joe. You'll keep me posted on your investigation."

Joe noticed it wasn't a question but more of a command. *How can I say no to such a beautiful woman?* "Absolutely. I'll call you either way, as soon as I get back to L.A."

As the pilot lifted the stairs, Joe could hear Jill say, "Arrivederci."

"Sayonara," he replied. Joe walked back to the FBO as the rain fell even harder.

<14>

It was late Sunday night and Jack Williams was suddenly feeling tired. He struggled to keep his eyes open and yawned as his brain begged for more oxygen. An oncoming vehicle failed to dim its high beams. Jack flashed his headlights at the car. Both vehicles passed one another on the narrow strip of rural New Jersey road as each driver shielded his eyes from the other's opposing glare. Jack shook his head in disgust and yawned again. He thought he probably shouldn't have drunk that last glass of wine after dinner. He couldn't wait to get home and into his soft bed.

Though the evening had been enjoyable and somewhat entertaining, Ross Nickels still hadn't been able to convince Jack to stay with the StratoShares program. Jack managed the estate of his eighty-year-old mother who lived in Saddle River, New Jersey. The invitation to dinner in the City with William Price and Tony Folino was a last-ditch effort on their part to keep Jack from selling back his mother's shares.

Ross Nickels had known exactly where Jack stood before he accepted the invitation. Jack had told the closed-minded Nickels that his decision was not likely to change. Jack had dealt with Ross for nearly two years and found he had selective hearing. Ross was not a good listener; Jack could eventually get through to him, but it always took a while. Just like Nickels' promises. He was always true to his word, but you had to keep after him before he'd finally come through.

Anyway, it really didn't matter. Jack's mother had been in the StratoShares program for twenty-four months, so she was guaranteed they would buy back her shares. Jack didn't feel like he could lose. He even got a great dinner at Tavern on the Green.

Once again, the evening had been first class. They had a superb five-course meal in the Tavern's Park Room with its fifty-two-foot mural depicting Central Park at the turn of the century, and antique Baccarat chandeliers.

Ross Nickels, who was his own biggest fan and never at a loss for words, spoke first and introduced everyone in the prestigious group of forty men and women. They consisted of existing owners in StratoShares as well as new prospects for the program. Many in attendance were the decision makers like himself and not the actual end users of the StratoShares product.

In Jack's case, his mother was the only user of the program. She used her StratoShares to travel around the globe for personal pleasure. Being an only child, she had recently inherited a small fortune including her StratoShares fraction, when her father, Jack's grandfather, passed away at the ripe old age of one hundred. She had never owned an airplane before, but had flown on her father's many times. Strato-Shares was her only exposure to a private jet. She knew it was an extravagance, but felt like she deserved it. She had waited a long time for her father's fortune. For the past two years she had traveled regularly to several locations overseas.

Jack struggled to keep his eyes open.

So, his mother didn't know any different when the StratoShares service was substandard or less than convenient. She thought the limitations, demands, and changes they made to her international trip schedules were normal. As far as she was concerned, everything was fine.

But Jack had been the CFO of a large corporation for many years before going out on his own. One of his responsibilities at that time had been managing the company aircraft, including the fractional shares they owned to supplement their fleet. As a result he had become familiar with what was, and wasn't, good service. He was now using that experience in his mother's best interest.

Jack's entire body jerked. He reflexively pulled at the steering wheel as the Saab started to cross the double yellow lines. He rubbed both eyes, blinked several times and yawned again. Jack couldn't believe he had just almost fallen asleep behind the wheel; he couldn't recall ever having done that before.

He turned off the heater and opened the power windows halfway on both sides of the car. He felt an instant blast of the cold night air as it roared noisily through the windows helping to keep him awake.

He went back to his thoughts of earlier that evening. After Ross Nickels had finished speaking, Tony Folino spoke. This was the first time Jack had ever met Folino. It was his understanding that Tony, at fifty-five, was just a couple years older than he was. After seeing him, though, Jack wouldn't have guessed Folino was a day over fifty.

Jack sensed that even though Tony had been born and raised in the United States, his Italian heritage ran deep. He briefly spoke of his father, the son of an Italian immigrant. He had come to America with only a few dollars and became a self-made man. The way Tony carried himself and spoke told Jack that Tony Folino had come from the "old school."

Jack's first impression had been that Folino was probably a man of few words, but that was quickly negated. Tony answered every question posed to him like a diplomat. He articulated on everything down to the minutest details. It was obvious Folino's involvement with the company was very hands on, all the way to its lowest level.

Yet when asked about his tremendous success, Tony was humble. Though he gave William Price some credit for the financial wherewithal, he sincerely thanked his mother and father for instilling in him the work ethic and values necessary to become so successful in today's business world and society.

Jack glanced up and flipped the switch on his rearview mirror. Someone was following closely behind him with the high beams on. *What is it tonight, with these people and their headlights?* he thought. Jack suddenly realized he was cold so he closed the windows and turned on the car's heater. He knew in a few moments he would probably get hot again and need to reopen the windows. It was a vicious cycle, but at least it was keeping him awake.

He looked at the illuminated numbers located on the information display. It was now 11:00 P.M. He had been driving for an hour and still had another half-hour before he would arrive home.

Jack allowed his eyelids to close ever so slightly as the leather interior warmed and his body once again became relaxed. *Sleep would be so nice,* he thought. His car again gravitated across the broken yellow lines. Jack's whole body shuddered as he jerked the steering wheel and the import veered back into its own lane.

"Damn it!" he said aloud. He couldn't believe he had almost done it again. Twice he had started to doze off. *I could sure use a cup of coffee or some caffeine or something. Unfortunately, there aren't any gas stations or fast-food restaurants on this stretch of country road. Besides, they probably wouldn't be open at this hour on a Sunday night.*

Jack reached down and turned on the radio. His ears were greeted with the relaxing sounds of a famous Mozart selection. He certainly didn't need to be anymore relaxed and quickly changed the station from 96.3 WQXR, his favorite classical music station. He pressed the search button until he reached 92.7, one of New York City's popular modern rock stations. He turned up the volume as the song's pounding bass shook his entire body. It actually made his head hurt. He hated the noise of rock music, but if it would help keep him awake, he'd put up with it until he arrived home safely.

His thoughts drifted back again to the evening's dinner. Bill Price had spoken next. He addressed the group like only he could do, delivering innovative but sound advice on fractional ownership with a helping of wit on the side. He kept the audience enthralled as they hung on his every word.

Jack's eyelids, feeling heavy, succumbed to the unrelenting feeling of sleepiness. His head and body slumped forward. His hands loosened their tight grip on the steering wheel. The shoulder belt stretched forward and kept him from falling completely frontward. Thoughts of dinner slipped from his mind as his entire body relaxed and he descended into a deep sleep.

A few seconds later Jack's foot slipped off the gas pedal. The black Saab 9-5 Aero veered off the desolate two-lane road and traveled about twenty yards over an embankment before driving head-on into a grove of sassafras trees.

The car following Jack slowed down and pulled over to the side of the road. The hum of the passenger side power window could be heard as it slowly went down and both occupants stared into the trees. The Saab's right headlight partially illuminated the large, deeply furrowed tree trunk that the car enveloped. The driver turned off his engine as they listened in silence. The only sounds they could hear were an occasional crack and pop from the car's mangled engine. As they watched, the remaining headlight noiselessly went out and the car was engulfed in the darkness of the surrounding trees.

The driver finally spoke. "Do you think he's dead?"

"I dunno, Bruno, probably," the passenger replied. "I don't see any movement down there. The way the car's wrapped around that tree, I would say he has to be dead."

"Maybe you should go have a look, Jimmie."

"No fuckin' way! What if somebody came along and saw us? Let's get the hell out of here. Now!"

Bruno started the car and slowly pulled back onto the road.

<15>

On Tuesday afternoon when Joe sat down at his office desk in the spare bedroom of his new home, he looked around at the clutter of boxes. "No rest for the weary," he said aloud. He had lived here about three weeks and still hadn't finished unpacking.

It seemed there was always something to pull him away from the miserable job. Dan and Nancy had helped him pack and move, but Joe would not allow them to help with the unpacking. Thinking about it now, he should have given in to their generous offer; but at the time, he didn't want to impose. He was getting tired of living out of boxes and continually having to rummage through cardboard containers in search of things.

The only items Joe had unpacked were the contents of his desk, toiletries, clothing, linens, and kitchen utensils. As he sat back and thought about it, he wondered why he even needed anything else.

Joe knew he was going to like it here in Venice. He had recently sold his condominium located on the other side of town. It took Danny to point out the only reason he was living there was because it was closer to Susan. Since things were now over between them, he had decided it was as good a time as any to move.

In addition there had been some security issues there. Someone had gained access to Joe's condo through the crawl space above his unit. After that incident he decided he needed to own his own place.

At less than twenty years old, the house was a quaint two-story white stucco with a composition roof. Its 1,700 square feet of living space with three bedrooms and two and a-half baths was more than enough space for Joe. Some of its other amenities included a wood-burning fireplace, two balconies and a two-car garage. Joe felt the garage was a must to protect his Lexus and motorcycle from the ocean's salty air, which was just a few blocks away at Marina del Rey.

Joe loved running and biking along the water. He had already gotten in a good workout this morning. Joe had taken a long aerobic bike ride along the coast and exercised at a medium intensity of about sixty-five percent of his maximum heart rate. Tomorrow he would get in a short run along with some strength training, and the following day he would get in a long aerobic swim. The Boston Marathon was only a few weeks away, but Joe's real focus remained on the Ironman Triathlon. He couldn't wait to once again tackle the Kona Coast.

Yet, as much as he enjoyed the nearby water, the best thing about Joe's new place was the fact that Danny and Nancy lived only a couple blocks away. They had lived in Venice for the past ten years and even had a boat docked at the marina not far from Joe's house. They were the closest thing to a family that Joe had, aside from his grandfather in Oahu.

Joe noticed that the sword fern on the plant stand beside his desk was badly in need of water. He loved tropical plants, but sometimes his extended absences would take their toll. This plant needed plenty of water and from the appearance of its sagging leaves, it was evident he had been gone most of the week. Joe poured the tall glass of water that was sitting on his desk into the plant's large white pot. He then went back and forth between the kitchen and bathrooms as he walked from room to room, watering all of his plants. When he was finished, he went back to the kitchen and filled a clean glass for himself.

Back in the office he sat down at his desk and turned on the Gateway monitor. Joe noticed some paper on the fax machine beside his desk. He reached over and lifted four pages off.

The first page was a cover sheet from Ross Nickels. Joe put that aside and read the next page. It was a thank you from Ross for taking the demonstration flight and coming out to tour their facility. He also apologized for not being able to meet with Joe during the visit, and was sending him an invitation to join him at the Toyota Grand Prix of Long Beach. Joe glanced at the third page, which was the invitation.

It said that he and a guest were cordially invited to join Ross Nickels of StratoShares and members of the Folino Racing Team at the event, which was scheduled for the third weekend of April. Seats would be provided in the grandstand on race day, along with hospitality at the team's tent throughout the race.

Joe was surprised; he had no idea that Tony Folino owned Folino Racing. He should have made the connection. He glanced at the last page. It listed the entire year's calendar for CART, including the season's first race this weekend in Miami.

Joe hadn't followed racing in about twenty-five years, back when it was called the U.S. Auto Club. Sometime in the late seventies it changed to CART, Championship Auto Racing Teams. He could remember watching the likes of A. J. Foyt, Mario Andretti, Bobby Unser and Al Unser.

It's a nice invitation, Joe thought. StratoShares spared no expense in trying to get people into their program, and Ross Nickels obviously thought Joe was a prospect. Depending where he stood with the investigation as the California event drew closer, Joe would keep it in mind as to whether or not he'd attend.

He reached down and pressed the button that booted his computer hard drive. Joe was fanatical about paying bills on time and wanted to get his personal business out of the way first.

He had been away for five days. After spending the day in Indianapolis on Saturday and touring the Jet Divide facility, on Sunday he had flown to Wichita, where he toured the operations of one of the manufacturer-owned fractional programs. From there he flew down to Dallas for his final tour, and then returned yesterday evening on another Strato-Shares plane. Each company had been quite impressive as they all put on their best dog-and-pony show. There was no doubt in Joe's mind that the StratoShares program stood out as the biggest and the best.

When Joe was finished with the bills, he would review his notes and give Danny another call. He was curious to know if he had any new information. They had spoken briefly on Sunday evening while Joe was overnighting in Wichita. Danny didn't have anything new, but said he had several people working on it. At the same time, Joe had added several items to Danny's long list of things to do. He informed him of QCI's fractional yacht program called OceanShares and requested that he perform the same due diligence on that program as well as any similar competitor programs.

Joe looked through his stack of mail. It appeared to be mostly junk, with numerous solicitations for credit cards. One letter, though, was handwritten and caught Joe's attention. He decided to open it first and was surprised to find a personal check from Nicholas Perrino. It was made out to Joe Hara, for five thousand dollars. A brief handwritten note on Perrino's personal stationery thanked Joe for his assistance and explained that the money was an advance to help cover any expenses that Joe might incur during his investigation.

Joe placed the check and the letter off to the side. He opened the file drawer to the right of his desk and pulled out the manila folder containing the upcoming month's bills. He paid his bills when they were due instead of doing them all at one time. He had it down to a science, knowing exactly how long it would take a check to get to its destination. Joe held onto his money as long as possible, since all his bank accounts were interest bearing.

He had even learned a trick that allowed him to earn interest in two money market funds on the same money by switching the money from one fund to another. While it takes several days for money-fund checks to clear, Joe could earn daily interest in two places with the same money. He was most successful when his checks were credited on a

Friday because the money doesn't come out of the other fund until the following Tuesday.

Joe pulled out his checkbook and methodically went to work. He finished about an hour later and slipped a brown rubber band around the stack of white envelopes, then placed them on the far left side of his desk. Joe glanced at the time in the bottom right corner of the computer screen. He still had plenty of time to get them to the mailbox so they'd be postmarked for that day.

From his briefcase he removed the leather-bound notepad containing the notes he had taken for the Folino investigation. Joe read through them.

When he finished, he placed the black leather notepad back on the desk. He picked up his tall glass of ice water and reclined in his chair. He noticed most of the ice in his glass had melted. He took a large drink and placed the glass back on the cork coaster. Joe wiped the condensation from his hand onto his right pant leg.

He clicked the phone tools icon on his computer. Danny's number popped up on the screen, along with half a dozen of Joe's most recent calls. Joe moved the mouse until the arrow was on Danny's number. Joe clicked and the modem began to dial.

Joe sat and waited as he heard the phone ringing through the computer's acoustic speakers.

Danny answered, "Daniel Froberg."

"Danny, it's Joe. How's everything going?"

"Hey Hara, you back in town?"

"Yep. Got anything new?"

"As a matter of fact, I was just getting ready to call you. We've contacted a couple aviation research companies. One is located in Oklahoma City and the other in Cincinnati. Between the two of them, they've provided us with lists of as many owners as possible in each of the fractional programs."

"How accurate do you think the lists are?" Joe asked.

"Well, they tell me people leave and join these programs almost daily. They supposedly update their information

126

monthly and apparently get their information directly from the FAA."

Joe was familiar with the Federal Aviation Administration, from when he was a younger man taking flight lessons. They're the branch of the Department of Transportation responsible for all civil aeronautical activities in the United States, and one of their responsibilities is keeping records on aircraft ownership.

"Although the information is available to the public, it made more sense to use a consulting firm that had already gathered as well as updated the information. We've taken the lists and started using our available resources. We also divided the lists with the guys on the force up north in Perrino's hometown. They're helping with the calls.

"Like you requested, we're trying to confirm whether any of the fractional owners in each of the four programs has had any employee deaths within the past couple years. Then we're checking to see the nature of their death and whether or not they had any involvement with their company's fractional aircraft. As you can imagine, Joe, it's an arduous process. But believe it or not, we already have some preliminary information. Ironically, the company with the used aircraft."

Joe cut Danny off. "Jet Divide?"

"Yeah, Jet Divide. They were the easiest to go through because they have the newest program and fewest owners. It seems that the only owner in their program that had any employees die, well, they died on one of the Jet Divide airplanes. About one year ago. They lost six middle managers in a crash during some bad weather."

Joe picked up his notepad and jotted this down. He didn't recall anybody at Jet Divide mentioning the accident, but then again he probably had forgotten to ask. "Did any of the managers that were killed have anything to do with their company's airplane?"

"No, not at all."

"What else you got?" Joe set the notepad down on the desk and reached for his glass of water.

"We're about halfway through the owners of the one manufacturer-driven program. So far they have only had two owners die. One was a chairman emeritus that rarely used the company airplane."

"How did he die?"

"He had a heart attack. Seems they were having a family reunion last summer at his estate on Martha's Vineyard. The whole family had been together for several days. He was on the beach playing volleyball when he suddenly dropped dead."

"Everybody saw it?"

"Yep, his kids, grandkids, and even a few great-grandkids."

Joe cringed at the thought. He saw death all the time and knew the hardest part of it all was watching the family try to deal with it. *What a terrible thing for the family to have witnessed*, he thought. *It's something they will never forget and will have to live with for the rest of their lives.*

Danny continued: "The other death was an executive secretary at a large corporation that used the program to supplement their existing flight department. She was in her late fifties and died of cancer. She never had anything to do with the aircraft. Turns out the executive that she assisted was claustrophobic and wouldn't even get on an airplane."

"So, nothing appears unusual about any of the competitions' deaths."

"No, not yet, at least. Like I said, though, we're only about halfway through the one manufacturer program's owners list and we're just getting started on the other."

"What about the StratoShares owners list?" Joe asked anxiously.

This brought a smile to Danny's face. "Well, let me just say I think we're on the right track."

Joe picked up his notepad, pushed his chair back farther from the desk, and leaned back to put his feet up. With pen and pad in hand, he was ready to write.

"We already had the Johnnie Perrino and J. Edward Chambers deaths to look into. Now we've got a couple more deaths and they're not just owners.

"It seems last spring, a forty-five-year-old man by the name of Chet Warner went out for a run in the park not far from his home in Reston, Virginia. He never came back. When his wife reported him missing, the local police and park rangers started to look. Search dogs found him lying unconscious in a creek bed at the bottom of a one-hundred-foot ravine. He apparently had fallen off the cliff while running on the trail above. The trauma unit—"

"He was still alive?"

"Yes, he was. The paramedics had him airlifted to Shock Trauma Center at the University of Maryland Medical Center in Baltimore, where he died several hours later. He never regained consciousness."

"So he might as well have been dead."

"Yeah. The doctors said they think he was probably comatose from the second he impacted with the ground."

"And what was his role with the company?"

"He was chief financial officer. One of his responsibilities was the corporate aircraft. I spoke briefly to his wife Cindy. She said she wasn't certain what it was, but knew something at the office had been troubling him. She said it most likely had something to do with the company plane. She said that seemed to be the biggest source of irritation for him over the past few years."

"What about his death? What did she say about that?"

"She said it didn't make sense. She said Chet ran religiously in the park. There was no way that he would have fallen off a cliff. She said she has always been suspicious of the accident, but didn't know of anyone that would possibly want to hurt him."

"Does his company still have an airplane with Strato-Shares?"

"Absolutely. The chairman is the primary user. Chet never even flew on the plane. He was just the decision maker."

"Have you spoken to the chairman?"

"No, not yet. I've got a call into his office. He's been out of town. I'll let you know as soon as I hear from him."

"Okay, so what else you got?"

"I found out that QCI has had several employee deaths. Two from the StratoShares program and one that worked for OceanShares."

"How did they die?"

"Well, you know Folino has that posh training facility in Colorado not far from Durango. It seems a couple of new-hire pilots were in a rental car on a snow-covered road not far from the facility. It was apparently snowing heavily and they were traveling at a high rate of speed. They lost control of their vehicle and slid off the road over the side of the mountain. They weren't found for three days."

Joe recalled Travis mentioning the accident. "Three days? Why so long?"

"Well, the state highway patrol informed me that the rental car agency had reported the car missing. The pilot had put StratoShares as his employer on the rental agreement. When the state police came to Folino's facility, they were informed that both men had been gone for several days. They didn't know where they were. They had chalked them up as being AWOL. They figured they must have quit. They said it's happened before."

Joe thought that was odd. He recalled Travis McGee's comment of how the pilots and detailers never quit. "Why didn't anybody see any tracks?" he asked.

"Apparently the heavy snowfall the night before covered their tracks. It was a private pilot in a small single-engine plane flying nearby a couple days later, who notified the state police. He noticed the sun reflecting off something protruding from the snow about halfway down the mountain-side. Turned out to be the twisted fender of the car."

"Have you talked to the relatives of either of the victims?"

"Again, I've left messages and am waiting to hear back."

Joe paused and thought for a moment. "So, what's this about an OceanShares employee?"

"I'm still working on getting a list of their owners, as well as their competitions' owners. I don't think there are nearly as many in the fractional yacht programs. Anyway, the employee that died was a detailer. They train at Folino's facility in West Palm Beach. Seems the guy was alone late one night, cleaning a yacht, when he somehow fell overboard and drowned."

"Sounds like he took a long walk off a short pier."

"That would be my guess too, but without any witnesses, what can you do."

"So, those are the only new deaths that you've found?"

"Yep, but we're still looking. I suspect we'll find more. Oh yeah, and you were right, Joe."

"About what?"

"The California Highway Patrol got a couple tire tracks in the mud and after a second search, also found a bullet in a wooden guardrail post. They were both about a hundred yards north of where Perrino ran off Highway 1. Ballistics is looking at them now."

Joe chewed on the black plastic cap of a Bic pen as he thought. "Danny, that's good stuff. Now, what about J. Edward Chambers? Did you find any more about his death?"

"Hold on just a minute, Joe. The chief's got something for me."

Before Joe could respond, there was a click, then silence on the line.

Joe sat and waited. He pulled the pen cap out of his mouth when he realized what he was doing. *What a nasty habit,* he said to himself. He thought about the mysterious deaths and wondered how many more hadn't been discovered yet.

Danny's voice came back on the line. "I just got some more information, Joe. The car that the lawn tech saw behind Randall Johnson's house? Turns out it belongs to the son of a neighbor. He lives just north of Trenton, not far from Princeton, New Jersey. He was just passing through the area and had stopped by to say hello to his mother who lives next door."

"What does he do? Does he have a record?"

Danny laughed. "No, Joe, he doesn't have a record."

Joe detected the mockery in Froberg's voice. "So, are you going to let me in on what you think is so funny?"

"He's a Roman Catholic priest. His name is Father Matt Kennedy."

"And priests aren't capable of killing? You should know better than that, Danny." Joe knew you couldn't remove anyone from suspicion. The elderly grandmother who was walking to the grocery store, the young boy playing stickball in the street, the beautiful young woman who volunteered at the local nursing home—they were all capable of murder. Joe knew because he had seen it many times.

"Joe, I know exactly what you're talking about, but it just doesn't seem likely. He's head pastor of his church and also teaches at Princeton Theological Seminary. The guy's record with the church is exemplary, and he does have an alibi. He was with his mother the entire time. He had spent the night and the next morning as well. The old woman said he never left her sight. He left to return home just before noon."

"It's his mother, Danny. What do *think* she's going to say?"

Danny raised his voice a little. "He's a *priest*, Hara. For Christ's sake, get real here."

"Didn't the Boston detectives ask her about the car when they canvassed the area?"

"They did, but she forgot to mention that her son was there. She didn't know he had parked around back or even what kind of car he was driving. It wasn't until she had spoken to her son yesterday and thought about asking him what type of car he had. After he told her, she immediately called the Boston police because she was concerned for him."

Joe took his feet off the desk and sat upright. He had already convinced himself the driver of that car was the murderer. He knew he had a tendency to let his imagination get carried away sometimes, but it was that creativity that helped him solve so many murders. He didn't like to allow himself to get boxed in or focused on any one thing. He knew Danny was probably right, but asked one more question anyway.

"What did his mother think of Randall Johnson? Were they good neighbors?"

"Hell, Joe, I don't know. I didn't ask her that. How do you think this has anything to do with all the deaths?"

Joe calmly replied, "I don't think it has anything to do with all the deaths." Joe heard Danny let out a heavy sigh.

"Okay, so now you've lost me, Hara."

"I think Randall Johnson's murder was committed by someone else. I don't think it was done by the same person."

Danny was silent.

Joe said, "First, tell me what you found out about J. Edward Chambers' death, then I'll tell you what I'm thinking."

"Okay. I spoke to Chambers' son, who told me he didn't have any problems with the StratoShares program. He did say, however, that his father had some problems and that he'd been thinking about leaving the program. His father had conveyed his dissatisfaction when he'd called and spoken to him about an hour or so before the accident."

"What did he say, specifically?"

"He told his son he was tired of the frustrations and inconveniences he'd been experiencing with StratoShares, so he was going to sell back his shares and join another program."

"And did his son follow through after he died?"

"Nope, he's still in the program. Like I said, he wasn't the one having problems with StratoShares. In fact, he sold his father's yacht and bought shares in QCI's OceanShares program. He even joked with me about it. He said his dad would probably roll over in his grave if he knew he was buying more shares in another one of QCI's programs. He said his father had heard Folino might have ties to the Mafia."

"He said that?" Joe scribbled as Danny kept going.

"Yeah, and I also spoke to the late Mr. Chambers' secretary, Barbara. She said Chambers had left her a self-stick note on the desk lamp on the night he died. He asked her to pull the StratoShares file and forward the contracts to his legal counsel. After he died, it just sort of got pushed to the back burner. Since everything was fine with his son's travels, they decided not to do anything."

"Did his son give any indication as to why he thought his father had problems with StratoShares and he didn't?"

"I asked him that very same question. His son seemed to feel that maybe it was because he typically would schedule his international trips well in advance and never make any changes. Whereas his father was always changing his plans. Also, the son primarily used commercial for most of his domestic travel. After his father died he sold back one-eighth of their half-share interest, but still uses the StratoShares aircraft for all his international trips."

Joe nodded his head after hearing the reoccurring fact that owners who changed their plans had problems.

"Finally, I called both of Chambers' ex-wives and what was soon to be his third wife. She sounded to be about half his age. Both exes couldn't shed any light, but his young fiancée did. She told me his attorney had been drawing up a prenuptial agreement for them. She also confirmed he had called her on the night of his death. She stated he was very upset with QCI and told her he was going to leave the StratoShares program."

"That was all she said?" Joe asked, surprised.

"That was all. She said Chambers didn't get any more specific. So now that I've told you everything—"

"Danny, hold on a minute." Joe looked at his notepad, glancing at the names he had written down. There were a total of five StratoShares owners, two StratoShares employees, and one OceanShares employee, who all died of unnatural causes. From the list of owners, four of the five deceased were not the primary user of the aircraft, but were solely the decision maker. The other one was both the only user and decision maker. His death didn't seem to fit the pattern.

Next, the two StratoShares employees and one Ocean-Shares employee were part of two exclusive groups, the pilots and detailers. The only reason Joe considered them exclusive was because they were the only employees that got to go to Folino's retreat-like training facilities.

"Okay, kid, here's what I'm thinking. Even though the StratoShares program is much larger than their competitors' programs, it's already becoming obvious there's a high number of people within their program dying of unusual causes. With the exception of Randall Johnson, all the other owners had two things in common. They weren't the primary user of the aircraft, but they were the decision maker. Randall Johnson, on the other hand, was the only user and sole decision maker."

Joe continued as Danny sat behind his desk and absorbed what Joe was saying. "As far as the pilots and detailer, well, they were all part of an exclusive group."

"And what group is that?" Danny asked.

"It's the group that Folino allows into his private training facilities in Miami and Durango. Tell me, Danny. If what you've told me is correct, why is security so tight at those facilities?"

"I'm not certain. Maybe he has proprietary information or industry secrets that he doesn't want anyone else gaining access to."

"Could be," Joe replied, "but my guess would be he's trying to hide something. So I'm thinking we need to get somebody inside one of those facilities."

"Maybe I could somehow get into the Florida facility when I'm passing through Miami later this week."

"You're going to be in Miami this week?" Joe asked, surprised.

"Yeah, Hara. I know I told you," Danny said, slightly irritated.

Joe had a habit of not always hearing what Danny would say—kind of like a father. Danny was used to it by now, but still couldn't help getting annoyed.

Danny continued but spoke more slowly, as if talking to a small child. "Nancy and I are taking a cruise to the Caribbean. We're going to Antigua and several other islands in the Lesser Antilles. We're first flying to Miami this Friday, then on to the Bahamas. We'll depart Saturday on one of those Windjammer Barefoot Cruises. It's the first cruise we've taken in a couple years. I thought we'd do something special for our tenth anniversary."

The mention of a cruise caused Joe to recall his first cruise to the islands. He and Susan had also gone to the Caribbean, but on a Carnival Cruise ship. They were gone for just over a week, stopping at several ports, sometimes for only a few hours and other times for the entire day. He quickly learned that the days cruise ships pulled into port, the price of many tourist-related items, taxi rates, and other services were inflated. If you wanted to save money, you had to learn to negotiate.

Joe also couldn't believe that Dan and Nancy had already been married for ten years. It seemed like just yesterday when he and Danny had shared an apartment together.

"You probably told me and I just forgot," Joe replied.

"How about I leave tomorrow and go down a couple days earlier. I can somehow try and get inside."

Joe was quick to respond to the younger detective's suggestion. "No way, Dan. It's too dangerous."

"So what do you suggest?"

"Well, I think it's a good idea. I mean, your going down there a day or two early. Maybe you could stop by the OceanShares facility for a tour and learn some more about their program. You know a little something about boats, don't you?"

"Just a little." Danny laughed. He had practically grown up on boats, and Joe knew it. Dan's father had been in the Navy and loved the water. He could never get enough of it. As a result, his entire family had spent a lot of time on the water. Danny learned some of his first knots by the age of four. Sailing had been the family's activity of choice, but Danny had always been fascinated with yachts.

"I thought you might like that. Maybe you could say you were looking at the program for your father. He's got enough money to be a legitimate prospect. Does he still have that yacht in Lincoln Harbor?"

"Yeah, he does. That's probably not a bad idea."

"You know what else you could do?" Joe didn't wait for a reply. "You could do a little recognizance work. Maybe stake out the FBO in Palm Beach. Travis McGee told me that most of the StratoShares owners fly in and out of Five Star Aviation to clear customs. You could check things out and see if you notice anything unusual."

"Let me call Nancy to see if she can be ready by tomorrow and if we can move up our airline tickets."

"Did you ever speak to Buchanan's friend who's the chief pilot at Adventure Studios?"

"No, I didn't. I left a couple messages for the guy, but he never got back to me."

"Well, never mind. Especially if you're going to leave tomorrow for Miami. I'll go out to the airport either later today or tomorrow and pay him a visit."

"What about trying to get somebody inside one of Folino's training facilities?" Danny reminded Joe.

"Let me think about that some more. If we could get somebody inside, I think I would want it to be at the Colorado facility. I'm still really suspicious about the two pilots that died there." Joe could hear someone in the background on the other end of the phone shouting Danny's name and telling Froberg he had an urgent call.

"Hold on again, Joe."

Joe waited while Danny took the other call. Joe didn't notice he had stuck the pen back in his mouth as he thought about whom he could send into Folino's facility in Colorado.

Joe removed a brown leather-bound atlas from the pine bookshelf behind him. He placed the atlas on his desk and flipped through the pages until he found a map of Colorado.

He looked for Durango and located it on the map. He scanned the nearby towns and noticed Telluride about sixty miles or so to the north. Joe knew a private investigator that resided in Telluride. His name was Mark Grady and he specialized in catching unfaithful spouses and their lovers.

He had once helped Joe catch a gray-haired, white-collar executive who was operating a large prostitution ring. It all started when a suspicious husband, who questioned his wife's frequent so-called business trips, hired Mark. The guy had no idea his wife was selling her body for a living. When the woman turned up murdered in L.A., Joe ended up investigating the homicide.

Mark usually worked for bitter wives who suspected their executive husbands of having an affair with a secretary or someone else in their employ. But sometimes, as in this case, it was the suspicious husband who would hire him to find out if his beautiful wife was doing somebody.

Occasionally Mark would accidentally stumble on a recognizable face, and would double as a paparazzo, selling any photos he could take, to the grocery store tabloids.

Aspen, Vail, Gunnison, and Telluride were all great places for a secluded weekend romance. Many of corporate America's richest executives had second or third homes in those locations. Joe realized this wasn't the typical case for Mark, but maybe business was slow. At worst, maybe he knew of someone else who could help.

Hara heard a click through his computer speakers as Danny came back on the line. "You aren't going to believe this, Joe."

Joe started to speak, then realized he had the pen in his mouth. He removed it. "What?"

"I just got a call from the Napa police. Like I told you, they're also calling the names on the lists of owners. Well, they just called the office of a man by the name of Jack Williams. Turns out he managed his mother's estate and she owned a share with StratoShares."

"You said managed as in past tense."

"That's right. He died in a car accident on a rural stretch of New Jersey highway Sunday night. And you'll never guess where he was coming from."

Joe hated it when Danny did this to him. "Where?"

"A dinner in the City with William Price, Tony Folino, and about thirty-five other people. He was a guest of Ross Nickels, and Jill Riley was there too."

"Jill Riley? What was she doing there?"

"I don't know. Maybe a story for the *Gazette*?"

"Of course," Joe replied after thinking it made sense. "So, what exactly happened?"

"The New Jersey State Police said he apparently fell asleep behind the wheel of his car. He drove off the road and struck a tree. It killed him instantly. The police said his blood alcohol level was close to the legal limit, but not quite over."

"And what are the guys in Napa doing about it?"

"Well, they immediately contacted the New Jersey State Highway Patrol and told them about the case they're investigating. The guys in New Jersey are now reviewing and discussing the results of the autopsy, though the coroner felt it was strictly alcohol related."

"They should recheck his blood for any other substances, you know, in case somebody slipped him something during dinner, like a sleeping pill."

"I'm sure they're probably discussing that even as we speak," Danny commented.

"Do you have anything else?"

"Yep. They also spoke to his secretary. She was still in the process of cleaning up his office. Seems the same night he died, his office was broken into."

"Anything missing?"

"His computer, briefcase, and some files were stolen."

"Did his secretary know which files?"

"They said she wasn't certain yet. I asked them to call her back and see if the file for his mother's share with StratoShares was still there. The local police said that whatever it was they were looking for, they must have found it."

"Why is that?"

"Because they said he had two vertical filing cabinets with four drawers each. They only broke into two of the drawers."

"Maybe something scared them off."

"No, they didn't seem to think so. I said the same thing. His office was in an old farmhouse without any type of security system. It was about a quarter-mile back off the road."

"Well, based on that, they probably could have taken as long as they wanted," Joe commented.

"That's exactly what the local police said."

"What's next?"

"The Napa police are going to call me back after they speak to the coroner and William's secretary. I'll let you know as soon as I hear anything."

"Okay. And I thought of somebody I could call who doesn't live far from Durango. Do you remember Mark Grady?"

"Isn't he the private investigator that helped you collar the guy running that prostitution ring?"

"Yeah, that's him. I thought maybe he could somehow get inside Folino's Colorado facility. I need to think of an MO. Maybe he can help me with that—if he's available."

"Well, I'll let you know if I can get to Miami tomorrow. I'm calling Nancy as soon as I hang up."

"You'll brief the chief on what you've got, Dan?" Joe asked.

"Yes, I will."

"I'll let him know what I've found out now. Is he around?"

"Yeah, he just walked by my desk. I think he was going toward the head. I heard him grumbling something about rusty pipes. You probably know about that, don't you, Joe?" Danny chuckled.

"No I don't, wise guy." Danny was always making geriatric cracks about Joe's age and no part of the anatomy was too sacred for comment, including the prostate. "Ask him to give me a call, if you don't mind. I'll wait to hear back from you."

"Sure, Joe. Oh yeah—one other thing. I checked with the Department of the Interior regarding Folino's endangered species."

"And?"

"And everything checks out. Folino is listed as having several species of endangered birds in captivity and has all the necessary licensing permits. I got it from a reliable source that a guy of Folino's wealth and stature could probably cut through the thousand-step process and a lot of red tape with one call to his friendly U.S. Senator or Congressman. So I guess he's got all his ducks in a row."

Joe replied to Danny's weak attempt at being humorous with, "You quack me up, Dan. Don't quit your day job." Although disappointed again, Joe was pleased with Danny's results.

As they said goodbye, Joe slid the computer mouse across the pad and clicked on the icon to end their phone connection. Joe hoped Mark Grady was available. He decided he should call him right away. Joe opened his address book and flipped through the pages as he looked for the PI's number. After calling Grady, he would place a call to Ross Nickels.

Things were really starting to come together. Everything was pointing to Folino, but Joe needed more. He needed something he could get an arrest warrant on and an indictment from a grand jury. It had to be something that would stick with the DA's office.

<16>

Joe clicked on the motorcycle's left turn signal as he approached Walgrove Avenue. It was a beautiful Southern California morning without a single cloud in the sky. Joe had been itching to take his bike for a spin and today's weather was perfect. The three-mile ride from Joe's front door to the Adventure Studios hangar at Santa Monica Municipal Airport would take less than ten minutes—too short a time and nowhere near the distance needed to appreciate the performance of such a powerful motorcycle.

The 1973 Kawasaki Z1 at one time had been the fastest motorbike on the road. Joe had only ridden this one a few times, having just recently acquired it. The thirty-year-old cycle was in excellent condition and had the original and most collectable color scheme of root beer and orange.

Joe's last bike, ten years newer, had been an '83 Kawasaki GPZ1000. Regrettably, though, that bike was destroyed when someone had tried to make a hit on him. Fortunately, or unfortunately—depending how he wanted to look at it— Joe hadn't been riding the bike at the time. Danny had borrowed Joe's bike at the last minute and taken it for a spin, traveling north up Highway 1. He wanted to see what the bike could do, knowing it was capable of speeds in excess of 161 miles an hour.

Danny was mistaken for Joe and was intentionally run off the road. The killers had left him for dead. Luckily, Danny only suffered a minor concussion, multiple scrapes, and a broken arm. Joe still felt bad for Dan, but was thankful the injuries hadn't been more serious.

Joe maneuvered the classic bike through traffic as he accelerated the powerful engine, traveling north one and a-half miles toward Airport Avenue. He had called Chief Buchanan late the previous afternoon to reconfirm whom he was supposed to see at Adventure Studios. Joe hoped this Max

142

Wells could shed some light on QCI and the StratoShares program.

The way the chief understood it, Wells, like many other flight departments across the country, used StratoShares to supplement their present aircraft. Adventure Studios owned a Challenger 601.

Some flight departments, though, would sometimes sell an underutilized aircraft or one they weren't flying enough, and replace it with a fraction of a StratoShares airplane. By doing that, they eliminated the majority of the operating costs associated with owning an entire plane. They then only had to pay for the smaller fraction they used with Strato-Shares.

It was also Joe's understanding that many companies would use their StratoShares plane to fly one-way legs or trips that resulted in them ferrying or deadheading an aircraft. This typically occurred when a passenger had already been at a location for an extended time or possibly arrived there by another means of transportation. The flight department would have to send or ferry an aircraft from its present location to pick up the passenger and bring them back.

In the same manner, if the passenger only needed to be dropped off and not returned, they would have to bring the airplane back empty or deadhead it. Since StratoShares didn't charge for that service, flight departments would use a fractional share for those legs and help keep the overall operating costs down on their own aircraft.

Joe turned right on Airport Avenue and began looking for the studio hangar. He traveled another half-mile and saw the hangar on his left as he approached Donald Douglas Loop South. He turned left onto the road, and then left again into the Adventure Studios parking lot.

He rolled his bike into a visitor parking space near the front door of the hangar. He shut down the engine, got off the bike, and removed his black helmet, which he carried in his right hand.

Joe never left his helmet with his bike anymore. He had learned his lesson the hard way, having had one of his nicest helmets stolen about ten years before. He should have known better, but because he'd been in a wealthy neighborhood, he figured it was safe.

He was wrong and still not sure what he'd been thinking at the time. All he could figure was he must have had a brain fart. Joe knew he should have known better. He had lived in Los Angeles long enough to be aware of the fact that crime had no boundaries.

He walked across the concrete sidewalk toward the single glass entrance door emblazoned with the studio's trademark palm tree logo. He looked up toward the top of the old glass hangar and saw the same logo, only larger, painted across the building's exterior.

Inside the big, empty hangar, Joe didn't see any airplanes and wondered where the company's Challenger was. Across the way, one of the hangar's large sliding doors was ajar. Joe could see out onto the ramp, which also was vacant of aircraft. He could hear another plane's engines running at full throttle as it roared down the runway and departed the noise-sensitive Santa Monica Airport.

The airport had noise restrictions that limited the times aircraft could arrive and depart. Joe had read somewhere that the entire country, not just Santa Monica, was becoming more sensitive to aircraft noise pollution. The article said that most airports are developed first, and then the people move in around them. As a result, many airports around the country were needing to implement restrictions regarding the use of older and noisier aircraft. These restrictions typically came in the form of altered departure and arrival times or patterns.

He glanced around and wondered if Max Wells was out flying a trip. He noticed another glass door on an inside wall with a sign above it that read Office. Joe called out, "Anybody here?" His voice echoed in the hollow structure.

He walked along the inside wall until he reached the office door. Inside, Joe could see a slightly balding, gray-haired man with silver-rimmed bifocals. He was wearing jeans with a white cotton shirt, and laughing heartily into the telephone. With both legs outstretched, the man's alligator-skin boots rested on the desktop. Joe knew the man had seen him when he read his lips as they said into the phone, "I gotta go."

The man swung his boots off the desk and stood up to his full six-foot, four-inch height. He motioned for Joe to come inside. When Joe entered the small office, his attention was immediately diverted to a gold nameplate on the man's desk. It read Max Wells.

Joe switched the helmet to his left hand as he extended his right and stepped forward. "Max Wells?" Joe asked.

The man nodded and smiled.

Joe said, "Hi, I'm Joe Hara."

"Mr. Hara, I've been expecting you. Frank called me yesterday and said you'd be stopping by." He shook Joe's outstretched hand.

Joe noticed the watch Max was wearing, a nice, black Fortis pilot's watch with a black embossed leather strap.

"Please, have a seat." He gestured toward a chair. "Can I get you some coffee or something, Mr. Hara?"

"No thank you, I'm fine. And please call me Joe."

"Fine, fine. Just as long as you call me Max." He sat down behind the mahogany desk.

Joe glanced around the small, plush office. Deep pile carpeting extended wall to wall. The chairs and sofa were of genuine Italian leather. The walls were adorned with several aviation related pictures, professionally framed and matted. A half-dozen lush tropical plants, including several varieties of cactus, were positioned about the room.

It seemed out of place compared with the rest of the building. From what Joe had seen so far, the exterior of the building, along with the inside of the hangar, appeared to be somewhat dated, maybe even antiquated.

"And how are things with the Los Angeles Police Department? It must be a kind of difficult time right now, huh? I mean, a lot of questions and such?"

Joe was puzzled. "In regard to what?"

"In regard to the allegations and investigation of corruption on the force. Is there anything else in the local news right now?"

"Oh, that."

Max was the first person to confront Joe with the question, even though the scandal was now old news. Joe tried not to think about it. To the best of his knowledge, it hadn't affected any of his cases and since he was retired, it was easier to forget about it. Nonetheless, he was embarrassed by the question.

There was an ongoing corruption probe that officers had lied under oath, falsified reports, planted evidence, and even shot unarmed suspects. So far, twenty officers had been either suspended or dismissed and the number was climbing. Likewise with the forty or so convictions that had since been overturned.

"You know, Max, it's really sad. It's a shame the public thinks a few bad eggs can spoil the whole bunch. I'm retired now, so it really doesn't affect me. But in my twenty-five years or so on the force, I saw a lot. It's really hard out there, especially for some of the younger guys without supervision. The temptations of drugs, money and sex are tremendous. I've seen good cops destroyed by undercover work, especially working narcotics and vice."

"Oh, I agree with you, Joe. I've witnessed the same thing in the entertainment industry. I can't tell you the number of times I've seen a new, young actor or actress submit to the temptations of drugs and sex as a result of their newfound wealth. Then I'd watch as everything, their entire world, would come crashing down around them in a single instant. It's a real shame."

Joe shook his head in agreement as Max switched the conversation to the matter at hand.

"Frank told me about the case that the two of you are working on and I have to say I wasn't at all shocked to hear about his suspicions. I've been looking forward to your visit, and think you'll find what I have to tell you, very interesting." Max again placed both feet on his desk and reclined in his chair while locking both bulky hands behind his head.

Joe placed his motorcycle helmet on the vacant seat beside him and leaned forward in his chair. He had one question first, and spoke up. "Where's the studio's plane?"

Max unclasped his hands and lifted them into the air. "It's gone."

"Gone where?"

"Gone as in 'for good.' The chairman got rid of the plane. That's what I think you'll find so interesting. The chairman sold the plane, fired the entire flight department—except for me—and replaced the plane with StratoShares."

"How long ago did this occur?"

"It's been about two months now, I'd say. I'm surprised you didn't read about it in any of the industry rags. Are you an aviation man, Joe?" He looked inquisitively at Joe over the top of his bifocals.

"No, can't say that I am."

"Well, I am," Max said proudly, raising his voice. "Was born and raised to fly. My grandfather flew, my daddy flew, and all four of my older brothers flew. It gets in your blood like a disease. I got started when I was ten and have been flying ever since." He reflected for a moment. "I guess it's been nearly fifty years now."

Joe reached inside his windbreaker and pulled out his notepad and pen. "I hope you don't mind if I take a few notes."

"Absolutely not. You go right ahead. Are you ready?"

"I'm all ears."

"Well, you see, Joe, it's like this. I wasn't an advocate of StratoShares or any other fractional ownership program. I saw it like so many other flight departments see fractional ownership."

"And how is that?"

"We saw it as the end of our jobs. StratoShares or another company would come in here and take away our jobs. We would all be replaced."

"Really?" Joe asked. "Why? I mean, if you're operating your aircraft efficiently and utilizing the plane enough hours, why would you be concerned about a fractional ownership program?"

"Because the airplane salesmen lie. They'll tell the chairman anything to convince him they can do a better job and save the company money."

"So then, why did he get rid of the Challenger and join StratoShares?"

Max took off his glasses and dangled them in his right hand, swinging them back and forth like a pendulum. "Well, for starters, we were already using StratoShares for supplement before he sold the Challenger." He folded the glasses and placed them in a black case on top of his desk.

"How did that come about? I mean, you buying into the program for supplemental lift."

"Somebody from their company contacted our chairman directly. They mailed him several nice gifts as part of an elaborate marketing scheme. You know, things like expensive cigars in a mahogany humidor, an expensive, limited edition aviator's watch, and a model airplane. They all came with some catchy phrase, making comparisons to the Strato-Shares product and the enclosed gift."

Max shrugged his shoulders. "Even though I discouraged it, the chairman bought into their bullshit and agreed to a meeting with one of the company's young sales reps located here in Los Angeles. Gary Milner was his name. The kid must only be in his early thirties. I sat in on the meeting when they met for lunch at the Polo Lounge at the Beverly Hills Hotel. That's where Folino was staying and it isn't far from my chairman's home. Tony Folino was supposed to join us, but got tied up elsewhere in the city and never made it to the meeting. Anyway, the kid didn't know the first thing about aircraft."

"Why did the chairman buy into the program, then?"

"All I can figure is because the kid was a namedropper. He mentioned several other people in the industry that were already using StratoShares. It turns out the chairman was personal friends with each of them and gave them a call. They gave StratoShares glowing reviews, so he decided to give it a try. That was the beginning of the end for my flight department."

"But doesn't the chief pilot of a flight department usually make the decision whether or not to use another provider? Isn't that your job?"

"Up until this instance, yes. The chairman had always gone with my decisions and what I said, stood."

"How long have you been with Adventure Studios?"

"'Bout ten years, I guess."

"And how long have you been using StratoShares?"

"One year now."

Joe said, "Did they know you were opposed to their program?"

"Hell, yes! I made it very clear what I thought of them and their program. That's why they decided to go around me. They had contacted me first and I refused to give them the time of day. It was then they started sending things in the mail to the chairman."

"What are your company's travel patterns?" Joe asked.

"Well, we have the studio nearby in Century City, as well as one on the East Coast in West Palm Beach. There's a lot of travel back and forth between those two locations, as well as New York. We also do frequent travel into Mexico because so many of our films are Westerns shot on location there."

Joe jotted down a couple notes. "And what exactly happened that caused your chairman to get rid of the entire flight department?"

Max shook his head, obviously frustrated, and took a deep breath. "QCI or StratoShares, whatever you want to call them, well, they sabotaged my airplane. Somebody came in here after hours and messed with the avionics onboard the Challenger. The chairman and crew, including myself, were almost involved in a midair collision."

"But why would they do that?"

"Because StratoShares knew I was going to somehow convince the chairman to sell back his shares and leave their program. When it appeared that the maintenance on the Challenger was less than perfect, the chairman decided to get rid of the plane and replace it with StratoShares."

"No offense, but why didn't he get rid of you too?"

"We've become close personal friends. I've been his chief pilot now for ten years and he values my opinion. He doesn't blame the near miss on me, but blames it on our former director of maintenance. He said he still needed somebody to supervise the operation of the company's fractional shares and if I didn't mind not flying, I was welcome to stay onboard at the same salary. So I said yes."

Max looked around the office. "I've given up on trying to change his mind about the StratoShares program, but I continue to be a thorn in their side. I know they were somehow responsible for our near miss accident. I'm just sitting back and waiting for them to cook their own goose."

"Do you know who you almost collided with? I mean, who did the aircraft belong to?"

"It was a Gulfstream IV that belonged to a guy named Angelo Procaccino out of West Palm Beach, Florida. He had chartered it out for the day. I can give you all the information I have, if you like."

"I'd appreciate that." Joe knew what he was going to do as soon as he was finished here. He was going to place a phone call to the precinct requesting a background search on Procaccino.

"Are you sure I can't get you anything to drink, maybe a Coke or something?"

Joe continued to scribble down notes as he shook his head and replied, "No, thank you, I'm fine."

"I can't tell you how excited I got when Frank called me yesterday and told me about his suspicions. I mean, who does this Tony Folino guy think he is, anyway?"

"I'm not certain, but I intend to do my best at finding out. Are there any other instances or times that you can remember where anybody from StratoShares might have acted strangely or possibly did something that might have aroused your suspicions?"

"Actually, yes. A couple things come to mind. Once when I was in Miami, I decided to pay a visit to the Strato-Shares training facility located there. Have you seen the place?"

Joe replied, "No I haven't, but I understand it's very impressive." That reminded Joe he hadn't heard from the private investigator who lived in Telluride or from Ross Nickels, either. He had left messages yesterday for both of them on their voice mail. He would have to give them each another call if he didn't hear back from them soon.

"Very impressive is an understatement. I'm not exactly sure what it is. I mean, it looks like a lot of different things."

"Such as?"

"Such as a prison, maybe, or some type of compound, maybe a resort, or even a military base. I don't exactly know how to describe it. It looks like a half-dozen different things all rolled into one. I mean, there's a mansion on the grounds that's bigger than either the Playboy mansion or Aaron Spelling's place in Bel Air."

Joe was familiar with both Hefner's and Spelling's spreads, so it was easy for him to visualize the enormous size of Folino's facility.

"Anyway, one day I stopped by unannounced and asked for a tour of the facility. I told the security guard at the front gate who I was and that I wanted to see where my Strato-Shares pilots trained. Well, you would have thought I had been standing in front of 1600 Pennsylvania Avenue asking to see the president!

"When they finally realized I wasn't going to leave without a tour, the director of training came out to the front gate and escorted me into the facility. He gave me a whirl-wind tour from a golf cart as we hastily drove around the compound."

"Compound?"

"Yeah, that's what I'd call it. It looked and felt like some type of military compound or installation. The security inside was like nothing I'd ever seen before, anywhere. There were checkpoints with guards everywhere, electric fences, and security cameras. The employees even had badges that gave them limited access to certain parts of the facility."

"And the whole place looked like that?"

"Not quite the whole place. The area around the large mansion where visiting employees obviously stayed, relaxed, and entertained, looked much less secure. Obviously, too much security in that part of the facility would have taken away from their rest and relaxation."

"So, overall, what was your opinion?"

"Well, it did look like pilots were training there. I saw several aircraft doing touch-and-goes, missed approaches and so forth. We walked into one building where a small class of new hires was in training. I was also shown the hangar that housed six flight simulators. All were in operation for recurrent training. The place was a bustle of activity.

"There was one building and area, though, that I thought looked a little unusual. It resembled a movie studio back lot like you'd see here in Hollywood. I asked the guy what it was and he said that's where they trained the airplane detailers. He said they had set up a generic-looking FBO and ramp area where detailers could go through the motions necessary to prepare an airplane for its next flight."

"Why do you think that's unusual?"

Max chuckled. "Because for supposedly being a generic FBO, it sure looked a hell of a lot like Five Star Aviation in West Palm Beach."

"How much is a hell of a lot?"

"Put it this way. You know how sometimes you can get that feeling of déjà vu? Well, I got that feeling. It wasn't until after I had left the facility that I figured out which FBO it had actually reminded me of.

"So all in all, I'd say my tour lasted all of twenty minutes. The director of training made it obvious he didn't have time for me and that I clearly was an interruption of his work, whatever that might have been. So without further ado, he drove me back to the front gate and dropped me off. He didn't say goodbye, kiss my ass, or go to hell."

Max laughed heartily. "I'm telling you, these guys just don't like chief pilots. They know we don't trust them and that we know them for the lying and conniving job stealers they are.

"Oh, they may have convinced a few chief pilots. I know a couple guys that had their flight departments shut down because of StratoShares, so they went to work for the company in an operational capacity. I also know they have since jumped ship and are back with real flight departments."

"You think they're really training pilots there?"

"Based on what I've seen, I'd say they are doing some training at the Florida facility. But I also think they're doing something else. Why else would security be so tight?"

Max leaned forward in his chair. "As far as the place in Durango, well, let's just say that seems fishy to me also. I've flown in and out of Durango-LaPlata Airport before, and both the altitude and afternoon temperatures can be severely limiting on the performance and operation of a jet aircraft. Based on that, it makes no sense to place a pilot training facility there."

"Interesting," Joe mused. "Could we find out the number of daily operations for StratoShares aircraft?"

"That might be difficult since Folino's airstrip is private. Would you like me to call a friend of mine at the FAA?" Max offered. "I could see if he can find out anything."

"If it's not a problem for you, that could be a big help."

"No problem at all."

"Can you think of anything else that sticks out in your mind as odd or unusual in regard to your experiences with StratoShares?"

"Hmm," Max said aloud as he sat there rubbing his chin with his right hand. "You know, there is one other thing that happened a couple times and I thought it was strange. . . . Yeah, twice. I had a couple trips that the chairman needed to cancel, so I called and told StratoShares that we didn't need the plane. Both times I called at least a day before our scheduled departure." Max sat, silent.

"And?" Joe asked.

"And they sent the planes anyway."

"You mean they sent them here?"

"Here and there," he said, and laughed. "Both times the dumb fucks brought the aircraft into the hangar the night before, prepared it for the trip, and then departed the following morning at the scheduled departure time."

"To where?"

"Miami and New York."

"But that wasn't where you were supposed to go, right?"

"Sure it was. The trips had been on the books for several months. Our trips there were on the same days every month. For meetings."

Joe crossed his arms and leaned back in his chair. "You're telling me that StratoShares flew two trips for Adventure Studios that you had called and cancelled."

"They didn't fly them for us."

"Well then, for who? Was there anybody on board the aircraft?"

"Not from our company. But the StratoShares passenger manifest said there was. I called regarding the flight plan they had submitted because I was curious. Come to find out it listed our chairman as the only passenger." Max laughed. "Oh, and it gets even better. They've sent me a couple invoices billing our account for the trips. Of course I haven't paid them."

"This is interesting. And again, how far in advance did you say you booked the flights?"

"Months, I tell you. The trips to Miami and New York are regular as rain," Max said in his smooth Texas drawl.

"Was there any chance they were just ferrying or repositioning the aircraft for another owner's trip in each of those locations?"

"Not very likely. They couldn't stay in business long if they were sending empty airplanes coast to coast. The operating costs would eat up their profits."

"Can you think of anything else?"

Max reflected for a moment, then replied, "That's all that comes to mind right now. Of course, if I think of anything else I can always give you a call."

Joe stood and picked up his helmet off the chair. "Max, this is good information. You've been a big help. If Frank or I can ever do anything for you, just give us a call."

"Thanks, I certainly appreciate that. I'm just glad to help out. I don't particularly care for those folks at StratoShares. Just in case you couldn't tell."

"I won't tell them how you feel," Joe said.

Max patted Joe on the back as he turned to go. "Oh, you don't need to tell them. They already know. I don't hide my feelings very well."

He walked Joe into the hangar. "You know the way back out, right?"

"I do."

"Well, I'll give my friend at the FAA a call and see what he can find out about the number of operations at Folino's so-called training facilities. I've got your number. I'll call you as soon as I know something."

Joe turned and shook Max's hand. "Thanks again. I enjoyed talking with you. I'll wait to hear back from you."

"No problem." Glancing down at Joe's helmet, he asked, "What kind of bike you got?"

"It's a '73 Kawasaki Z1."

"You're kidding! Those are a classic. You ever take it up to the Angeles Crest Highway?"

"Only every chance I get. Why? You have a bike?"

"Yeah, I just got a new Yamaha, a YZF-R1."

"Now, that's a nice bike. I've never ridden one but I've seen a few around," Joe stated.

Max started backing toward his office door. "Well, give me a call sometime and we'll go riding. I'll let you take her for a spin."

"I'll definitely keep that in mind."

As Joe strode across the large, empty hangar, he twirled the helmet on his fist. When his cell phone rang he reached inside his windbreaker pocket and pulled it out. "This is Joe."

"Joe, this is Jill. How are you?"

"I'm fine, Jill. I'm looking forward to seeing you again."

Joe turned back and waved with his hand that was holding the helmet. Max nodded through the glass as he closed his office door.

"Where are you, Joe? I hear an echo or something. It sounds like you're in a tin can."

"I'm inside the Adventure Studios hangar at Santa Monica Airport. I just met with their chief pilot, Max Wells. His company owns shares with StratoShares. I can tell you about it when I see you."

Joe waited for Jill's reply but only heard silence. "You still there?"

"I'm here," she said.

"We must have a bad connection or something. Let me go outside." Joe stepped into the late afternoon sunshine. "Is this better? I said I'm looking forward to seeing you."

"Me too," Jill replied. "That's why I'm calling you. I just had some things moved up on my calendar and wondered if you could come to Rhinebeck before the marathon instead of after it."

"When were you thinking?"

"Like this Friday? Pleeeease," she whined.

"Let me think." Joe didn't hesitate. "Okay." Then added, "That is, of course, if I can find a flight."

"I'm sure you won't have any problem. There are tons of flights."

"All right. I'll call you later and let you know what time I should be arriving."

"That's fine. You do that. I have to go now. I'll talk to you soon."

"Goodbye," Joe replied as he heard their connection end.

After putting the phone back in his jacket, Joe climbed on the motorcycle and slipped on his helmet. He was very pleased with his day so far. Max Wells had turned out to be a good lead and in addition, Joe was going to see the beautiful Ms. Riley several days sooner than he'd anticipated.

<17>

American Airlines flight number 898 touched down at Miami International Airport at 3:37 P.M. local time. Dan and Nancy Froberg had departed Los Angeles on the Boeing 767 a little before 8:00 A.M. Nancy had been successful in moving up their airline reservations by two days so that Dan could spend the next forty-eight hours on the case. Chief Buchanan had agreed to compensate Danny for the difference in price that occurred from changing his airline tickets.

They had each already rented a car and checked in at the Hampton Inn & Suites about three miles southeast of the airport. Nancy was going to spend the rest of the day doing some shopping. She said she wanted to go to the chic Bal Harbour Shops in North Miami Beach. She loved the numerous designer fashion boutiques of Cartier, Saks Fifth Avenue, Charles Jordan, Hermes, and Gucci. She said she might also check out the Mayfair Shops down in Coconut Grove.

Nancy sensed Danny's concern at hearing the names of such pricey and upscale shops, so she assured him she would only be looking. She was ultimately headed for the Sawgrass Mills mega-mall that was located about a half-hour west of Fort Lauderdale. It was the world's largest outlet mall with more than two hundred stores including Ann Taylor and Nine West.

Whatever floats your boat, Danny thought. It definitely wasn't his idea of a good time. He said, "I'm sorry I won't be able to join you for dinner, but Joe mentioned a place you might try. It's in Coconut Grove at the Mayfair Shopping Center. He knows you're a mallrat and thought you might go there. The place is called the Chiyo Japanese Restaurant, or something like that."

Nancy stepped closer to Dan. "Mallrat?"

"He said it, I didn't," Danny quickly replied as he threw up both hands with his palms facing forward ready to defend himself.

Nancy pretended to be upset by the comment. "I'm hurt."

"Yeah, right." Danny laughed. "The only thing that hurts when you go shopping is my wallet."

Nancy stepped closer and wrapped her arms around Danny's slim waist. She gazed deeply into his blue eyes as she placed a hand on the back pocket of his black jeans and felt his bulging wallet. "Then let me relieve some of the pressure by taking some of that money out of your wallet."

Danny leaned forward to kiss her soft lips but she pushed away haughtily and said, "That's okay, I'll just use a charge." She turned away giggling as Danny sighed, frustrated.

"You are such a tease. Come here and give me a kiss."

Nancy walked back and, reaching up, wrapped her arms tightly around Danny's neck. She gave him a deep French kiss that seemed to last forever. When she finally pulled her lips away, she replied, "A tease, huh?"

Danny just smiled. "How much money would you like, dear?"

They both laughed. It sure didn't seem to Danny they had been married for ten years. He was still as much in love today as he had been ten years ago. He never even looked at anyone else.

"You be careful tonight, Daniel. What time do you think you'll be back?"

"I'm not sure. I'm going to drop by the OceanShares facility in West Palm Beach, then maybe if time allows, Folino's training facility, and finally to Five Star Aviation at West Palm Beach International. I'm going to do a little late night surveillance work there. Apparently, that's where Folino's airplanes have the most activity in South Florida, though we're not exactly certain why. I probably won't be back until morning. Don't worry, though. I don't expect any trouble."

"That's easy for you to say."

"I know." Danny knew it had to be difficult being married to a detective. The long hours and late nights on stakeouts had to be stressful. She never knew what was going on or when he would return. But he was always good about calling her. "I'll call you if I can."

"I know you will, but I'll still worry." She let go of Danny and walked over to the chair beside the armoire that held the room's television set. She picked up her purse, then fluffed up her hair as she passed by the mirror.

Danny preached, "You be careful, okay. Remember, if anybody flashes their lights at you, don't pull over. It's a well-known ploy that robbers use to trap tourists. And don't you flash your lights for somebody to let you pass on the interstate. People have ended up getting killed just for doing that down here. It's a territory thing or something. Just give them the lane."

"I know, Danny. I'll be careful. I'm a big girl."

"So do you need any money?"

She laughed as she gave Danny a soft peck on the cheek and headed for the door.

"What's so funny?"

"No, dear, I don't need any money. I've got my own." She paused as she opened the door and looked back. "Plus what I took out of your wallet while you were asleep on the plane. I love you, dear, be careful." She closed the door and Danny could still hear her vivacious laugh as she walked down the hall toward the elevator.

Danny reached in his back pocket and pulled out his brown leather wallet. He looked inside to find just what he had suspected. Nancy hadn't taken any money. She was just clowning around as usual. She loved being blond and always played the part to the hilt.

Smiling, Danny closed his wallet and shouted through the door, "Well, I hope you at least left me enough for dinner."

* * * * *

About an hour later Danny pulled into the visitor parking lot of the OceanShares headquarters in West Palm Beach. The greenish blue numbers of the car's dashboard clock read 5:30. He was right on time. After his conversation with Joe yesterday, he had immediately called the Ocean-Shares office and spoken briefly with a young woman who arranged a tour for him with the company's sales rep for the area, Rick Garcia.

Danny was prepared for their meeting. He had read the information he'd pulled off the OceanShares website as well as the StratoShares packet Joe had forwarded him.

Danny picked up the Yankees ball cap from the passenger seat. He pulled down the car's sun visor and flipped open the mirror. He adjusted the navy wool cap until it rested straight on his head. Several curly blond hairs protruded from each side. He slapped the mirror shut and pushed up the visor as he climbed out of the black Grand Am, closing the door behind him.

His nostrils were immediately greeted by the smell of salt water. Danny took a deep breath and enjoyed the ocean air. He looked down toward the dock where there appeared to be some type of ceremony occurring. There looked to be about two hundred full finger slips with vessels ranging in size from forty to one hundred twenty feet in length, and a face dock that could handle even larger yachts.

Dan noticed a tall, stocky man walking toward him. If he had to guess, he would say it had to be Rick Garcia. The man had dark brown, wind-blown hair and wore round wire rim glasses. His skin was dark tan. He appeared to be in his early to mid-fifties and was puffing away on a cigar.

"Daniel Froberg?" the man asked.

"Yes, that's me. You must be Mr. Garcia."

"Yup, that's me, but please call me Rick." Leaving the cigar in his mouth, he extended his hand for a shake. "I hope you'll excuse the cigar. We were having an informal party down on the dock. Did you have any trouble finding the place?" The man spoke accent-free, but had a raspy voice that was obviously the result of years of smoking.

160

"No, not at all. I mean it would be kind of hard to miss. This has gotta be the largest facility around on the water."

"Well, I hope you haven't been here too long. I was down on one of the docks. We were christening another ship. We just took delivery today and have several of its new owners here. We always throw a little party and do the customary breaking of a champagne bottle on the prow of the vessel."

Danny was familiar with the modern custom. "Well, we certainly wouldn't want to deprive any gods of their libation, now, would we?" Danny commented.

Rick laughed. "No, we wouldn't at that." He looked at Danny momentarily as if sizing him up. "Why don't we go inside and sit down for a while. We can have a cold drink and discuss the program in more detail. I can find out exactly where your interest lies and see if OceanShares can be of service to you."

"That sounds fine."

"Good. Then when we're finished, I'll give you a tour of the facility and show you some of our yachts. Who knows, maybe the next ship we christen will be yours!"

"One can hope," Danny said, trying to sound excited.

Rick turned and walked toward the two-story glass structure. "So tell me a little bit about yourself and what you think your needs might be."

Danny followed close behind as they walked across the newly paved asphalt parking lot. Danny almost hated to walk across the pristine black pavement with its freshly painted yellow stripes. The contrast was so strong, it looked like you could reach down and peel the stripes up.

"Well, as I stated yesterday on the phone, I'm looking at this for my father. He's retired from the Navy and owns a small export business. He already owns a 1992 70' Hatteras CPMY that he births at Lincoln Harbor Yacht Club and Marina just across the Hudson from midtown Manhattan."

"Lincoln Harbor Yacht Club. Yes, I'm very familiar with it. We have several OceanShares owners located there.

Let's see, Harold Jones is one and Jerry Wiley is another," Rick commented. "Do you know them?"

"I can't say that I do, but my father might. Anyway, the boat has low hours and he wants to consider trading it in for a newer and larger one. Maybe an OceanShares one."

They entered through the building's glass double doors and into a large open atrium with a reception area in the center. Hundreds of tropical plants throughout gave the place the appearance of a conservatory. Danny couldn't name a single one; plants weren't his thing. Nancy had the green thumb at their house. Dan remembered Joe's description of the StratoShares facility in Newark and figured this must be similar, but on a smaller scale.

They climbed an open staircase off to the right. At the top of the stairs they entered a small conference room with glass walls. One side looked out over the lobby while the other gave way to a spectacular view of the slips and yachts.

"I'm sure we could discuss brokering his yacht and possibly rolling those proceeds over into the purchase of an OceanShares. You know, a like kind exchange." He rolled one of the high-backed leather chairs across the carpet and away from the table. "Please, have a seat, Daniel. Can I get you something to drink?" He slid a nearby ashtray across the small conference table and scrunched out his lit stogie. The last swirls of smoke rose as the pungent smell lingered.

"No thank you, I'm fine."

"Well, I'm going to have a glass of ice water. Let me know if you change your mind." As Rick poured some water from a nearby pitcher, the ice cubes clinking and rattling into the glass, Danny started asking some questions.

"So, how long have you worked for OceanShares, Rick?"

Rick took a drink as he walked back to the table and sat down beside Danny. He pushed a small stack of magazines aside and placed his glass on the wooden table. "I've been with QCI for about ten years now. I started selling with the StratoShares program, but more recently switched over to OceanShares."

"Why is that?" Danny asked.

"Well, I was tired of the travel. Since I can basically work out of West Palm Beach with OceanShares, I decided to give it a try. I've been selling yacht shares now for about two years. I also have a Hatteras, but mine is a few feet longer and a little newer than your father's. I keep her tied up down in Fort Lauderdale. It's been great for entertaining the ladies. Say, I know of a good place to stay, if you're going to be in the area for a while."

"Actually, I'm just passing through with my wife. We're leaving tomorrow for a cruise to the Caribbean." Danny paused, then said, "It's our tenth anniversary."

Rick suddenly looked solemn. "My condolences. You'll have to pardon me if I'm not overly appreciative of the accomplishment. My experiences with women have been less than favorable." He paused for a moment, then added, "Actually, they've sucked."

Danny laughed and so did Rick.

"You certainly don't mince words, do you, Rick?"

"Well, I think I'll probably live a lot longer as a result. At least I hope that's the case. It's not good for your health to keep things all bottled up inside, so I just let it out. I say whatever I'm thinking. It makes me feel better. Course, sometimes it gets me in trouble but . . . oh well."

"So, tell me, Rick. What type of guy is Tony Folino? To work for, I mean. What do you know about him?"

"Tony is a great man. He's probably one of the most astute entrepreneurs in America. He should have written the book called *The Art of the Deal*, not Donald Trump. I remember watching him several times negotiating airplane deals. You should have seen him. He can really beat up the manufacturers when he purchases twenty-five, fifty, sometimes even a hundred planes at a time. It's a wonder they make any money. It's one of the places where Tony makes a profit. He sells the shares to you at a fraction of retail, but retail isn't even close to what he pays for them.

"Anyway, I've worked with him about eight or nine years now. He's always been a good friend to me. Why do you ask?"

"Well, my father was just curious. He had heard some rumors that Mr. Folino might have ties to organized crime. Dad certainly wouldn't want to buy into a program that had any ties to the Mafia. You understand."

"I've worked for Tony for many years and never once heard anyone imply such a thing. What did you say your father did again?"

Danny shifted in his seat. "He owns a packaging company. You know, packing and crating, shipping cases, pallets, those sorts of things. He has annual sales of about one hundred million a year and about two hundred employees. You can check it out if you like. He can afford Ocean-Shares if he wants to do this."

"And what do you do, Danny?" Rick took another drink of water while he waited for Danny to reply.

"Me, uhm, well, I'm vice president of sales for the West Coast division of the company."

The answer seemed to satisfy Rick. He pushed a thick, full-color magazine across the table. "Here's our latest issue of *OceanShares Magazine*. Have you seen it?"

"No, I haven't." Danny flipped through the pages. "Wow, this is a gorgeous piece of literature. This must have cost a fortune to produce."

"Well, Tony always likes our marketing to be the nicest. Besides, it helps when you own the publishing company."

Danny turned back the glossy pages looking for the editorial page. About three pages in, he found what he was looking for. It listed AMF Publishing, Inc., out of New York as the publisher. His jaw practically dropped. AMF was one of the biggest newspaper/periodical publishers and printers in the country. He had no idea Folino owned the company and he was certain that Joe probably didn't know either.

"So, how did you find out about the program?"

Danny laid down the magazine. "Can I keep this?"

"Absolutely."

"An acquaintance of mine from New York, J. Edward Chambers III. He told me about it."

"Oh yes. I facilitated the transaction and handled the purchase of his father's boat in exchange for an Ocean-Shares. Terrible thing, what happened to Joseph's father, truly bizarre." Rick shook his head and silently looked down, appearing saddened at the thought. After a moment he raised his head. "Do you understand how the OceanShares program works?"

"Well, I went onto your website and reviewed the information. It was self-explanatory. The way I understand it, I can become an owner in a crewed yacht and use it for upwards of twenty-five weeks each year depending on my share size. And I pay only a fraction of what it would cost to own the entire yacht."

"That's right," Rick said. "You're not responsible for the operations, maintenance, repairs, fuel, clean-up or bookkeeping. Those sorts of things."

"The concept is really very similar to your StratoShares program."

"Oh, you've been considering that program for your father as well?" Rick asked, sounding skeptical again.

Danny continued to fabricate his story. "No, not for Dad, but for me. My sales territory is about eight states on the West Coast. I decided to look into it for myself."

"Oh. Well, whom did you speak with at StratoShares?"

Danny quickly scanned his brain trying to remember the name of the guy that Hara had spoken to. The name Ross popped into Danny's head. "If I recall, I think his name was Ross . . ." Danny paused, allowing Rick to finish the name.

"Nickels."

"Yeah, that's him. I also talked to Joseph Edward Jr. about it, too. Anyway, I found it to be too cost prohibitive for me. I've decided to continue flying commercial."

"And how many hours does your father think he'll need with OceanShares, and what are his destinations?"

"Well, the hours are low on his Hatteras, but the overhead is ridiculous. He thinks he'd probably like to start traveling a little more for pleasure. He's got a second home in Coral Gables. He'd probably just use it to go back and forth between the two places."

Dan noticed Rick watching through the glass as several young ladies walked down the hall just outside the room. They were obviously going home for the evening. Still gawking, he got up from his chair and replied, "Why don't we go down to the docks and I can show you some of the yachts that we have. You said he wants something larger than he already has, right?"

"Yeah, that's right."

"Well then, follow me. Are you sure you wouldn't like something to drink?"

"No, really, I'm fine." Danny got up from his chair and followed Rick from the room. "So, what is OceanShares' safety record? I understand there was some type of accident sometime back."

"Accident," Rick repeated as they exited the room and headed down the open stairwell. "No, I'm not aware of any accident. Unless you're talking about that poor young man that fell off the dock late one night and drowned."

"Yeah, maybe that's what I heard about."

"Yes, that was unfortunate, his getting in a scuffle with a thief, then falling overboard. But it really has nothing to do with the safety of our program. He was just a yacht cleaner—or detailer, as we call them."

Rick now had Dan's attention because his story was obviously different from the one he had heard earlier. "What exactly was stolen?"

"I was told some avionics. Another detailer witnessed the attack and saw the assailant running away from the yacht with something tucked under his arm. Our security department was taking care of the matter. I haven't heard anything about it since."

Danny decided that as soon as they were finished, he'd place a call to the local police. He was curious if they had found the thief and exactly how the incident with the detailer had been reported to them.

The men continued past the dense foliage of tropical plants and across the atrium lobby. After exiting through a set of double glass doors at the back of the building, they stepped directly onto a boardwalk that led to the face dock. Danny glanced down at his gold Rolex and grinned. He had only been here a half-hour and already had some great information. As they headed for the yachts, Danny smiled and wondered what else he would learn today.

<18>

When Joe entered the lobby of the Beekman Arms Hotel, he was greeted by a structure of strong oaken beams and wide plank floors. He found Jill waiting near the large stone hearth where a small fire softly burned. She welcomed Joe with a peck on his cheek.

Having already checked them both in, she took Joe by the arm and gave him a brief walking tour. Jill explained how the inn was constructed back in 1766 and that it was the oldest in America. It reminded Joe of something one might see in Colonial Williamsburg, Virginia. When they were finished looking around, she took him to their room. It too dated back to 1766, but had recently been renovated. Jill stated she thought the room's décor, with its warmth and intimacy, made it historically romantic.

Joe agreed as he strode across the wooden floor while admiring the fireplace. He placed his bag on the quilt of the four-poster bed, unpacked his clothes and hung them in the closet. He kept his running gear stuffed in a large black leather duffel. Because of the time change and long flight, Joe had gotten up early and taken an early morning distance run.

Joe put on a fresh dress shirt and chose a casual corduroy jacket with elbow patches. He sat down in an antique wingback chair and watched as Jill searched for a pair of shoes. *She must have brought a dozen pairs*, he thought.

After what seemed like an eternity, Joe got up from his chair and walked across the room. As he passed Jill, who was questioningly eyeing a pair of heels in front of an old-fashioned freestanding mirror, he sarcastically asked, "Exactly how long did it take you to get dressed?"

Jill lifted her right leg and drew it back as if she was going to kick him in the groin.

"Hey, be careful with those heels. I might still like to have kids someday."

"Very funny."

"Maybe you had better go with a pair of flats. I know I'd feel safer. Anyway, when you're finished, I'll be waiting down in the lobby."

"I'm coming, I'm coming," Jill whined as she kicked off the heels and slipped on a pair of flats that she had been wearing minutes before.

Joe waited by the door as Jill quickly transferred some personal items into a matching handbag. As they were about to leave the room, Joe wrapped his left arm around her waist and glanced down at her shoes.

"Don't say anything," she snipped as they proceeded downstairs.

Just outside the doorway to the 1766 Tavern, Jill realized she had forgotten something. She asked Joe to go ahead and get their table and she'd be right back.

"Can I order you a drink?"

"Sure, I'll have a gin and tonic with a twist of lime."

"You got it."

The hostess seated Joe at a small, round wooden table near the brick fireplace of the hotel's restaurant. Hanging above the wooden mantle was an oil painting of George Washington.

After ordering drinks, Joe thought to himself, *Friday night and I'm once again having dinner with the beautiful woman who has suddenly begun to occupy my thoughts. It's the start of a great, long weekend. Maybe many, I hope.*

Though Joe had plenty of time to think about the case on the five-hour Continental flight from Los Angeles and he was now here with Jill, he still found himself obsessing over the case.

He had checked his voice mail immediately after landing in Newark and was surprised to find several new messages, all related to the case. Unfortunately, none of the news was particularly good. With each voice mail he listened to, the case became even more confusing. However, one thing did become clear. QCI and Tony Folino were definitely up to something and Joe wasn't going to rest until he found out what it was.

The first message was from Mark Grady in Durango, finally calling back. The message said that he wouldn't be interested in any investigative work. His part-time hobby of photography that supplemented his income had become a full-time job. He said he was now working as a photographer for a subsidiary of AMF, Inc. He provided compromising photos of politicians, Hollywood celebrities, and other high net worth individuals for a couple of their supermarket tabloids.

Joe had to admit he was a little surprised. Contributing to supermarket tabloid journalism was quite the contrast to having previously been a police detective. He still wanted to speak with Mark. With Folino's training facility located nearby, Mark might have some dirt on him. Joe decided he might try calling Mark again later to let him know more about the case.

Joe found the next message on his voice mail to be somewhat concerning. It was from Chief Buchanan. He called to tell Joe that Max Wells' wife had called him that morning and reported Max missing. She told Frank that Max had received a strange call late the previous night after he had gone to bed. He quickly got himself dressed and left for the hangar. His wife said Max seemed really concerned about something, so she asked him if everything was all right. He had said, "Yeah, I think everything will be fine. I'm just needed down at the hangar."

Max's wife didn't think it was odd because even though he no longer had a plane, the StratoShares aircraft still always arrived and departed from the old Adventure Studios hangar. It wasn't until he didn't call and never came home that she began to think something was wrong.

She called the chairman's office at the studio and was informed they had no flights either the previous night or early that morning. The office also said they were not aware of anybody having contacted Max. After hanging up, she immediately called Frank.

Frank said he sent a couple men out to investigate, but so far they hadn't found anything. There was no evidence that anybody had been at the hangar the previous night or earlier in the morning.

The next message was from a young female lieutenant on the LAPD who was doing the background search for Joe on Angelo Proccacino, the guy whose plane had the near midair collision with Max Wells' aircraft. The one piece of information that caused Joe to sit up and take notice was the fact that she said Angelo was the vice chairman of AMF. It was the second time he had heard the company's name that day.

Jill was in the industry. Maybe she could help. When she returned to their table, Joe got up to pull out her chair. He couldn't help but think that each time he saw her, she appeared more stunning than the time before. As he pushed in her chair, he smelled the honeysuckle fragrance from her vibrant auburn hair. Joe sat down as she picked up her gin and tonic.

"Why, thank you, Mr. Hara. It's so refreshing to see that chivalry still exists."

Joe smiled. "What was it you said to me? Oh yeah, flattery will get you everywhere, Ms. Riley."

Jill laughed vivaciously.

As they sat there smiling, Joe picked up his scotch glass. "I don't mean to change the subject, and I promise not to dwell on the case this weekend, but I've got a question."

"What?" she asked, smiling.

"What do you know about a publishing company called AMF?"

Jill chuckled. "You're kidding, right?"

Joe took a drink.

"That's Tony Folino's company. AMF stands for Anthony Massimiliano Folino."

Joe had to catch himself as he practically choked, almost spitting out his drink.

"Why do you ask?"

Joe turned his head and coughed as he regained his composure.

"Are you all right?"

"Yeah, I'm fine. Sorry about that. I guess it went down the wrong pipe. I knew that."

"Knew what?" Jill asked, confused.

"Knew that AMF was Folino's initials. I was just seeing if you knew."

"No you didn't," she said, shaking her head, obviously not believing him. "I'm really beginning to wonder just how good a detective you actually are."

Joe decided this was a good opportunity to change the subject even though he knew now it would be even more difficult not to think about the case. "You're right. Detective work isn't my specialty. That's why you invited me up here this weekend. You know . . . to show you what I'm really good at."

Jill laughed again. "What—cooking?"

Joe frowned. "Oh, you are funny." He rebounded with, "Actually, yes, cooking," then paused and added, "but not just in the kitchen."

Jill was now smiling ear to ear. "I'll be the judge of that—again." She reached down and picked up her menu. "Let's hurry up and order. I suddenly feel very hungry."

Joe picked up the wine menu and looked it over. "Would you care for some wine?"

"That would be wonderful, but please, let me choose. After all, you are my guest. I invited you. Tonight is my treat."

Joe thought about it for a moment. He would have preferred to pick up the tab just because it was the gentlemanly thing to do. But nowadays buying dinner, or even sometimes just a drink for a woman, often implied that she was somehow indebted to you, with the ultimate form of payment being sex.

Now, Joe was quite certain, since she had invited him for the weekend, the sex part was a given. That was of course barring any piece of embarrassing behavior on his part, which he knew he was always capable of.

"Only if tomorrow night is on me."

"Okay," she conceded.

Joe passed the wine menu across the table as Jill outstretched a long, slender arm. He sat across the table admiring her elegance and beauty while she scanned the wine list.

Joe thought she was possibly the most beautiful woman he had ever known. Her toned, golden bronze skin emphasized her sleeveless black dress. This was accented by a large gold herringbone necklace that hung elegantly around her neck and was accompanied by medium-sized gold rectangular earrings and a gold Audemars Piguet watch. Joe had noticed earlier that both pairs of flats she had deliberated over for so long and matching handbag were Chanel. He had also noticed when they were in Boston that she had the finest taste in clothing and accessories. He thought to himself, *She probably never wears the same thing twice.*

He wasn't obsessed with these things, but observation had simply become second nature to him. He always made mental notes of everything. His powers of observation were critical in his detective work. Unfortunately, it became such a habit that it carried over into his personal life.

As a result he couldn't help but wonder if he could afford her standard of living. Not that Joe's standard was anything to be ashamed of. Joe had done very well for himself and lived quite comfortably. But Jill obviously aspired for the best of everything.

She laid down the wine menu and slightly raised her right hand and first finger to motion for the waiter. He was standing near the bar, speaking to the bartender. He noticed immediately and briskly walked over to the table.

The young man was getting ready to speak when Jill spoke first. "We would like a bottle of wine," she said, pausing as she looked at his name badge, "Phillipe."

The young, blond, wavy-haired waiter focused his blue eyes on her and said, "What would you like this evening, madame?" His accent was obviously French.

"Please bring us a bottle of your finest Château Margaux."

"Oh yes, madame. Château Margaux. That is an excellent choice. I will be right back with that." The waiter turned and briskly walked away.

"Excellent choice indeed," Joe stated. Her choice confirmed his thoughts of only seconds before; she liked the best of everything.

The waiter returned shortly and Jill asked Joe if he would like the honor of tasting the wine.

"I would be delighted," he told her with a smile. He went through the usual ritual and then stated, "Thank you, Phillipe. It has a nice balance and intensity of character in the finish."

"Oui, monsieur. Would you like to order now or do you need more time to look over the menu?"

Joe looked across the table at Jill.

"Whenever you're ready, Joe. I know what I want."

Normally Joe would order for his dinner date, but since this was Jill's treat, he replied, "Then you go first."

Jill placed her order, then Joe followed suit.

A few moments later their salads arrived and they began enjoying their meal. They conversed about the hotel as Jill spoke of its fascinating history. She was telling him how Franklin Delano Roosevelt had been a frequent guest there and had concluded all his campaigns for both governor and president by speaking from the front porch.

When their entrees were served and Jill stopped speaking momentarily, Joe took the opportunity to try and change the subject.

"I know we said we wouldn't talk about work, but I was just curious how your story was coming."

"What story? I mean, which one?"

"Which one?" Joe looked confused. "The one about the wealthy and their toys."

"Oh, that one. Of course. It's almost finished." Jill picked up the wine bottle to pour herself another glass. "Would you like some?"

"No thank you, I'm fine."

"Let's see, now where was I. Oh yes, Franklin Delano Roosevelt." Jill continued where she had left off.

It suddenly became obvious to Joe that Jill didn't want to talk about the case or her story. He couldn't help wondering why, but decided not to press the issue.

When they were both finished eating, the waiter removed their dinner plates and asked if they would like an after dinner drink. "Perhaps a port?" he asked.

Jill asked, "Do you have Fonseca Port?"

"Yes we do, madame, Fonseca '94."

Jill looked at Joe, who nodded again in agreement at her fine choice.

"Then we'd like two glasses, please, Phillipe."

"Oui, I'll bring back the dessert menu as well."

After the waiter had left the table, Joe asked if he could be excused for a moment. He got up and walked to the men's room. About five minutes later he returned. Joe noticed two glasses of the exotic fruit port sitting on the table.

"Let's drink a toast," Jill said as she raised her glass.

Sitting down, Joe replaced the white linen napkin on his lap and picked up his glass. He extended his arm across the table.

"To good health," Jill proposed, smiling.

"To good health," Joe repeated as their glass rims clinked.

Joe raised the glass to his lips and drank. He thought the port wine tasted slightly bitter, but figured it must be because of the breath mints he had popped into his mouth just before returning to the table.

The waiter returned five minutes later to take their dessert order. The menu selection looked very tempting, but both of them, feeling full, declined. The waiter left the table once again.

Joe shifted in his chair as he started feeling strange. He turned his body sideways in the chair and accidentally knocked over his half-empty glass of port. It immediately transformed the white tablecloth crimson. Jill quickly scooted backwards in her chair until she was well out of harm's way. She appeared agitated by the incident.

"I'm sorry," Joe said. "I tell you, I can really be a klutz sometimes. Did I get any on you?"

"No, I'm fine," Jill replied, sounding unsympathetic.

Joe wasn't certain what was happening, but he felt a tightness in his throat and was suddenly finding it difficult to breathe.

"Is something wrong, Joe? You look a little flushed."

"You know, I think there is. I'm suddenly not feeling very well." Joe scratched his chest and arms and could feel large, itchy lumps forming on his skin. "If you'll excuse me, I think I should be going."

Joe started to get up but quickly sat down. Abdominal cramps were kicking in, as well as a nauseous feeling. The itching was intense and he was finding it extremely difficult to breathe.

Quickly rising from the table, Jill said, "Maybe we had better get you back to the room, where you can lie down." She went over and tightly grabbed Joe's arm.

Joe pulled his arm away. "I don't think so, Jill." Joe could feel his face and hands swelling. "Please ask the waiter to call for help. I feel like I'm starting to suffocate."

As Jill hurried off to the reception area, a man at a nearby table hurriedly came to Joe's side. He quickly surmised it was an allergic reaction of some type and feared Joe was going into anaphylactic shock.

The slightly balding, black-haired man reached into his coat pocket, removed his cell phone, and punched in 911. Joe could hear him anxiously saying, "Yes, this is Doctor Trent. I'm at the 1766 Tavern at the Beekman Arms Hotel. I have a man who appears to be going into anaphylactic shock. Yes, that's right. Thank you."

The doctor put the cell phone back in his jacket pocket. Jill returned with the manager, who was quickly briefed by the doctor. Jill watched in horror as Joe's face swelled and became distorted. She couldn't believe it; it didn't even look like Joe anymore.

A woman who had been watching from a nearby table got up and hurried over with her bottle of Benadryl allergy medicine. The doctor kindly thanked her and explained that the bottle of pink syrup would not be of any benefit. He stated that only cases of mild allergic reaction could sometimes be prevented with a medication such as Benadryl. Joe's symptoms were that of anaphylaxis, which was on the extreme end of the allergic spectrum.

The doctor helped hold Joe upright in his chair as Joe continued leaning on the wine-stained table for support. His broad chest heaved as he struggled for air.

In a slurred and barely audible voice, Joe uttered, "How far to the hospital?"

"Not far," the doctor replied. "Don't worry, the life squad should be here any moment."

Seconds seemed like minutes to Joe. He felt extremely weak and started to think that this might be it for him. In twenty-five years of police work, he had been shot multiple times, stabbed, clubbed on the head, run over, and even fallen two stories. And not once did he think he might die. He thought he heard sirens as he closed his eyes and rested his head on the table.

He also thought he heard a cell phone ringing, then Jill's voice, but wasn't certain. It sounded like a whisper.

"This is Jill. Max? What? Oh, don't say that, Max. You know I lov . . . "

Her words trailed off as Joe collapsed from the chair and lost consciousness.

"I'll call you right back," she whispered. Jill stood by looking anxious and uneasy. She couldn't believe what was happening. *And what does Max want,* she wondered.

She stared down at Joe, who appeared unconscious. In a trancelike state, Jill watched Joe and the doctor. After asking her twice to step aside and getting no response, the two paramedics on the scene gently moved Jill away and started administering to Joe.

<19>

Danny shut off the Pontiac's headlights as he turned from the service road and drove alongside the small vacant building. The parking lot was empty so he opted to park around back. Danny didn't want to draw attention to his presence. He turned off the engine and sat in the darkness. A not quite full moon shone brightly over the airport illuminating the West Palm Beach sky.

He reached under the front seat and removed the black case that contained his night scope. He had brought it along specifically with this evening's rooftop surveillance in mind. He slipped the leather strap over his left shoulder and looked outside the vehicle to make sure nobody had noticed him.

After his meeting with Rick Garcia, Danny didn't have enough time to check out Folino's training facility, so he proceeded directly to Five Star Aviation at West Palm Beach International Airport, or PBI, as it was more commonly known.

After parking his car and walking past the landscape of palm trees, Danny entered the two-story Mediterranean-style structure with its masonry and stucco facade. He walked around the waiting area appearing to be a passenger or somebody meeting an arriving flight. He wasn't questioned and nobody standing around or sitting there paid him any attention.

He didn't notice anything particularly unusual. There were the typical early evening arrivals and departures of private jets with visiting businessmen and West Palm Beach's wealthiest residents.

Dan stood and watched as several StratoShares aircraft arrived at the facility over the course of an hour or so. He tried his best to overhear the pilots as they spoke with the women working the front desk, but heard nothing out of the ordinary. Apparently, all the StratoShares aircraft were going to spend the night on the ramp with no further trips until the following morning. He overheard the pilots saying the StratoShares detailers would arrive during the middle of the night to clean and restock the planes.

Everything certainly appeared normal until he walked past a pilot's lounge. Danny noticed the door was cracked slightly open and he could see inside. What he saw surprised him. He recognized a StratoShares pilot who had arrived a short while earlier with passengers from the Caribbean. He was now passing something, during a handshake, to another man with a briefcase. It appeared to be a sizeable wad of cash. The man was dressed rather casually in white twill pants, a light blue button-down shirt and a navy sports coat.

Danny reached inside his windbreaker pocket and pulled out a small brown leather address book. He stood at an angle so he could continue to watch inside the lounge while appearing to be flipping through the book. Out of the corner of his eye, Danny saw both men walking in his direction. The young pilot was laughing and patting the other man on the back. Danny quickly moved toward the nearest telephone. From there he watched as the men turned and walked toward the front doors of the lobby.

Danny recognized the person with the StratoShares pilot. He too had been hanging around the lobby of the FBO; he appeared to have been waiting for someone. Both men exited the building. Danny quickly walked over to the counter where he got the attention of one of the older women working there.

"Excuse me, but maybe you can help me. I'm looking for a gentleman that should have arrived on a StratoShares flight from Nassau. I just saw the captain leave through those doors." Danny pointed in the direction of the double glass doors. "I was wondering if that might have been the man I was looking for."

The dark-eyed Italian woman replied with a distinct high-pitched New Jersey accent. "Oh no, sir. I believe the passenger who arrived on that flight left immediately. If I'm not mistaken, the gentleman you just saw leave was Larry Hill, our customs agent."

"Oh?" Danny paused, acting confused. He lifted the ball cap from his curly blond hair and scratched his head. "Well, I guess I'll just have to try and reach him on his cell phone. Thank you for your assistance."

"You're welcome. I hope you find who you're looking for."

"I'm sure I will. Thanks again." Danny turned around and walked toward the doors. He suddenly had several calls he needed to make.

That was a couple hours ago. After placing the calls from his car, he left the FBO and scouted out this vacant building for the night's surveillance. He determined that the roof would give an unobstructed view of Five Star's ramp area where several StratoShares aircraft were parked for the night.

Dan ate a late supper just a couple miles away at a restaurant on South Dixie Highway called Craig's - An American Bistro. He enjoyed a burger with everything on it while he thought about the last call he had placed. He spoke to somebody on the West Palm Beach police force and found that the OceanShares employee death had been reported as an accidental drowning. The report made no mention of any type of robbery. Danny found this puzzling and had been thinking about it ever since.

After dinner he called to check on Nancy. It was ten-thirty when he spoke to her. She had just gotten back to their hotel room and sounded exhausted. She had gone to three different malls around the city. He was happy to hear that she hadn't bought much since she would have plenty of time to shop on the cruise.

He wondered if Nancy knew about Worth Avenue in West Palm Beach. It was similar to Rodeo Drive back in Beverly Hills. He hadn't thought to mention it to her and only remembered it himself when earlier he had driven past its many shops distinguished by early twentieth-century Mediterranean architecture. If she had known, she would probably have driven all the way up there. He thought it probably best not to mention it now.

After a brief conversation regarding the case, he wished her good night, sweet dreams, and told her not to worry. He would see her in the morning sometime.

Danny, on the other hand, was wired. He wasn't at all exhausted and his body was still on Pacific Standard Time; to him it was only about eight in the evening.

He got out of the car, locked the door, and walked quietly along the back wall of the vacant building. Security lights on tall metal poles illuminated the perimeter of the lot as well as the corners of the building. The two-story white stucco structure appeared to be one of the area's older buildings, and it was still in excellent condition.

A high chainlink fence with barbed wire across the top separated the FBO's ramp and operations area from the general public. An electronic sliding gate was used to allow vehicle access to the facility's ramp and aircraft parking apron.

He thought the For Lease sign out front might have been posted prematurely. A construction dumpster in the parking lot was overflowing with the protruding remnants of all types of building materials including drywall, lumber, and rolls of carpeting. The facility had obviously been remodeled before being listed on the market.

If Danny had to guess, he would say the previous tenant had been a fixed-base operator that just couldn't afford the overhead. Probably a mom-and-pop business that couldn't compete with the likes of their nearby neighbor, Five Star Aviation, just across the ramp.

Danny reached the steel rung ladder he had noticed earlier. It was attached to the side of the structure and led to the flat roof. After looking around again to make sure no one was watching, Danny climbed the ladder as the sound of a jet's engines roared its departure on a nearby runway.

When he reached the top he pulled himself over the two-foot wall and stepped down onto the roof. He squatted, and then bent down, placing both hands on the roof's loose gravel as he bear-crawled across to the other side.

When Danny got there, he noticed a square black seat cushion laying close by. It was the kind a person would use at a football game. It looked practically new and its un-weathered appearance told him it hadn't been lying there long. He pressed his hand in the center and determined it was dry. Danny sat down on it and crossed his legs. He noticed an empty yellow Juicy Fruit gum package and several wrappers on the gravel nearby as well as an empty Diet Coke can. He thought to himself, *Somebody must come up here to sit and watch planes.*

Danny looked around and immediately understood why. The roof was a great place to watch from. It offered an unobstructed view of all three runways and most of the airport. It was better than he had imagined.

Danny slid the black case off his left shoulder and removed the night scope. After looking through it a couple times, he made a couple adjustments until he was satisfied. He was now ready to watch the StratoShares aircraft sitting on the Five Star Aviation ramp.

He glanced down at his watch. The moonlight was sufficient for Danny to make out the time—eleven-thirty. He didn't know how long he'd have to sit there and wasn't certain what he was looking for, but that was typically the case with stakeouts. You never knew what to expect. Many times you were disappointed and other times you were pleasantly surprised. He would sit and watch until the aircraft cleaners arrived to prepare the planes for the next day's flights.

Danny didn't have to wait long. It was just after midnight when he noticed the first signs of activity.

The hangar door slid open as a tow motor used for pulling airplanes drove across the ramp to the first plane. At the same time, another man exited the FBO and walked over to assist. Both men were wearing navy blue walking shorts and white, short-sleeved dress shirts with the blue StratoShares logo on the pocket. They removed wooden chocks from the fore and aft of the plane's main gear wheels. Next they pinned and locked the tow bar to the aircraft's front wheel. One worker climbed into the cockpit while the other climbed back on the tug.

The two men pulled the Citation X aircraft into the Five Star hangar and a few moments later closed the door behind them. The other four StratoShares airplanes sat idle on the ramp along with several other aircraft. There was nothing else happening around any of them.

Almost one hour later the doors to the hangar opened. The same aircraft was pushed back onto the ramp to its previous position and its chocks were replaced. Immediately, the next aircraft in line had its chocks removed and was pulled inside. Again like clockwork, one hour later, the second aircraft was brought back onto the ramp.

And so the process continued. Danny couldn't tell what was going on inside the building, but thought the activity looked suspect. All the while he continued to scan around the airport with his night scope and saw no indication of any other similar procedures. Several planes at other FBOs were also obviously being prepared for early morning departures. The difference was their preparation was being done on the ramp. If it had been rainy or cold, Dan could have understood pulling the aircraft into the hangar, but since it was a clear night and the temperature was mild, he was suspicious.

The last StratoShares aircraft was being pulled into the hangar when Danny heard an unsettling sound. It was a crunching noise coming from behind him. The sound happened suddenly, then stopped. Danny didn't turn around until he heard it for the second time. As he clumsily spun around from his sitting position and lifted himself off the foam cushion, he stumbled to his feet. He stood totally erect on the roof of the vacant building. The outline of his body on the rooftop could be seen all over the airport.

But so could the dark outline of the man who stood across from him on the rooftop. From the distance of about fifty feet, Danny couldn't make out the man's face but could make out the outline of a gun. Danny suddenly felt anxious when he realized he had forgotten his guns, both of them. Usually even when off duty, he still carried a revolver tucked in his waistband or ankle holster. But now he was totally unarmed.

Danny remembered there was a short section of cast iron pipe lying on the ledge behind him. He had noticed it there while he sat. It was apparently a remnant left behind from some electrical work. The pipe was evidently being used as conduit to house or hide electrical wires for the building's exterior lighting. Dan had noticed most of the lighting appeared new.

The unidentified man spoke first. "Who are you and what are you doing here?"

Always a wise guy, Danny replied, "Oh, I'm sorry. This must be your seat."

The man ignored Danny's comment and said, "You're the guy I saw earlier this evening hanging around Five Star."

Danny strained to make out the man as he approached even closer with his gun extended. He didn't recognize the voice, and his brain worked frantically as it tried to place the man from earlier that evening. The sound of the rooftop gravel, which had given away his presence, became louder as it crunched beneath his feet. When the man stopped about ten feet in front of Danny, he was able to make out the man's face in the moonlight. It was the customs agent he had seen taking money from a StratoShares pilot.

"I'm going to ask you one more time. Who are you and what are you doing here?"

Danny again ignored the question as he cautiously moved backward one step and brought his right hand within inches of the steel pipe. He wasn't exactly sure what good the pipe would do him. At ten feet away, it wasn't likely he was going to deflect any bullets with it. His only other option was to go over the wall, but the twenty-foot drop to the asphalt below was equally unattractive.

"If you're going to kill me, you won't get away with it. I saw what you did tonight and I've already placed calls to the authorities. StratoShares is obviously paying you to look the other way, but for what? What are they up to?"

The man said, "First of all, you don't know what you're talking about and you don't know who I am. Now, nobody said anything about killing anybody. I'm just not going to let you fuck up my last nine months' work!"

Dan thought for a moment while deciding what to do. If the guy was in cahoots with Folino and he told him his suspicions, the man would no doubt waste him without blinking an eye. On the other hand, if he wasn't who Danny thought he was, and what he had told Danny was correct, then maybe they could help each other. Danny's instincts were usually good; for some reason he didn't think this guy was a killer.

"My name is Detective Daniel Froberg with the Los Angeles Police Department. I'm investigating QCI and Strato-Shares in conjunction with the mysterious deaths of several owners in their program."

The man lowered his gun and placed it inside his navy sports jacket. He walked another two or three steps toward Danny, extending his right hand, and said, "Name's Larry North with the U.S. Drug Enforcement Administration. I think we need to talk!"

<20>

Joe turned onto Interstate 87 and headed south toward New Jersey. He was feeling much better after having spent the previous night and that morning at Northern Duchess Hospital in Rhinebeck.

Joe still couldn't believe what had happened the night before. Anaphylaxis was the most severe allergic reaction that a person could have, and Joe had never experienced it before. The paramedics had given him an adrenaline injection and loaded him into the ambulance. Five minutes later on the way to the hospital, he showed no signs of improvement so they gave him a second injection. That did the job.

He remained at the hospital for the remainder of the night and continued to improve. The first thing in the morning, a couple nurses ran a battery of tests trying to determine what caused the reaction. With Joe having no past history of anaphylaxis, the doctor was somewhat baffled. He recommended an allergy clinic for Joe when he returned to L.A.

The doctor told Joe he should consider wearing a Medic Alert bracelet and carry an adrenaline kit with him wherever he went. Since Joe was already in his late forties and had never had a reaction before, he didn't think a bracelet was necessary, but told the doctor he would keep the adrenaline kit nearby.

Ironically, what was bothering Joe the most was the embarrassment aspect. He couldn't imagine what he must have looked like last night as he lay unconscious and swollen on the restaurant floor beneath the painting of George Washington. *I must have looked like a blowfish out of water. Real attractive,* he thought.

Then, add the fact that they had cut their weekend short and he and Jill hadn't gotten to spend any more time together. He told her he didn't feel up to anything today and that she should just return to the City. Though she seemed concerned and somewhat distraught over the situation, she agreed she should probably go.

Isn't it ironic? Yesterday I visited the nearby Culinary Institute of America, then had dinner at the 1766 Tavern with cuisine by noted Chef Larry Forgione. Shortly thereafter, I'm in the hospital with some type of food allergy. At least that's what I think it was.

Joe's cell phone rang and he picked it up off the passenger seat. He hoped it was the hospital lab with the results of his blood work. He pressed the button. "Joe Hara."

"Hey Joe, it's Danny. Where have you been? I've got all kinds of information."

"Well, it's about time, kid. What have you got for me?" Joe asked. Danny could sense that Joe was smiling on the other end of the phone.

"First, where are you? I called the inn and they said you had checked out."

"I'm driving in the rental car heading south on I-87, toward New Jersey."

"Is Jill Riley with you?"

"No, we called the rest of the weekend off after I got sick. She headed back to the City this morning."

"You got sick? What happened?"

"I'll explain it all later."

"Okay. Well, I just spoke to a detective on the San Francisco force. It seems that a couple of their uniformed officers in a squad car arrested the guys driving the vehicle that chased Johnnie Perrino."

"How did they manage that?"

"Well, they noticed a car that fit the description parked on a street near Fisherman's Wharf. They sat and waited for the driver to return. A short while later two guys got in and drove away. They also fit the description that Johnnie had left for his father on his father's voice mail.

"Anyhow, the goons ran a red light and that was all the officers needed. When they started to pursue them, they attempted to elude the officers at high speed down several side streets. They eventually pulled over feigning ignorance and saying they didn't know the officers wanted them to stop. When they opened the trunk, they found a MAC-10. The gun has already been tested in the ballistics lab and matches the .45 caliber bullet they found in the guardrail post along Highway 1. They got a match also on the tires from the tracks they found."

"So did they confess?"

"Yeah, they confessed. They said they received cash for the job. It was dropped on a bench in a fast-food bag on Pier 55. They said a woman contacted them. They don't know who and they don't know from where. They couldn't tell us anything about her voice other than she sounded rich and distinguished. They couldn't recall an accent, either."

"How the hell do you sound rich?" Joe asked. He moved the phone over to his other hand as he switched hands on the wheel.

"They're a couple of hired thugs, Joe. What do you expect? Besides, they weren't supposed to kill him."

"What do you mean, they weren't supposed to kill him?"

"They said they were just supposed to scare him. They said they could have hit him with the bullets if they'd wanted to. How did they know that truck was going to be around the bend?"

"This just isn't making a whole lot of sense, now, is it?" Joe commented.

"You know, if they are telling the truth, I can't help but think how unfortunate this whole thing is. I mean, do you realize Johnnie Perrino was the last of the line. He was an only son and his father only had sisters. The Perrino name will end with his father since Johnnie is now dead and can't have any kids."

Danny's statement made Joe think about a similar comment he had made to Jill, when she had playfully acted like she was going to kick him with her heel and he had said, "Be careful, I might still like to have kids someday." Joe just shook his head as he thought about it. She was ready to kick him like a dog.

Then suddenly it hit him. Danny was still talking but Joe hadn't heard a word. Joe interrupted him. "Danny, where are you?"

"I'm at the precinct. Why?"

"Let me call you right back."

"But I've got more to tell you."

"You can tell me when I call you back. Don't go anywhere."

Joe pressed the Off button and set the phone between his legs. He pulled his address book from his coat pocket that was draped over the back of the passenger seat. He quickly found the number for the veterinarian who had looked at Randall Johnson's dog, Lady. He punched in the number.

A young lady answered the phone. "Dr. Martin's office."

"Could I speak to Dr. Martin, please?"

"May I tell him who's calling?"

"Yes, tell him it's Detective Hara."

"One moment."

As Joe waited, his mind raced. He truly hoped he wasn't right.

A few seconds later Dr. Martin answered. "Detective Hara, how can I help you?"

"Do you remember the puncture wound on Randall Johnson's dog, Lady?"

"Of course I do. I'm still not certain what caused it, though."

"I think I know," Joe quickly replied. "I think a woman kicked Lady. I think the spike of a woman's high heel is what caused the wound."

"Hmm," the doctor commented as he thought about the possibility. "You know, if a woman had kicked at the dog and missed, then maybe the tip of the heel could have found the dog's underside on the way up. The angle would be just right for a wound the nature of Lady's. You know, you might just be right, Mr. Hara."

"Thanks, Doc. Thanks for all your help. I'll talk to you later." Joe pressed the button to end the call.

Joe knew he was right and he didn't like the direction his thoughts were taking him. Now he knew why the dog had become excited in Jill's presence. Joe thought about what he should do next as he held the phone. It rang in his hand.

"Joe Hara," he anxiously answered.

"Mr. Hara, this is Dr. Lennox at Northern Duchess. We've gotten the results of some of your blood work. Have you been taking any medications recently that were prescribed or non-prescribed, for that matter?"

"No, absolutely not. I prefer to never take anything." As a competitive athlete, Joe had always felt strongly about not taking medications. He took a more holistic approach and avoided prescription drugs.

"Interesting." The doctor paused and then continued: "Well, I think you had an allergic reaction to a drug called chloral hydrate. The lab found traces of it in your blood."

"What?" Joe couldn't believe what he was hearing.

"Someone apparently slipped you a Mickey, Detective Hara."

Joe wasn't quite sure what to say. He knew a bit about chloral hydrate from a couple college psychology courses. He had taken a class on addictive behaviors and another on drug and alcohol education. "You're certain about this, Doctor?"

"Oh, quite certain. Chloral hydrate is a hypnotic drug that commonly comes in a liquid form. That's where it got the name 'knockout drops.' It induces sleep shortly after a normal therapeutic dose. It's potent, quick acting, but can also be lethal. You didn't get enough, though, for it to have its full effect, but you apparently got enough for an allergic reaction. And a bad one at that," he added.

"Now, we didn't run enough tests to be a hundred percent certain that's what caused the anaphylaxis, so I still recommend you go to that allergy clinic as soon as you get home."

"Okay, Doc. I appreciate your timely follow-up and response. I may need documentation on your findings at a later date."

"That's certainly not a problem. Please don't hesitate to give me a call."

Joe thanked him one last time, then turned off his cell phone. He began to play back yesterday evening's dinner in his mind.

He had returned from the restroom and taken maybe two or three swallows of wine before accidentally spilling the glass. The waiter had poured him a fresh glass. *Something must've been slipped into my drink while I was away,* he thought. He remembered the bitter taste and how he had attributed it to the breath mints he'd taken while in the men's room.

That had to be it. Now Joe definitely didn't like what he was thinking.

Jill had proposed a toast to his health and they had clinked glasses. Joe shook his head as he thought about the irony.

Clinking glasses was a custom of mutual trust, an ancient ceremony that dated back to the days of frequent poisonings. As a result, drinkers would pour some of their wine into the other person's cup. This would show that they didn't have it "in" for each other. Today it had simply evolved to the touching of rims.

It just can't be true. I refuse to believe it!

Then Joe remembered something else. Or had he simply dreamed it? He could remember having lain somewhere and hearing a lot of commotion, lots of different voices talking. He heard Jill on the telephone. Somebody named Max had called her and she said she loved him . . . or something.

It must have been right before he lost consciousness.

"Max?" Joe said aloud to himself. "Max Wells, maybe?"

Joe suddenly realized that he hadn't spoken to the chief since he had received his voice mail the previous evening. He wondered if Max Wells had turned up. Picking up his cell phone, Joe quickly redialed Buchanan's number back in L.A. He answered on the first ring.

"Buch here."

"Frank, it's Joe. I got your message yesterday about Max Wells. Any new developments?"

"You mean you haven't heard?" The chief sounded surprised.

"No. Heard what?"

"Max Wells is dead. A uniformed officer found his car in the main terminal parking lot at Santa Monica Airport. When they opened the trunk they found his body. He had a bullet in his head fired at point-blank range. It looks like a Mafia hit. There's no doubt in my mind the type of people we're dealing with here. We searched his office at the hangar but didn't find anything."

Shit, Joe thought, *he must have gotten whacked because I spoke to him. But how did they know? Nobody knew I met with Max.* Then Joe remembered Jill's call while he was at the hangar. *Oh shit,* Joe thought.

"Have you spoken to Froberg?" the chief added.

"Actually, he started briefing me a few minutes ago. I need to call him back."

"Well, call him. Then call me right back so we can discuss your thoughts. This thing is apparently bigger than we ever imagined."

Joe thought for a moment about this most recent revelation. "When did the coroner estimate the time of death for Max Wells?"

"Just a minute, I've got it right here on my desk. Let's see, it says here . . . approximately nineteen-thirty. Why?"

"Let me give Dan a call first, then I'll call you back and tell you what we've got."

"Okay, I'll be waiting."

Joe hit the End button on his phone and redialed Danny. He thought again about yesterday evening's dinner. *It was probably about seven-thirty last night when I had the allergic reaction. That would make the time on the West Coast, four-thirty. The coroner's report estimated the time of death to be about seven-thirty Pacific Standard Time.* Joe mused while the phone rang.

So that means it could have been Max Wells that called Jill Riley last night. But why? Joe wondered. *Why would Max Wells be calling Jill? It doesn't make sense.*

Then another memory flashed through Joe's mind as he recalled his past conversation with Jill over dinner in Boston. He had asked her if she had ever been to Valentino in Santa Monica and she had said, "Max took me there a couple times." *What the hell is going on,* Joe wondered.

After several more rings, Danny answered.

"This is Froberg."

"Danny, it's Joe."

"Where you been, man? I've been waiting for you to call back."

"You go first, Dan. Finish telling me what you've found."

"Okay, but you're not going to like it."

"C'mon Dan, I'm a big kid. I can take it. Whadda ya got?" Joe hoped he sounded unconcerned because he knew if Danny said he wasn't going to like it, then he probably wasn't going to like it.

"Well, it turns out that Folino is in bed with the media."

"What are you talking about? I know he owns a publishing company called AMF that publishes a supermarket tabloid, among other things," Joe stated.

"Yeah, but he also owns many of the reporters and journalists that work for other publications. Not just across the country but around the globe. That's how he controls what goes into print. Especially the investigative reporters that report on homicides and drugs and any other nastiness he might be involved with."

Danny paused, so Joe knew he was about to drop the bomb.

"And there's one name that keeps coming back to us. Apparently she's his biggest supporter."

Joe felt a lump the size of a baseball welling up inside his throat. Barely audible, Joe said, "What's her name?"

"It's Jill Riley, Joe."

He suddenly felt lightheaded and thought he might get sick. He quickly pulled the car over to the side of the road. He didn't say anything. He couldn't say anything. He rested his forehead on the steering wheel as other cars drove past.

"Joe, you okay, man?" Danny paused. "Because there's more. Folino and she have apparently been sleeping together."

Joe tried to regain his composure. "Are you certain about this? I mean, what exactly do you know?" Joe sounded anxious now.

"Well, they apparently spent considerable time together during one of Ms. Riley's visits to Italy back in the late seventies. She was on a summer college trip when somehow the two of them met. Apparently, Folino was attracted to her and became her personal tour guide. After returning to the states, they continued to see each other on and off for the next five or six years. Apparently, right up until the time when Folino married Maria."

"So, have they seen each other since?"

"They've been seen together since, but nobody is certain whether or not they are having a relationship. My source says he doesn't think so. He said to the best of his knowledge, Tony has always been faithful to his wife and is a devoted family man. So if that's the case, their meetings must be business related. Apparently, though, Folino has gotten Jill every job she has had since college."

Joe sat still as a mannequin as he recalled his dinner conversation with Jill a couple weeks before in Boston. She had actually told him a lot of this already. She had just left out a few things. In particular, Tony Folino's name. Now a lot of this was starting to make sense to Joe. Jill Riley was still in love with Tony Folino. Joe had seen it in her eyes that night when she spoke of Italy.

Danny sheepishly asked, "How much have you told her about the investigation, Joe?"

"Practically nothing. Well," he said, and took a deep breath, letting out a heavy sigh, "except for Randall Johnson's death. I told her exactly how he was murdered. She must have been going nuts sitting there at dinner and listening to me recreate the murder from earlier that day."

"What do you mean?"

"Because she's the one who killed him. I mean, I didn't know for sure until just a few moments ago. You know, when I had to call you back. You said something that made me recall a conversation that Jill and I had earlier. I called the vet up in Boston who'd checked Randall Johnson's dog. He confirmed that the puncture wound on the dog's belly could have been caused by a woman's high heel."

"So, how do you know for sure it was Jill?"

"I'll tell you that later. What else have you got? Any more information?"

"As a matter of fact, yes."

Joe turned off the engine and turned on the emergency flashers. After glancing out the window to make sure he had pulled far enough off the road, he picked up his notepad as Danny started to speak.

"I ran into a special agent for the DEA in West Palm Beach. The guy's name is Larry North. We talked about the case and he told me they already have a guy on the inside."

"Well, who is it?"

"Travis McGee."

"You've got to be kidding me. That baby-faced bullshitting little dork with the bad complexion is the DEA's inside guy? I don't believe it!"

"Believe it. McGee used to work at an airport near Knoxville, Tennessee. After McGee graduated from college, he got a job as a flight instructor at a local FBO where StratoShares aircraft would frequently fly in and out. Over time, he noticed a pattern of suspicious activity while the StratoShares aircraft sat on the ramps and were prepared for their next flights.

"Anyway, late one night, Travis somehow found several kilos of cocaine being smuggled on board one of the Strato-Shares aircraft. The temptation was too great and he took it. In his haste to get home with the goods, he drove a little too fast through a residential neighborhood. A police officer who lived in the subdivision was approaching in the opposite direction and clocked him on radar. When he turned on his lights, Travis attempted to elude but was unsuccessful. When McGee finally pulled over and the officer opened the trunk, he found the drugs.

"After listening to Travis' story, the police realized this might not have been an isolated incident and that Folino's operation might be much bigger than anybody realized. So they contacted the DEA.

"When the DEA checked with the FAA, they found that the plane had started its day in Miami. This immediately got their attention and they decided to try and build a case against StratoShares. When they mentioned possibly putting somebody on the inside, McGee graciously volunteered. He fit the description of probably ninety percent of Strato-Shares' employees. He had a four-year college degree and a couple years of work experience, more specifically in aviation. The solution for McGee was simple. He plea-bargained.

"The bottom line is, though, it's now been almost nine months and they still haven't been able to nail Folino or any of his men. It seems every time they try to bring him down, something goes wrong. It's like they always know when the Feds are coming," Danny said.

"So, what does that tell you, Dan? You know how it is with any confidential informant. We can never be quite sure who they're being loyal to."

"You think McGee is working both sides? Larry North told me McGee is pretty intelligent and graduated at the top of his class in high school and college."

"I think he's weasely enough," Joe added. "He probably makes a good salary with StratoShares, *and* gets paid handsomely by the DEA. In addition, he could anonymously be getting paid by Folino for passing along information regarding the DEA. My guess is Folino would kill him if he knew McGee was giving any information to the DEA. Unfortunately, the little prick will probably get away with it and when it's all over, he'll write a book and make millions."

"You know, Joe," Danny said, changing the subject, "I was also thinking about Jill. If she killed Randall Johnson, what's to say she didn't make the call that led to Johnnie Perrino's death? I mean, based on what those two goons told the police."

"You might be right, Danny. Why don't you see if you can get a subpoena to obtain Jill's phone records. If we can find the number for the two goons in Northern California, then maybe we can give the Napa police sufficient probable cause to pursue a warrant for her arrest."

"Good idea."

"I'm also curious if she received or placed any calls around seven-thirty or later last night with her cell phone. Particularly to or from Max Wells. You know he's dead, don't you?"

"Of course, it's all the talk around here today," Danny replied. "Do you think he's part of this?"

"I'm not certain yet. I need to keep checking. In the meantime, I've got another idea I'm working on. Give me the number for your contact at the DEA, Larry North."

<21>

Jill Riley sat on the soft Italian leather sofa in the living room of her Greenwich Village apartment. Tears were rolling down her cheeks. She downed another glass of straight whiskey, then placed the glass on the coffee table in front of her. She held the white mobile phone to her left ear. She leaned forward and waited while drumming her right-hand fingers on the glass top.

She was scared. *What have I done?* she asked herself. *What was I thinking? I have to talk to Max. I have to tell him I still love him, no matter what.*

Jill heard the familiar tone she had heard at least a hundred times before. There was no message on Max's voice mail.

She instantly started to ramble: "Max, it's Jill. It's about three in the afternoon. Oh God, I'm so sorry. I know you didn't mean what you said last night, but I got upset. And I was still upset this morning when that little prick Travis McGee called.

"Oh Max, I'm afraid I might have said some things that I shouldn't have. But you have to understand, you hurt me." She paused momentarily and sniffled. "He tricked me, Max. He said he had evidence of what you were up to. He acted like he knew everything and got me to confess to some things. I even think he might have recorded our conversation. Oh, Max, I'm so sorry," she said through her sobs.

"Please don't hate me. I don't hate you. I could never hate you. I know deep down you feel the same way I do. I've seen it before. We can have it again. Maria will never love you the way I do. It's not too late for us, Max. Oh sweetheart, you'll see."

Jill's voice changed and she became more perky. "I can kill McGee for you, Max. I've killed before, I can do it again. I'd do anything for you, Max. Oh, can't you see that," she whined.

Jill sniffled a couple more times, then sat upright as she tried to pull herself together. "I'll be here, Max," she said softly. "I won't go anywhere. I'll wait for you to call. Please call me." Her voice got even quieter. "I love you," she whispered.

Feeling the emotion swelling inside her, Jill laid the phone on the coffee table. She sobbed convulsively as the tears poured down her cheeks. Drawing both legs to her chest, she hugged them tightly and fell sideways curled up on the sofa.

<22>

Joe was heading toward the City. He pressed in the phone number for Larry North in West Palm Beach. Larry had been expecting Joe's call. After a brief conversation he gave Joe the telephone number where he could reach Agent Hogan who was heading up the investigation out of New York City. Several minutes later Joe was speaking with Samuel Hogan.

The two quickly decided they should meet as soon as possible. They arranged a meeting at One Police Plaza in the City. Joe was getting anxious. Between the information he and Danny had gathered and the information the DEA had obtained, Joe felt certain they were now going to bring down Folino, and fast.

Less than two hours later Joe was sitting with Sam Hogan in an office at One Police Plaza. Joe explained everything he and Danny had found so far in their investigation. Danny had already conveyed a lot of information to Agent North, with the exception of Joe's most recent revelations. Joe was glad to hear Hogan had already expedited the subpoena for Jill Riley's phones and obtained the records that were being scrutinized as they spoke.

What Joe found most surprising was that both the FBI and DEA were not aware of the unusual deaths and their connection to Folino's organization.

Joe continued: "I think the fact that Travis McGee didn't say anything to you about the mysterious deaths confirms that he was withholding information from you. He obviously took the pictures of the deceased StratoShares owners off the wall of the boardroom so as not to draw further attention."

Joe's information obviously fueled Hogan's fire. He looked like a man on a mission. Hogan was a short guy, just over five and a-half feet tall. But what he lacked in height he made up in muscle. He was thick and stocky, without an ounce of fat. Joe thought he wouldn't want this guy as an enemy.

Hogan sat there with the sleeves of his white dress shirt neatly rolled up above his elbows. The shirt was unbuttoned and a tie hung loosely around his neck. Large wet circles of perspiration stained the armpits of his shirt. His short brown hair stuck up in several places where his hands had crept through it while he was deep in thought.

He leaned forward in his seat, with arms resting on the table and his hands folded. "Now let me tell you what we know," Agent Hogan began. "Are you aware that Strato-Shares had an accident about three years ago?"

"No, I didn't know that."

"Well, they did. A Challenger of theirs went down just off the coast of Boston as it was returning from Italy. The only passenger was Tommy Barconi, chairman of a big Italian clothing company here in the City."

"Now that you mention it, I think I remember reading something about it. What happened?"

"The plane apparently got caught in some clear air turbulence that sent the aircraft spiraling out of control. After a review of the cockpit voice recorder, the flight data recorder and the crash site, the FAA determined it was basically a freak accident and really wasn't the fault of the company or pilots. It could have happened to anyone."

"So, what significance does this have on the case?"

"Only a few items were recovered from the wreckage, but one of the items they retrieved, floating in the water, was one kilo of cocaine wrapped in plastic. Since those were the only drugs they found, we assumed it belonged to Barconi. Especially since he had a prior for cocaine possession. But now, in light of what we've found out, it could have been some that Folino had been smuggling. Unfortunately, everybody died so we'll never know. Based on what we do know, we have to wonder whether there could have been a lot more and it just got destroyed in the wreckage."

Joe said, "You would think that after finding the cocaine, StratoShares aircraft would have been under a lot tighter scrutiny when clearing customs."

"You're right, and they were for a while. But you have to also remember, Folino's fleet was much smaller a few years ago so it was much easier. Its size has nearly tripled each year since."

Hogan leaned back in the chair and crossed his arms. "Ironically, a few days after the accident, Folino's pilots, who at that time were working without a contract, decided not to show up for work."

"Yeah, Travis McGee mentioned that to me."

"Well, both the accident and work stoppage cost him a lot of money. So what did Folino do? The very next day he reached an agreement with the pilots that included the construction of two new training facilities. Then he immediately hired a company here in New York to do background searches on all StratoShares prospects as soon as they start to execute documents. We found this out from an informant of ours that works there. He said if any drug violations show up, Folino wants to know."

"Apparently," Hogan continued, "Folino must have been surprised to find out about Barconi's prior charges for cocaine possession. But as luck would have it, it worked out for Folino because it cast a shadow of doubt on exactly who the drugs belonged to. Nonetheless, his planes then had to deal with the closer scrutiny of customs agents for a short period of time."

Hogan uncrossed his arms and leaned forward on the table again. "Folino didn't want that happening again. The last thing he wanted was to be flying an owner in his program that might be a suspected drug trafficker. Therefore, the background search."

"We also have it from our source that over the past two years, they found six different StratoShares prospects that had drug priors. Folino obviously found some way to discourage them from joining because to this date, none are in his program."

Joe shook his head. "Well, McGee never mentioned the accident to me, but I guess that's understandable. It's definitely not something you would want to point out to a potential prospect of your program."

"Well, I'll tell you. McGee has given us some great information and supposedly has more on the way. One of the things is a special owner list that comes directly from Folino. He distributes it throughout operations where everybody has strict orders to accommodate their requests. McGee told us the employees don't know the real reason for the list. They think Folino just doesn't want to lose the owners."

Joe jumped in. "But the real reason is because Folino doesn't want to lose those owners and the routes that they travel. It would mess up his drug trafficking."

"That's exactly what we think. After North spoke to your partner Froberg down in West Palm, we compared the names of the people you thought had died suspiciously. Every one of them was on Folino's special list—at least at one time or other. A couple of them were removed from the list after the deaths occurred. We wondered why they were taken off, but didn't know about the deaths. Now it makes sense."

Joe was getting excited. By combining the DEA and FBI's information with that of Joe's, they were finally getting a better picture of what they were dealing with. "Keep going," Joe said. "What else have you found out?"

"McGee has also provided us with information that shows the number of sell-offs in dollars that occur at Strato-Shares. Last year alone the company spent millions on sold-off or subcontracted flights. Based on what the company reported as earnings, there is no way that Folino could or would continue to operate unless there was some other source of revenue for him.

"We suspect the reason they sell off or subcontract a lot of the domestic StratoShares owners is because they specifically want the StratoShares aircraft to do international or other domestic trips that involve drug trafficking."

"And McGee has given you this information?" Joe was surprised at the kid's cooperation and still questioned his loyalty.

"He has. The special owner lists are copies of an original that's distributed internally and the number of sell-offs is in a report that's created by one of the managers specifically for Folino. We still don't have anything in writing about any drug involvement, though. We do of course have the drugs that McGee took from a StratoShares aircraft about nine months ago."

Joe sat and listened intently as Hogan continued.

"In addition to the sell-off information, he's given us information showing that StratoShares aircraft do an extremely large number of ferry legs for international trips. We think this is when they smuggle a lot of their drugs in and out of the country. It's probably also why they want clients that travel internationally. They stand to make a lot of money on the international trips by moving drugs."

Joe chimed in. "I remember when I spoke to the pilots on my flight from L.A. to Newark. They seemed to have a keen interest in my international travel. Likewise in the boardroom at their facility. The chief pilot seemed only interested in the details of my international travel."

"It's also quite similar with the OceanShares program," Hogan added. "We had one of our agents pose as a prospect for one of the yachts and he too said they were mostly interested in any international travel that he might have.

"We're also trying to tie him to the transporting of drugs through his racing teams. Folino owns several teams in Formula One, CART, and the IRL, and they all compete internationally. We suspect Folino might somehow be using the racing car transports to smuggle drugs. We're going to be keeping a close eye on Folino Racing this weekend when the CART season begins down in Homestead, Florida."

"Ross Nickels invited me to the Long Beach Grand Prix in a few weeks. Maybe I can go to that race and see what I can find," Joe commented.

"I'll keep that in mind, but I hope to be done with Folino by that time. The case has already taken longer than I expected and as I said before, I'm expecting more information from McGee. Hopefully, it will be enough information to go to a grand jury and allow us to bring down his ring."

Hogan had no sooner finished the sentence when an agent rapped once on the office door before entering. "Sorry to bother you, Sam, but McGee still hasn't called in yet. I'm starting to get worried."

Joe was surprised by the agent's overweight appearance. He was quite the contrast to Hogan. He walked over to Hogan's desk and glanced at Joe. "Excuse me," the rotund man said. "This just came for you, Sam, by special courier." He gently laid a large, flat letter package on Hogan's desk and smiled.

"Who's it from?" Hogan asked.

"I don't know," the other agent replied.

"Well, why don't you be a pal and open it for me?"

"I don't think so." He laughed as he headed back toward the doorway. He stopped and stood just outside the doorway with his body shielded by the wall. "Okay, tear away."

"Real funny," Hogan said as he grabbed at the taped flap.

"No, wait!" the other agent said.

Hogan stopped and looked up.

"Can I have your Corvette if anything should happen to you?"

"Would you get out of here?"

Joe watched as the other agent turned and walked away laughing robustly. Joe remembered how Danny would do the same thing to him. He looked back at Hogan, who was opening the envelope.

Hogan commented, "It doesn't take a rocket scientist to figure out that we're not the most liked people on earth."

"And you think it's any different being a homicide detective?" Joe responded.

Hogan laughed. "Oh, yeah." He reached inside the brown envelope and pulled out several pieces of paper that were stapled together. As his eyes scanned over them, he continued speaking to Joe. "That's definitely not like him."

"Like who?" Joe asked.

Hogan looked up at Joe. "Like McGee. He has called and checked in every afternoon at the same, exact time for the past nine months. Without fail," he added. "It's part of the arrangement." He looked down and continued to read.

Joe couldn't help but wonder what exactly the arrangement was that the DEA and FBI had with McGee.

Agent Hogan said, "I think he must have known we were getting aggravated and suspicious. He hadn't given us anything recently and every time he did, Folino always somehow seemed to know ahead of time. When I talked to him yesterday, he said he thought he would have something big for me today, and here it is."

"That's from McGee?" Joe asked, surprised.

"Yep. But this is really unusual. McGee has never done this before."

"Done what?"

"Sent me information by special courier. He's always called me on the phone. Something must have scared him." Hogan smiled. "I think this is just what we were looking for. McGee says there's a large shipment of cocaine arriving in West Palm Beach tonight on several Challenger aircraft. The drugs will be distributed to the other aircraft on the ground for distribution across the country."

Hogan turned a page. "He says here that aircraft in the Miami and Jacksonville, Florida, areas will primarily be used to transport the shipment around the country. He goes on to say that the transports for Folino Racing, along with Ocean-Shares yachts, will also be used."

"What's the significance of Jacksonville?" Joe asked.

"Wait a minute. Let me read on a bit." Hogan mumbled as he read some more, then said, "McGee says the Players Championship is this weekend just south of Jacksonville, in Ponte Vedra Beach at TPC Sawgrass." Hogan shook his head. "Of course. I can't believe we never thought of that!"

"Thought of what?"

"The professional golfers. StratoShares has many of the PGA, Senior PGA and LPGA golfers as owners in their program. You figure after each event, either they or their significant others probably take a StratoShares plane back home, creating the perfect distribution network for Folino."

Joe said, "Don't forget about the other StratoShares owners who fly into town for some of the events, especially ones like the Masters Tournament or the U.S. Open. That would significantly increase the number of StratoShares planes available for Folino's smuggling activities."

"This is all starting to make sense now," Hogan said. "The shipments arrive the night before and the detailers, while preparing the planes for the next day's flights, transfer the drugs to the appropriate aircraft for their flights the following day."

Joe asked, "But how did McGee get all this information, and what took him so long?"

"I don't know, since this information has obviously been typed on a computer by him. Maybe we should swing by his apartment in Newark and find out. If this information is correct, we should get McGee into a safe house as soon as possible. You want to come with me, Joe?"

"Yeah, that's probably not a bad idea. We can continue to discuss the case on the way."

"You got a permit to carry a concealed weapon in New York?" Hogan asked.

Joe's pause answered the question and before Joe could respond, Hogan said, "That's okay, I'll get one for you."

Joe knew the procedure and even though he typically carried an off-duty revolver inconspicuously tucked in his waistband or ankle holster, he didn't always get a permit.

"Thanks," Joe replied. "Does McGee happen to mention who or where he got some of his information?"

"As a matter of fact, he does. He says here he became friends with Folino's nephew, Donnie, who's also a pilot. He's been building his trust, and Donnie just now confided in McGee."

Joe recalled how Travis and Donnie had appeared to be friends when he had arrived in Newark. Joe looked at Hogan and could tell the man's mind was racing.

Hogan said, "Now I need to make some phone calls. I can't allow that much cocaine to be distributed around the country. It looks like we have no choice but to plan to bring down Folino tonight."

Joe detected disappointment. "Why do you say it that way?"

"Because we don't think Folino is the top dog. In fact, we know he's not. We think he just conducts and orchestrates his fleets of airplanes and yachts. If we capture him without any information on who's providing him with the drugs, then the smuggling will continue. Sure, it'll slow them down a while, but they'll eventually find another way. Whoever they are. They always do."

"Maybe Folino will cooperate and provide you with the names of his colleagues," Joe offered.

"That's exactly what I'm hoping too," Hogan said with a smile.

<23>

A half-hour later Hara and Hogan were leaving the City and heading for Travis McGee's apartment in Newark. They had only been in Hogan's late model Crown Victoria a few minutes when Sam noticed Joe eyeing his small statue of the Blessed Virgin Mother glued to the center of the car's dash.

"The guys call her Our Lady of Perpetual Motion because we're always on the move," Hogan joked.

As Joe chuckled, Sam's cell phone rang.

"Sam Hogan. Yeah. Okay. Folino, huh? But you didn't find any calls to or from Max Wells? Anything else unusual? Really? At the same time every morning? Okay, thanks." Sam put down the phone. "Good work, Hara. The lugs and tolls paid off."

"What'd they find in the phone records?" he asked.

"Jill Riley did place the call to the two hired hit men in California."

"What about Max Wells?"

"But not Max Wells. They didn't find any numbers that appeared to be to or from him on any of her phones, including the one you thought you overheard last night at the restaurant. You must have heard wrong."

Joe shook his head. He was certain he had heard her say the name Max. Joe shifted his feet to avoid stepping on an overstuffed Saborro's bag filled with fast-food trash.

Hogan noticed. "Oh, just throw that shit in the back. Sorry about that. I didn't see it down there."

Joe picked up the bulging sack overflowing with wrappers, napkins and a fast-food cup, and dropped it on the floorboard behind him. "So, who did last night's call come from then?" he asked.

"They're still trying to pinpoint it. What they did find, though, were tons of calls from Riley to Folino. But so far they haven't been able to identify any calls that might have come from Folino to her. Here's something interesting, though. Tell me what you make of this. Jill Riley phoned Randall Johnson every morning on the five days before his murder at almost always the same time."

"What time was that?" Joe anxiously asked.

"He said she always called between 9:10 and 9:20 A.M. Why? Do you think you know why?"

"I'm certain I know why. Randall Johnson died at 9:15 A.M. His housekeeper told us that he was a creature of habit and always did the same things at the same time every day. My guess is Jill Riley called every day to discuss their interview, but at the same time she was confirming where he was in the house and what he was doing."

As they drove past the tall, ornate steeple of a Roman Catholic church, Joe caught a glimpse of the sign out front. It read: Our Lady—of something or other. Joe hadn't been paying close attention. But it did make him think of Father Matt Kennedy. He was the priest that Dan said was visiting his mother next door, the morning Randall Johnson was murdered. His mother said he never left her sight, but maybe she had been mistaken. There was only one way to find out. It was worth a shot.

Joe removed his cell phone and held it tightly. He waited until they had exited the Holland Tunnel, then he dialed information. Hogan drove without comment. Moments later Joe had Father Matt on the line.

"Father Matt?"

"Yes, this is Father Matt," a soft voice answered. "Who is this?"

"This is Detective Joe Hara. How are you today?"

"I'm fine, Detective Hara. What can I do for you?"

"I'll get right to the point, Father. Your mother lives next to Randall Johnson in Boston. Is that correct?"

"Yes, that's correct." The priest's tone turned anxious. "Is everything all right with my mother? Is something the matter?"

"Your mother is fine," Joe quickly assured him. "My apologies if I scared you, Father. The reason I'm calling is in regard to your recent visit, though. You visited her a couple weeks ago. Is that correct?"

"Yes, that's correct."

"Well, I'm not sure if you are aware, but Mr. Johnson, Randall Johnson, your mother's neighbor. . . ." Joe stopped, waiting for acknowledgment.

"Yes, Randall Johnson. Mother told me he died in his bathtub. Electrocuted or something, right?"

"That's right. But just between you and me, Father, well, we think he was murdered."

"Oh my," the priest softly said.

"So the reason I'm calling is to see if you might have noticed anything or anybody at Mr. Johnson's house that morning."

"And what day was this again?"

"One week ago yesterday. Last Friday morning."

"Oh my," he said again. "Yes, well, let me think a minute and see if I can remember what I did, exactly."

Joe waited patiently while the priest quietly reflected. Joe could hear the sound of classical music playing in the background. He covered the mouthpiece of his cell phone and looked at Hogan. "He's thinking," Joe said.

Sam didn't turn but smiled in acknowledgment to Joe's comment. He too was deep in thought.

The priest finally spoke. "If my memory serves me correctly, I think I went out to my car to get some papers out of the glove box. It was parked out back of my mother's house. And now that you mention it, I do remember seeing somebody. In fact I saw them twice."

"Saw who?" Joe asked.

"Oh, I don't know who she was, but I saw a very pretty lady in a business suit and heels in the backyard at Mr. Johnson's house. Both times she was walking up the sidewalk toward the back door."

"Both times? What time do you think it was?"

"Let's see. The first time was . . . yes, I remember. It was just about nine or a little after. I remember because we had just finished watching my mother's favorite morning show and *Regis and Kelly* was coming on as I got up to go outside. She had gotten up to go to the bathroom, so I took the opportunity to go outside and get some papers that I needed out of my glove box."

"Did this woman see you?"

"No, I don't believe so. I hadn't stepped out the back door yet when I noticed her through the window."

"How about the other time. When was that?"

"That was when I left to return home. I would say it was just before noon sometime."

"Do you think you would recognize this lady if you saw her?"

"Yes, probably. She was, as I said, a very beautiful woman. God has definitely blessed her."

Regarding Father's last words, Joe thought, *We'll see how blessed she is when she goes to prison for murder.* He said, "Father, would you be willing to testify to what you saw, in a court of law, if necessary?"

"Yes, I would have to. It would be my duty as a good Christian and a good citizen."

"Thanks, Father. You've been a big help. We'll be in touch."

"Yes, well then, good day and God bless."

Joe turned off the phone and placed it on the seat between his legs. His right hand was red with an imprint of the phone where he had been gripping it so tightly. He felt a mix of feelings and wasn't certain exactly what they were. Excitement, disappointment, anger, hurt—he didn't know. Hogan's voice snapped him out of it.

"Well?"

Joe said quietly, in a monotone, "We got her."

"You don't sound very excited."

Joe realized he was slouching, and straightened up in his seat. He took a deep breath and changed his tone. "Oh no, I'm excited."

"So, the priest saw her there and is willing to testify?"

"You got it."

"That's great! Well, at least you've got a credible witness."

Hogan was right. So many times the only witnesses they would have at murder scenes were vagrants, crackheads, prostitutes and drug dealers. That is, if you were even lucky enough to have any at all.

"How much farther?" Joe asked.

"We're almost there," he replied. He reached down, picked up his cell and placed another call. "Larry, it's Sam. How are things coming down there?"

Joe stared straight out the windshield and caught a glimpse of Lady Liberty as they headed southwest toward Newark on I-78. He could hear Hogan talking, but Joe wasn't listening anymore. He was thinking about Jill and wondering how he could have been so stupid.

Ten minutes later they were passing Newark International on their left and exiting the interstate.

Joe heard Hogan saying he would wait for Agent North to call him back. He then said goodbye.

"I'm hungry. How about you, Hara?"

Joe glanced at his watch. It was already after six. "Now that you mention it, I am kind of hungry."

"We'll grab a couple sandwiches after we hit McGee's place, before heading back downtown, if that's okay with you. He's only a couple more blocks away."

"That's fine." Joe was surprised at the neighborhood. *It isn't exactly the type of area where I'd expect Travis McGee to live,* he thought. *It has to be quite the contrast to growing up on a farm in Tennessee. If both the DEA and Folino are paying McGee, he sure isn't spending it on housing.*

"North said everything is coming together in Florida. They've confirmed that StratoShares has several flights from the islands coming into multiple airports in the Miami, West Palm Beach and Jacksonville areas later this evening. Based on what McGee told us, those should be the planes loaded with drugs."

They pulled into the parking lot of an old, dirty two-story brick apartment building just as the outside security lights flickered on. It had already started getting dark.

"There's McGee's car over there," Hogan said, pointing at a late model Nissan Maxima near the end of the lot.

Joe noticed the car had been repainted. "It looks like he got the ninety-nine dollar paint special," Joe commented.

"Actually, I think it's more like a hundred and ninety-nine now," Hogan replied. Hogan pulled into the first open space.

"Really? Where the hell have I been? Shit, now I feel old." As they got out of the car, Joe asked, "So, Sam, what do you think? Is McGee a dork or what?"

Hogan and Joe walked toward the black Maxima.

Hogan laughed. "You know, I kind of wondered that myself for a while, but then I saw his girlfriend. She's a swimsuit model for an agency in the City."

"You're kidding me, right?"

"No, I'm not. I mean, you should see her. I tell you, I don't know how a guy like that does it. I think he looks and acts like a schmuck."

Hara and Hogan laughed loudly as they approached the car.

Joe walked around the back of the vehicle heading for the passenger side while Sam approached the driver's door. Hogan could not see inside the vehicle's lightly tinted windows. He reached for the door's handle and it lifted.

"It's unlocked. That's unusual," Hogan stated.

"Especially in a neighborhood like this," Joe commented. Joe reached out to open the passenger door but stopped before pulling it.

"Holy shit!" Joe heard Hogan exclaim. "Jesus!"

Joe let go of the door handle and hurried back around to the driver's side. Hogan was standing there shaking his head in disbelief. In front of them, on the driver's seat, was the head of Travis McGee, with genitals stuffed in his mouth.

"I'll get on the horn." Hogan turned to head back to his car. "So much for that burger," he mumbled as he hurried away.

Joe stared down at the bloody head, then leaned forward to get a better look inside the vehicle. It was meticulous; it appeared there wasn't a scrap of paper or piece of dirt anywhere. *The guy must have been a real neat freak,* Joe thought. He looked back at the decapitated head and felt sorry for the kid. *Nobody deserves to die like this.*

Joe noticed it was dark inside the car; the overhead light hadn't come on when they had opened the door. Joe leaned farther in and flipped the light switch. He pulled his upper body out of the car and squatted just outside the driver's seat. As he looked more closely, he realized that the blood on the leather upholstery appeared fresh. It hadn't dried yet or turned that familiar crimson red. It appeared to still be dripping.

Joe reached out and pressed on the side of the dead man's cheek with the back of his hand. A chill ran up Joe's spine as goose bumps formed on both arms and the hair stood on end. The corpse's flesh was still warm. McGee had just been killed.

Without thinking, Joe yelled, "Saaaammm!" Realizing he shouldn't have yelled, Joe got up and hurried toward their car.

Sam, running, met him halfway across the lot. "What's the matter?"

Joe spoke more quietly while looking around the lot. "McGee was just killed. Probably only minutes before we got here."

"That means they might still be here!" Hogan said excitedly. "I'll go to his unit and see."

"I'll come with you."

"No, you stay here and watch the body. Well, uhm, head."

"You can't go in there alone," Joe declared.

"Watch me. I'll be fine. Backup's on the way."

Sam pulled a revolver from a shoulder holster inside his sports coat. He quickly but cautiously walked up to the glass door and slipped inside the building.

Joe stood by the car and waited. He checked the revolver in his waistband and bent down to double-check his ankle holster. He straightened up and stood silently watching the door that Sam had entered. In the distance he heard the wail of police sirens.

Joe heard the crash of breaking glass and the clang of metal banging against metal. It sounded like it came from the other side of the building, but it was hard to tell in the darkness.

Seconds later, Hogan burst out the front door and yelled, "He went out the window on the other side of the building!" Hogan ran around the right side of the building and headed toward the back. "You go around the other way," he shouted back to Joe.

Joe knew it would be to no avail. While Hogan was hollering, Joe had heard the sound of a car door slam, followed by the roar of an engine and squealing tires.

Nevertheless he pulled out his revolver and headed around the other side. The sirens were getting closer. When Joe reached the back, he found Sam Hogan standing on a patch of worn grass and dirt, with both hands on his hips and breathing heavily. A fifties-style chrome chair with red Naugahyde upholstery lay on its side among the broken glass scattered on the ground.

Joe came up beside him. "You okay?"

"Yeah, I'm fine."

"Did you get a make on the car?"

"No, all I saw were taillights. That son of a—" but Sam didn't finish the sentence. Off in the distance they could hear the sound of several automobiles skidding, then the sound of a massive collision.

"They might have just gotten our guy," Joe said.

"God, I hope so. You should see it up there, Hara. I found the rest of McGee. It's a real butcher shop." Hogan nodded his head toward the ground floor unit with the broken window. "His body's laid out on the kitchen table with a meat saw beside him. I obviously interrupted his work. He wasn't done cleaning up yet."

"Then hopefully he didn't have enough time to get any evidence that McGee might have stashed in the apartment," Joe commented.

"Yeah, hopefully."

Joe had another thought. "I hope you didn't leave the door to his apartment wide open when you came running out." Joe smiled.

"Oh shit!" Sam bolted back around the building as the first squad car arrived at the scene.

<24>

Two hours later Joe and Sam were back in Hogan's car, leaving the run-down Newark neighborhood. McGee's apartment complex had become a buzz of activity after the police emergency service unit truck arrived. A telescoping pole with its bright halogen light lit up the crime scene like a Hollywood movie set. Both the crime scene unit and medical examiner's inspector were still busy doing their work while agents and detectives continued their canvass of the area. Joe and Sam had found all the information they needed.

Hogan's cell phone rang. Joe listened intently as Samuel Hogan sounded more and more excited. Several minutes later he hung up the phone.

"We hit the mother lode, Hara! That was North down in Florida. He said four different planes all landed from the islands within the past hour, two in Jacksonville and two in West Palm. They found hundreds of kilos on board each of the aircraft and one of the pilots was Folino's nephew."

Even though he was driving, Sam became more animated with hand gestures as he spoke. The men weren't headed for One Police Plaza, though. They were going to Tony Folino's residence on the Upper East Side. They had just found enough evidence and information in McGee's apartment to put Folino away for life.

"I can't believe it," Hogan said. "The little chump had all that information and wasn't giving any of it to us."

"You said he was smart," Joe replied.

"Oh yeah, real smart. Look what it got him."

"Well, it's obvious he was going to try and blackmail Folino. That's probably what got him killed. McGee must have contacted Folino and told him what he had. Folino probably didn't give in to his demands, and threatened him. Seeing that his plan wasn't going to work, Travis at the last minute decided to call you with all the information. Unfortunately, Folino got to him first." Joe sat silent for a moment, then commented, "The kid had no idea who or what he was dealing with."

"Actually, this might have all worked out for the best," Sam said.

"How's that?"

"I mean, if McGee hadn't done this and we hadn't come by when we did, we may have never gotten the additional evidence we needed."

"So, how do you think he did it? Surely he couldn't have gathered all that information by himself. I mean, how did he get copies of some of those documents, especially the ones with Folino's signature on them?"

"Don't forget," Hogan interjected, "he *has* had nine months to do it."

Joe continued, "And that taped conversation with Jill Riley was great! I wonder how he got that. I mean she practically confessed. It was obvious from what we briefly heard on those tapes that he must have bugged Folino's nephew's phone. That must have been why Travis got so chummy with Donnie."

"That is why." Hogan sounded aggravated. "We told him to become friends with Donnie Folino because it was our understanding he was the closest thing Tony had to a son. So when the time was right, we were going to put a wire on Travis and get everything we could on tape. Obviously the little shit had ideas of his own."

"And Folino was probably grooming Donnie to take over things. You know, run the family business." Joe laughed. "I even joked with the kid when he told me his uncle was Tony Folino. I said something about it being a family business."

Hogan's cell phone rang again. Joe listened as he tried to make out what was being said on the other end.

Sam ended the conversation with, "We're on our way." As Hogan hung up the phone, he drove past the interstate on-ramp.

"Where are we going?" Joe asked.

"We're going to the airport instead. My guys have been staking out Folino's place and say he's on the move. He just left his penthouse and is headed out of the City. It looks like he's driving toward Newark International. My guess is he has a plane there waiting to take him out of the country. He probably plans on heading for a country that doesn't have an extradition treaty with the U.S. Other units are already en route and we're all going to meet a couple blocks away. I just hope he doesn't put up a fight."

"Where's his wife and kids?" Joe asked.

"They're at his place in West Palm Beach on spring break. We've been keeping a close eye on them too." Hogan paused, then added, "You know, there's a new breed of Mafia women. It used to be they knew their place, but now many women are active participants in the Mafia, especially wives, sisters, and lovers. Police have tapped phones and heard women acting like bosses, even ordering killings. The Mafia will never admit it, though. Too proud, I guess."

Joe didn't reply to Hogan's comment because he already knew this all too well. He had just gotten his first taste of the new breed of Mafia women and her name was Jill Riley.

Within ten minutes Sam and Joe had gathered along with twenty other agents from the FBI and DEA. In addition, several local uniformed law enforcement officers and state police joined the effort.

Shortly thereafter, Sam received another call saying that Folino had stopped at an apartment in Greenwich, but was on his way again. They said Folino had waited in the limo while his driver went inside for a few minutes. When he returned he was carrying a large black chest. The doorman had helped him lift it into the limousine's trunk.

A plan was quickly strategized and everybody moved to their assigned positions. Fifteen minutes later, Tony Folino's sedan pulled onto the service road and headed for the Strato-Shares gate. Three unmarked cars pulled from alongside the road and tucked in a car's length behind him.

As Folino's car approached the gate and the left-turn signal came on, three cars approaching from the opposite direction stopped in front of the entrance to the gate as one pulled sideways across his lane. One of the agents that had been following behind Folino's sedan also pulled sideways across the other lane. Folino was boxed in without an exit.

Simultaneously, on the other side of the fence, four unmarked cars surrounded Folino's plane and stormed on board the aircraft.

As the airplane's engines could be heard shutting down, the rear passenger door of the large black Mercedes limousine swung open. Tony Folino stepped out and put his hands in the air. His driver followed suit.

With guns drawn, several agents approached the car with caution, confirming those were the only passengers. While several officers handcuffed Folino and his driver, Sam and Joe opened the sedan's trunk.

Inside was a large black and gold chest. The latch was closed but not locked. Joe flipped the gold-plated clasp and lifted the lid. Both Sam and Joe stared. There, with her hands and feet bound by rope and her mouth covered with duct tape, was Jill Riley. Her eyes were frantic with fear and her clothing was soaked with perspiration. Joe smelled alcohol and could tell from Jill's appearance that she had been crying. She also had another black eye. Joe wanted to slam the lid closed and walk away, but knew he couldn't.

"Who's that?" Hogan asked.

"Jill Riley," Joe said, his voice void of emotion. "Give me a hand, Sam."

He and Hogan reached inside and grasping her roughly under the arms, lifted her sweaty body from the chest and placed her standing on the street. Several agents rushed over to assist.

"Cuff her," Hogan said.

One of the FBI agents placed handcuffs on Jill Riley's wrists, then cut off the ropes while the other removed the gray tape from her mouth. Jill Riley was breathing heavily, but didn't say a word. Joe found he couldn't even look at her. He wiped his damp hand on the side of his pants, suddenly feeling soiled from having touched the woman's sweaty clothing.

As several officers read all three their Miranda rights and loaded them into separate vehicles, Joe watched Tony Folino and couldn't help but think he looked relieved.

<25>

Joe walked in with a Styrofoam cup of steaming black coffee and sat down in the old wooden chair across from Frank Buchanan's desk. Daniel Froberg sat beside him. Buchanan was sipping coffee from an old Dodgers mug that had probably been around since the days when Tommy Lasorda was a player with Los Angeles. Danny was getting his caffeine from a can of Coke. Joe never understood how Danny could drink that stuff so early in the morning.

They were eager to hear the details of Joe's collar.

"Let's hear all about it, Joe," Danny said.

"For starters," Joe said, "the prosecutors said they would recommend a lighter sentence for Folino if he cooperates. Nowadays, more and more of the Mafia are breaking with the mob and confessing their crimes. They're hoping Folino will be like Ralph Natale, the former Philadelphia mob boss who's been turning over compatriots in La Cosa Nostra since his arrest on drug charges."

"Or like Joe Valachi," Frank added. "I think he was the first to break the Omertá—code of silence—back in '59."

"As of late last night though, Folino still hadn't told them anything."

Buchanan picked up his coffee mug and slurped noisily. "So, what faction of La Cosa Nostra was Folino involved with and what was his position?"

Joe said, "The Feds still don't know for sure. And as far as Folino's position goes, the DEA thinks he was just a criminal associate or puppet of LCN, not a boss or chieftain. Although there is a slim chance he could have been a lieutenant or underboss. They hope the information and evidence that McGee gathered will help them figure it all out."

"So where was he going when you finally caught him at the airport?" Buchanan asked.

"Well, it wasn't West Palm Beach. He knew he couldn't fly there with everything that was happening. It turns out he intended to go to Belize or somewhere else in Central America that doesn't have an extradition treaty with the United States. He figured he'd somehow get his wife and kids there later."

"And how did you finally figure everything out?" Buchanan asked, taking another sip.

"Well, I certainly couldn't have done it without the FBI and DEA's help. It actually wasn't until we combined our information that everything started to fall into place. Then we found the evidence at Travis McGee's apartment. Several of the pilots they arrested, including Folino's nephew, are now talking, as well as two federal inspectors from the Immigration and Naturalization Service. And then there's Jill Riley, who is being very cooperative. She's filled in a lot of the blanks for us."

"She must have a death wish," Frank commented.

Joe shrugged his shoulders and snickered. "She's one irate bitch, that's what she is. After Folino's chauffeur chloroformed her and stuffed her in the trunk, she finally realized that Tony didn't love her, so she's been singing like a canary ever since.

"She confessed to having killed Randall Johnson and also claimed responsibility for the death of Johnnie Perrino. You see, Jill worked for Folino, but indirectly. When Tony Folino gave in and joined the Cosa Nostra about three years ago, Jill Riley said she was already on the Mafia's payroll, though she's certain they won't admit it. She's just one of many journalists and investigative reporters around the country that the organization owns. That way they can control what goes into print. They write stuff that diverts people's attention elsewhere and away from La Cosa Nostra's activities."

"So much for the Law and Ethics of Journalism seminar she took," the gray-haired chief quipped.

"Jill Riley says Folino put hits on all the other people, including a couple that we didn't even know about. There were a total of eight murders that he ordered over the past three years. But Jill murdered Randall Johnson on her own. She also hired a couple of goons to scare Johnnie Perrino, but he accidentally got killed in the process."

"Why did Jill kill Johnson and try to scare Perrino?" Frank asked. "I mean, surely Folino had to have known something about it."

"Tony Folino didn't have anything to do with either death and also wanted to know who made the hits. That's not to say he wouldn't have eventually killed Perrino, but it's unlikely he would have ever killed Johnson. He really didn't know what she was up to. Whenever she was away, he just assumed she was writing legitimate stories for the *Gazette*."

"So, why was she doing it?" the chief prodded.

"Jill did it because she was in love with Tony and thought she could help him," Joe answered. "She figured if she did this for him, he might love her more. She thought if she killed Johnson, it would show Tony how much she loved him and maybe he would leave his wife. She wanted to surprise him, but when Tony found out, he wasn't pleased. He had one of his soldiers rough her up early the next morning. That's when I saw her the next day with the black eye and a very tender arm. I was somewhat suspicious but believed her. She could be very convincing." Joe paused as he thought how he had mistaken feelings of lust for possible love.

Frank said, "What about my friend, Max Wells. Didn't you say you thought he called Jill at the restaurant the night you were having the allergic reaction? What was his involvement in all this?"

"That's what I thought, but it was a different Max that called. I guess I sort of jumped to the wrong conclusion there."

"Not like you've ever done that before," Danny commented sarcastically.

Joe ignored the dig and continued. "In addition to the call at the restaurant, Jill had also mentioned to me a couple weeks earlier that somebody named Max had taken her a couple times to Valentino in Santa Monica. Since Max Wells lived in Santa Monica, I started thinking it might be him."

Joe shrugged his shoulders and looked at the chief. "I'm sorry about your friend, Frank. He seemed like a nice man. Unfortunately, I think his only involvement was when he talked to me and that's what got him killed. The information he provided helped keep us on the right track, though. Especially the information about StratoShares continuing to fly trips that Max had cancelled and telling me the FBO at Folino's facility in Florida resembled Five Star's in West Palm."

"So, what was that all about, anyway?" the chief asked.

"I'll let Danny tell you about it. He was with North and the DEA when they raided the StratoShares facility in Miami."

"Folino had a hangar there surrounded by very tight security," Danny explained, "and on the inside, it was set up much like a Hollywood soundstage. They had replicas of several key FBOs around the country as well as mockups of all the StratoShares aircraft.

"The FBOs they duplicated were the organization's key entry points for their cocaine and heroin smuggling activities outside the country. The planes would typically fly into the actual FBOs the night before, sometimes with passengers, sometimes not. The detailers and mechanics would then unload the aircraft under the cover of the FBO's hangar. They would re-hide the drugs on other aircraft for transport around the country the following morning. Otherwise, they just left the stuff on board and sent it on its way the next day.

"Sometimes, though, if they got concerned, they would have the detailers carry it off to transport the drugs by car or be shipped by overnight carrier. If it needed to go somewhere along the coast, then they could always use the OceanShares yachts."

Buchanan sat there rubbing his chin as he processed all that he was hearing.

Joe resumed the briefing. "Anyway, getting back to Max. Another Max did call Jill that night on her cell phone.

After Danny got a subpoena for her phone records and they were examined more closely, it was found the number that called her came from Tony Folino's residence. You see, Folino's full name is Anthony Massimiliano Folino. Massimiliano is the Italian form of Maximilian and its diminutive form is Max. That's what Jill called him, Max."

"What did she call you, Joe," Danny cracked. "Almost done in by another beautiful woman. Hell, Hara, that's the second time your dick has almost gotten you killed. In less than a year, I might add. First there was Tokyo Rose and now Jill Riley."

Joe just shook his head at Froberg's comments. He was frustrated because he knew Danny was right. Tokyo Rose wasn't really her name, but an alias. She was an international hit woman who had seduced Joe during his previous investigation of a Japanese organization.

When will I ever learn, he wondered. He didn't even want to think about what Jill might have had planned for him if she had been successful with the chloral hydrate. The New Jersey State Police said Jack Williams' autopsy confirmed that he had been given the same thing less than an hour before he drove his car off the road.

"Anyway," Joe continued, "Jill was writing the story about Johnnie Perrino's death for the *Gazette*."

"Or in this case, writing for the Mafia," Frank added.

"That's right," Joe confirmed. "Anyway, she called Nicholas Perrino a day or two after the funeral and that's how she found out that I was investigating the case. It was sometime after you and I had spoken, Frank. You had already called Nicholas and told him I would help. Nicholas told Jill that he thought I was coming to New Jersey for a tour of the StratoShares facility. While she was conducting the interview, Nicholas confided in her and conveyed his suspicions about Tony Folino."

"So she knew all along that his son Johnnie had been chased down the highway by a couple thugs, but opted not to include that part in the story," Danny commented.

"That's correct, Dan. She was very vague in the article and made little, if any, indication that Johnnie's death was anything other than an accident. She then checked with an inside contact at QCI to find out when I would be arriving. Next she called Ross Nickels with the fabricated story that she was writing an article about the rich and their toys. Ross Nickels, like about ninety-five percent of the company, didn't know Folino was smuggling drugs."

"So, is it safe to assume Bill Price didn't know anything either?" Frank asked.

Joe took another sip of coffee, then shook his head. "Not even Price knew. The guy had no idea what he was buying into. Ironically, though, it was Price's deep pockets that enabled Folino to increase the size of his fleet and expand his smuggling activities around the globe."

"So, who within QCI knew?" Chief Buchanan asked.

Joe said, "Right now they think it's only a few select pilots, maybe thirty or so, along with some of the detailers and mechanics. Those particular pilots would fly all the drug trips with the airplane detailers and mechanics loading and unloading the narcotics on the aircraft under the cover of an FBO."

Joe leaned back in the chair and locked both hands behind his head. "The Caribbean was a common destination of many StratoShares owners. Columbian cocaine would come through the islands for shipment to Miami. The faction that Folino was involved with apparently had ties to Columbia. They transported the cocaine and heroin in concealed compartments of the aircraft like the auxiliary power units, bathrooms, and food service areas. It was always an area that was only accessible to the mechanics."

"And then there was Jill Riley," Joe added. "She also knew. When Perrino shared his knowledge of my involvement with Jill, she thought she could handle Joe Hara herself and make Tony love her more if she could eliminate a prying detective. She intentionally bumped into me during the tour so that we could meet later. Coincidentally, it worked out well for her that I was going to be in Boston the next day.

She thought calling me to the murder scene would help divert attention away from her. After all, who would invite a detective to investigate a murder that they had just committed, right?"

Joe stood and paced around the room while he spoke. "But Randall Johnson's murder didn't fit the rest of the deaths. Randall Johnson was not only the decision maker, but also the only user of the aircraft. So if he died or left the program, it would have disrupted some of the drug trafficking routes that Folino had established over the past several years from Johnson's regularly scheduled trips."

"So," Frank interrupted, "if Randall Johnson had been upset, Folino would have done everything in his power to keep him in the program. He wouldn't have killed him."

"That's right," Joe said. "Unfortunately, though, there was much about Tony Folino's dealings that Jill Riley didn't understand. You see, Jill only overheard part of a conversation between Tony and a couple of his soldiers, talking about how Randall Johnson was really fucking things up for them. So Jill called Johnson to ask for an interview under the pretense that she was writing a story about the rich and their toys.

"She called every day for several days before the murder. Randall always kept the phone by the tub so he could hear it and take any calls. While talking with him each day, he informed her he was taking a bath. She could also hear the radio blaring in the background and one day commented on the loud music. That's when he told her about his partial hearing loss."

Joe stopped pacing and leaned against the filing cabinet. "At some point, he told her he was thinking about getting some new toys and was presently reviewing contracts for a new boat and a new plane. He was apparently going to leave both the StratoShares and OceanShares programs. He agreed to the interview and informed her that Carmela, his housekeeper, would be out the next day. When we talked to Carmela, she told us Randall would have probably given Jill the security number for the front door and told her to just come on in and up to his office. The reason being because he would have never heard her at the door anyway.

"But Jill wouldn't have wanted to take a chance at being seen coming in the front door anytime before Randall Johnson's death. It just worked out well that the back door was already unlocked and partially open when she came the next day to kill him."

"You still haven't told me how you finally figured out it was her," Danny pointed out.

"It wasn't until I remembered how Jill had playfully threatened to kick me with her heel the other day that it clicked with me. We'd been puzzled by what could have caused the injury to Lady, Johnson's dog. The wound was too small to have come from the front of a shoe or boot. The angle and size of the puncture wound under the dog's belly could only have come from a woman's high heel. Since Carmela Gonzales, at age fifty, didn't wear heels, it quickly ruled her out. Also, the priest who was visiting his mother next door identified Jill Riley as having been at Johnson's house at the time of his death."

Joe slapped his hands together. "To top it off, we got a search warrant for Jill Riley's place. The NYPD confiscated every pair of high-heeled shoes they could find. The guys said you should have seen it. She had more shoes than Imelda Marcos."

Pausing while Buchanan laughed, Joe then added, "The lab examined the shoes and found traces of the dog's blood on one of the heels.

"Also, after the San Francisco police captured the two thugs Jill hired to scare Perrino, they confessed to chasing him and firing some shots, but said they weren't supposed to kill him, just scare him. When Jill later confessed, she said that was correct. She hadn't intended for them to kill Johnnie Perrino, just scare him. She was going to send him an anonymous letter telling him he should reconsider leaving the program. She was actually trying to help him. I mean, I'm sure she was smitten with him too. There probably isn't a woman in the country that wouldn't have liked to latch onto Johnnie Perrino. But when he accidentally died and she heard how upset Folino was, she knew she couldn't tell Tony."

"But how did she know Johnnie was upset with the program?" Buchanan asked.

"It turns out that she would check Tony's voice mail. She admitted watching and memorizing Tony's security code one night while the two of them were at dinner. He had called from their table to check his messages. Being an investigative reporter, it was just her nature to be suspicious of people, and she was of Folino's activities. She suspected he had ordered some hits on other people in the program. But again, she loved him and was only concerned for his welfare. She just wanted to help him.

"So, while he was in Europe, she checked his voice mail and heard the message from Perrino. That's how she knew Johnnie would be driving down the coast. She called the thugs in San Francisco and arranged to have some money dropped on a bench at Pier 55. They complied with the instructions and followed Johnnie."

Frank asked, "Why didn't they just take the money and run if they didn't even know who she was or where she was calling from?"

"Because the woman that called told them if they didn't follow through, they would have to deal with Tony Folino."

"So, what about Folino?" Frank asked as he reached into the right top drawer of his desk and took out a white plastic bottle of multiple vitamins. "What's his involvement with the Cosa Nostra? What all was he involved with?" Frank poured one of the round yellow pills into his hand and put the bottle away.

"Well, here comes the best part," Joe said. "Remember how I told you William Price didn't have any idea about what Folino was doing when he bought the company?"

"Yeah, go on," Buchanan practically insisted before he popped the vitamin in his mouth and reached for a cup of water.

"Well, it turns out that Tony Folino didn't know, either, when he bought the company about eight years ago."

"Okay, Hara, now you've lost me," Buchanan professed.

"It turns out Folino's grandfather fled Sicily in the mid-nineteenth century, like we suspected, to get away from the Octopus. He died of natural causes several years after arriving here. As Tony's father grew up, he too was pressured most of his life to join the Mafia, but never did.

"Well, where Tony's father and grandfather had succeeded, Tony failed. He didn't realize the company he purchased to start his fractional program about eight years ago was already partially controlled by the Mafia. The pilots, mechanics, and cleaners all belonged to a union that was secretly controlled by the Mafia."

Frank raised his eyebrows as Joe nodded his head.

"Their presence went unnoticed by Tony for the first five years or so. In fact, Folino had no idea until about three years ago, when the Italian clothing manufacturer, Tommy Marconi, died in a StratoShares plane crash and the Coast Guard discovered a kilo of cocaine floating in the water at the crash site. Even though Folino was suspected, he had no knowledge of the cocaine on board the aircraft.

"The DEA and FBI launched an investigation and Folino even helped. He wanted to clear his name as well as his company's name. That's when the Mafia made its presence known to Tony." Joe paused and took a sip of coffee.

"So, how did they do that?" Buchanan asked.

Joe answered, "They called Folino and told him that the cocaine wasn't Marconi's, but that it belonged to the Mafia. There was a lot more, but it apparently washed away after the crash. The union pilots were smuggling it into the country onboard the aircraft. They had been doing it for years, long before Folino even owned the company.

"As Tony grew his fleet of airplanes and fractional program, the Mafia's business grew too. It became perfect for their drug smuggling activities around the globe. The high-profile owners in his program often were never suspect by customs agents, so they would pass through security and customs at FBOs around the country with relative ease. The pilots also often took advantage of airports where the customs agents were inefficient and less likely to look inside the plane."

Danny tried to cover his mouth as he yawned and stretched, his body still adjusting to the time change.

"Even if they did come aboard," Joe said, "it was typically just to check for a customs decal or airworthiness certificate. The places where security was tighter, they simply bought or paid off the agents. Such was the case with the two Immigration and Naturalization Service inspectors they arrested during the roundup. Even Danny got to see this firsthand."

"Yeah," Dan added, "it turned out that Larry North's briefcase had a hole in the side not much larger than a pin. A 35mm camera inside caught on film every payoff to him while posing as a customs agent."

"That was great work you did, Danny," the chief said with a nod in his direction. "I know that cut into your vacation with Nancy. I'll be sure you get the time back, and then some."

Danny smiled. He and Nancy had cancelled their cruise as a result of the weekend's busts. Dan had ridden along with Larry North most of the weekend as they inspected all the drugs that were confiscated from StratoShares aircraft in Miami, West Palm, Jacksonville, and the surrounding areas.

The chief said, "So, that still doesn't explain why Folino decided to join forces with them. What happened that caused him to join their organization?"

Joe replied, "It was really very easy for the Mafia. After they told Tony Folino what they were doing, he threatened to expose them. As you can imagine, that didn't sit very well with the chieftains. So they decided to flex their muscle."

The chief jumped in with, "So, what did they do?"

"The pilots just didn't show up for work one day. There was a work stoppage. You see, the pilots had actually been operating without a contract for several years. During which time the StratoShares fleet had grown tremendously. That one day alone cost Folino a lot of money. It didn't take him long to figure out he could quickly lose everything. They had him where they wanted him. The Mafia knew that Strato-Shares was his lifeblood and they were ready to cut it off."

"He figured if you can't beat 'em, join 'em?" Danny asked.

"I guess so," Joe said. "Apparently, when he realized how lucrative a business it was, he decided to help grow it. He invested even more money and built two new training facilities with the sole purpose of training pilots, mechanics, and detailers on how to smuggle the drugs. Folino also began using his OceanShares yachts and found that the transports he used to move his racing teams around the globe were also perfect for drug smuggling.

"You see, Folino had an elaborate but proprietary system developed. The logistics alone of moving that many planes and boats are mind-boggling. There probably isn't a company in the transportation industry that wouldn't like to get their hands on it."

Frank chuckled and said, "Then add Bill Price and his very deep pockets."

"And you've got a very sophisticated drug smuggling organization," Joe declared.

"Unbelievable," Buchanan said. "So, explain to me some of the other murders."

"Well, from the information that Danny was able to provide me, we were able to put together a pattern. We determined the owners or decision makers that were being killed had all been in the StratoShares program for a long period of time, with very established travel patterns, many of which were so regular that Folino could count on them to smuggle his drugs. So, if any of them left the program, it would seriously disrupt his activities and cost him millions of dollars. That's why I said he probably would have eventually killed Perrino, if Jill hadn't killed him first."

Joe walked over and sat down again. He leaned forward and folded his hands together. "Their vineyards in France were located not far from Marseilles, where Nicholas Perrino would fly regularly. Remember the movie *The French Connection?*"

"Of course," Buchanan replied.

"Well, that's where part of it was filmed and Marseilles to this day still has serious drug problems. In the Middle East, the dried juice of opium poppy pods finds its way to Marseilles where it's refined into heroin and then sent off to America."

"So," Buchanan added, "Folino's program in the Middle East might have had something to do with that as well. Shit, officials over there would have beheaded Folino if they'd discovered what he was doing."

"Hell, his program everywhere—Brazil, Mexico, the Islands—all had something to do with it," Joe concluded.

Danny said, "Another example was Chet Warner. His chairman's trips always stayed the same and he never made any changes. They would typically schedule their international legs many months in advance and then never stray. His travel had been the same for years. No changes meant no problems for StratoShares."

Danny paused for a moment while he thought. "But the domestic trips were a different story. It was those trips with StratoShares where the company had the most problems. Chet's company's domestic legs served no purpose for QCI's drug smuggling activities so they had a tendency to abuse them. They would frequently sell them off or subcontract the flights to other vendors.

"That's why Chet wanted to leave the StratoShares program. Unfortunately, after Chet died, his actions went for naught. It wasn't the chairman that traveled on those legs anyway, but some of the other executives. The chairman wasn't aware of either Chet's or the other executives' frustrations, so he never left the program."

"Just like Folino had hoped," Joe added.

"You can't tell me that Folino put a hit on anybody that wanted to leave his program. I mean, surely other people have left the StratoShares program successfully," Buchanan commented.

Danny said, "Other people have left the program, but the difference is they were either the sole user of the plane or their trips were primarily domestic with travel between locations of no interest to Folino for his drug smuggling activities."

"So," the chief queried, "how did he always seem to know when an owner was upset enough to possibly leave the program?"

Joe answered, "We wondered the same thing and Travis McGee gave us the answer in the information that he sent to Hogan. It turns out Folino had somebody at StratoShares that was responsible for all of the company's telecommunications. All incoming and outgoing phone calls were recorded and monitored by that person. When you called StratoShares, a recording came on saying that your call may be monitored to insure quality customer service. That's how Folino was able to keep tabs on which owners might have been irate enough to leave the program.

"Then Folino would distribute a weekly list of owners' names throughout the operations and customer service departments, asking employees to take extra measures to insure those owners remained happy. They had no idea of the list's real significance. And if ultimately the owners still weren't appeased, well, Folino would somehow see to it that they were no longer a problem."

The chief sat there shaking his head. He said, "What an elaborate scheme. And they killed the DEA's informant, what was his name again, Travis McGee?"

"Yeah, because he was working both sides, taking money from the DEA but anonymously tipping off Folino's organization every time a bust was going to go down. When Folino found out through Jill Riley's phone call, McGee became a blown agent for the DEA and Tony took executive action."

Danny added quickly, "Yeah, bet the little dick never saw that coming."

Joe laughed lightly, as did the chief. If it wasn't for a little gallows humor, they would all go insane from the murders they witnessed daily.

Joe continued, "And as it turns out, McGee wasn't the first person within the organization that Folino exercised executive action on. Donnie Folino said his uncle murdered two pilots at his training facility in Durango and a yacht detailer in West Palm Beach. For some reason all three employees were going to talk, so he simply had them eliminated and made their deaths look like accidents."

Covering all the bases, Frank asked, "So, what about all his boats and planes—what's going to happen to them?"

"Both the FAA and Coast Guard have revoked QCI's licenses and the DEA has seized all of their planes and boats. They even seized his CART, IRL and Formula One racing cars and transports. The DEA also found cocaine hidden in Folino's transports in Miami. It had apparently come in on several earlier flights."

Danny added, "So far, U.S. drug agents have made about fifty arrests. Several were corrupt federal inspectors, but most are StratoShares pilots, mechanics, and detailers. All told, they've confiscated close to three thousand pounds of cocaine."

The chief spoke again. "How many people in the program has this affected? They've got to be pissed."

"All of them," Joe said.

"And Folino still isn't talking, right?" Frank asked, anticipating the reply.

"Not as of last night. Folino isn't telling the authorities anything because his biggest concern is his family. He doesn't want anything to happen to them and said he'll do anything to keep them safe."

Frank stood up from behind his desk. "Well, Joe, I think congratulations are in order again. Chalk up another collar for Joseph Hara."

"And Daniel Froberg," Joe added.

"Of course, absolutely," Buchanan emphatically stated.

They all stood to shake hands and give congratulatory pats on the back, when the phone on Buchanan's desk rang and he stopped to pick it up.

"This is Buch." There was a long silence as the expression on the chief's face suddenly became more serious. He motioned with his left hand for both Joe and Danny to sit down. He nodded his head several times and then said, "Thanks."

After hanging up the phone, Buchanan looked seriously at both Joe and Danny.

"I don't think I want to hear this," Joe mumbled.

Buchanan cleared his throat. "Well, Joe, you know how you were just saying that Tony Folino wanted to make sure his family would be safe?"

"What do you mean?" interrupted Danny.

"Well, you know the saying, dead men can't talk. The Mafia somehow got the message to Folino last night during his incarceration."

"What was the message?" Danny asked.

"They sent him a black leather belt."

"That was all?" Danny replied, still not understanding.

Joe looked at Danny and explained. "They were saying, 'If you don't kill yourself now, we will later.' You see, Dan, joining the Mafia is a lifetime commitment. You can never retire from it. The only way out is go to jail or die."

"He hung himself with it early this morning," Buchanan finally said.

"Shit," Danny said.

All three sat silent for a moment before Froberg spoke again.

"There went the possibility of bringing down more of the Mafia. This could have been one of the biggest busts in Mafia history if Folino had turned informant."

Joe slumped in his chair and stared at the worn squares of the linoleum floor. *How ironic,* he thought. *Both Folino's father and grandfather fought off the Mafia for years. Tony had only started working for the Cosa Nostra because he had no choice. He loved his family and didn't want to lose everything he had worked so hard for. He only wanted to protect them and ultimately had to kill himself to do it.*

Joe got up and walked to the window. His whole body felt numb. He looked out at the gray, overcast sky and took a deep breath. His chest heaved as he released a loud, heavy sigh and said, "But at least his family is safe now."